PRETTY SECRETS

PRETTY LITTLE DEAD GIRL

BOOK ONE

By
E. M. MOORE

Manufactured in the United States of America
First Edition February 2022

Cover Model Photographer :Michelle Lancaster/www. michellelancaster.com

Cover Model: Mitchell Wick

Cover by 2nd Life Designs

Edited by Chinah Mercer of The Editor & the Quill, LLC

PA's: Affinity Author Services (Bibiane Lybaek & Ashton Reid)

Jax

The Ballers of Rockport High Series

Game On

Foul Line

At the Buzzer

Rockstars of Hollywood Hill

Rock On

Spring Hill Blue Series

Free Fall

Catch Me

Ravana Clan Vampires Series

Chosen By Darkness

Into the Darkness

Falling For Darkness

Surrender To Darkness

Ravana Clan Legacy Series

A New Genesis

Tracking Fate

Cursed Gift

Veiled History

Fractured Vision

Chosen Destiny

Order of the Akasha Series

Stripped (Prequel)

Summoned By Magic

Tempted By Magic

Ravished By Magic

Indulged By Magic

Enraged By Magic

Her Alien Scouts Series

Kain Encounters

Kain Seduction

Safe Haven Academy Series

A Sky So Dark

A Dawn So Quiet

Chronicles of Cas Series

Reawakened

Hidden

Power

Severed

Rogue

The Adams' Witch Series

Bound In Blood

Cursed In Love

Witchy Librarian Cozy Mystery Series

Wicked Witchcraft

One Wicked Sister

Wicked Cool

Wicked Wiccans

USA *Today* Bestselling Author

E. M. MOORE

PRETTY

PRETTY LITTLE
DEAD GIRL

BOOK 1

Secrets

PROLOGUE

Eden

Fresh, raw grief snakes its way across my clammy skin. Hooks of incomparable sadness imbed into me like a psychopathic stalker who won't let go. I'm marked. From the crown of my head to the soles of my feet, despair bleeds into every crevice.

Dee is dead.

I feel it in my soul, accompanied by a darkness that threatens to take me under alongside her. She's everywhere, yet nowhere, and I don't know how much longer I can weather the storm raging inside me.

The wind picks up, tracking a stray strand of hair across my cheek. Crisp, autumn leaves rustle with the sudden burst, tumbling across faded green cemetery grass to nestle against a white casket. Of course it had to be white. Dee was nothing if not the light of our family. She was the happy, reserved one. If I had a penny for every time someone said our names should have been reversed, I'd have more money than my father. Delilah was far removed from the tempting, treacherous biblical figure that also bore her name. And I'm the opposite of Eden. I'm a goddamn heathen. If anything, I deserve to be in that casket. Not her.

Agony rips through me at the thought. The palpable, all-consuming pain tears me up inside. Grief is a spiked wrecking ball being wielded haphazardly and without warning. It comes on with tornado vengeance, ripping through everything it sees.

No one is a spectator to my true feelings, though. On the outside, I'm the picture of placidity. Especially now. *Especially* here. Funerals are for letting grief out, but I don't have that luxury. My life is a game, and my sister's death upped the ante.

All the major players are here, surrounding me in a semicircle. Old asshats with more money than God. Young fucks who grew up spoiled and coddled. Any one of them had the means to put my sister where she is. They're all privileged, living as if they're the only beings that matter. I despised my upbringing before, but I haven't hated my life more than the moment I took my first breath after learning Dee was gone.

Drowned.

Suffocated by murky river water.

Or if you ask me, the classification of "tragic accident" is extreme bullshit.

My sister doesn't go in the water unless she's forced. I'll never be convinced otherwise. If she was in that river, someone put her there.

It's everything I thought could happen in this fucked up world, only the reality is much, much worse.

To my right, my mother stands abruptly. I blink away the haze I buried myself under and watch as she takes a step forward in her black pantsuit, spinning the stem of a blood-red rose between her fingers. The priest has stopped talking. I'd tuned him out after he droned on about knowing Delilah is at peace in the afterlife. I disagree. The sunny sister I know, though pleasant in every way, doesn't go down without a fight. She's probably in death's cage somewhere, rattling the cell bars with carefully controlled anger.

"Edie..." a fractured voice whispers.

I turn toward the voice. Past my mother's now empty chair sits my father. As distinguished as our Astor background is, he's currently the living opposite. He spends his days crying into a bottle of brandy and his nights wailing into the ceaseless dark. The tear tracks down his face have etched new wrinkles in their wake like the glaciers carved the earth's landscape a million years ago. I'd always expected Dee was his favorite, but now it's been confirmed.

"Edie, honey," he chokes out. "Your flower."

Wordlessly, I stare down at the black rose gripped in my fist. My father chose white, signifying his precious angel. My mother red because she's nothing if not traditional. I chose black for the void now in my soul. Black for my sister's life unlived.

Black for my vengeance.

My mother presses a used handkerchief to her nose on the way back to her seat. She doesn't look at me when we pass, and I straighten my shoulders to show everyone here that there are some Astors who haven't lost their ever-loving mind to sadness. I need to be my family's sentinel; our show of strength. Because someone here, watching me place this midnight flower on this beautiful white casket, murdered my sister. Someone here is probably looking at us with relief, believing their crime will go unnoticed, unrectified...*unchallenged.*

They're wrong.

You don't just kill an Astor and get away with it. You don't kill my sister and have everything swept underneath a trough of tears and condolences.

For a moment, I lay my black-gloved hand on the

4

shining white surface of Delilah's final resting place. I close my eyes to the sun streaming down, heating my ever-frigid body just slightly. It's a different warmth than the West Coast. This one is laced by a chill I'll never be rid of.

I bite my lip until I taste the metallic tint of blood then make the silent oath that's been swirling inside me. *It's okay, Dee. I know I never stepped up when you were alive, but I'm here now. I promise you they won't get away with this. You will be able to rest in peace when I'm done. I swear it.*

A tingle starts in my toes. The wind picks up again, tracking another strand of hair over my lips as the buzzing sensation follows the curve of my calves, up my legs and hips, and settles in my heart. It's an aware-ness, a lighthouse beacon of strength that steals my breath.

Dee is egging me on, that's what this sensation says to me. She'll push my feet forward one step at a time. She wants this as much as I do.

Turning, I stare into the crowd. I memorize as many faces as I can, taking in their tight lips and solemn gazes. Most won't meet my eyes. I catalog their looks, their demeanors. I store them away for future use because I'm going to need a whole hell of a lot of help detangling the web surrounding my sister and her death. And I know just where to start.

Off along the far edges of the somber grouping is a line of men that are mostly my father's age or older, all sporting shiny cufflinks and matte black walking canes. The handles of those canes bear the Knights of Arcadia crest, their owners flashing it like a badge of honor. The Knights are unlike any men I have ever met. They're wealthy. They're prestigious. And have more to lose than any other.

That makes them dangerous.

And my sister—precious, sweet Delilah—walked purposefully into their snare.

Each of their unfriendly pairs of eyes meet my discerning glare with a hardness of their own. A chill skitters up my spine. If my sister is here, pushing me forward, the coldness sweeping through me is a warning. To turn back. To save myself.

I won't be doing any of that. My sister died on Devil's Night. And on Halloween, I vowed vengeance.

I'm here to fight for the truth. It's time for me to shed my West Coast persona and grab hold of the life I was dealt.

Secrets and parties, dresses and scandals, are all in my future.

I can hardly wait.

1

Leo

Ten Months Later...

Thumbing through my phone contacts is about as uninspiring as listening to one of my dear old grandfather's tiring lectures. The screen's harsh light makes me squint. I've been sitting in the dark with nothing but the soft blue glow from the electronics on my dash to light the interior of the car, waiting for this bitch to show up.

Imagine me back at Carnegie. The swelling anger inside me makes me scroll faster. I need a quick fuck to get all this aggression out. *Daphne?* No. Tight cunt, but she's got a little too much ass for my interest right now.

Gloria? She's a moaner, which is hot in the right time or place, but I want a quickie, and she has this annoying propensity to want to stay after I nut.

The fuck is wrong with some girls? Can't a guy just get in and out without strings?

Anne-Marie? Been there, done that plenty of times. She's exactly what I'm looking for—the kind of no-holds-barred fuck that's all about getting off and nothing else. My thumb moves to press her name, my dick already thickening, when headlights cascade through the interior of my car.

Glancing up, I watch as the lights from a Wrangler sweep the cobblestone pathways that crisscross CU's campus before landing on Jarvis Hall. The stone building my family built for the exclusive college almost a century ago is old world gothic. When I was a student here, I prowled the place, using my name to get some ass. Rule number one if you were staying in Jarvis Hall, you gave it up to me whenever I wanted it. Anyone who refused got kicked out and had to find other sleeping arrangements.

Welcome to the world of the elite.

A smirk pulls my lips apart as I think about the good ol' days. Jarvis hospitality, that's what I'd called it. Most girls were more than willing to go for a ride, threat of homelessness or not, but it was a good excuse to tell themselves so they wouldn't feel like the cheap whores they were.

Parked between two lamp lights, the Jeep door opens, and a single, toned leg searches for the pavement. I toss my phone down and huff. Looks like I won't be working this aggression out of my system any time soon. Duty calls.

I pull out the picture I threw in my glove box after the meeting with Grandfather yesterday. It's a family photo. Two stuck-up parents the same age as my own grin in the background while a pair of blonde girls are seated in front of them. One is smiling from ear-to-ear, a clone of her mother with her shoulders pulled back tightly. She looks like the kind of good girl I'd love to fuck the tension out of. The one who'll scream for my dick over and over again after acting all coy and innocent. The other sister looks bored as fuck. Sure, she's smiling because that's what's expected of her, but there's a hint of annoyance simmering under the surface.

There are hundreds of Jarvis family photos like this where I look the exact fucking same.

Tracking my gaze toward the younger sister's vehicle again, I find her on her tiptoes, digging into the back of the Wrangler with ripped shorts hugging her ass. My dick responds. It's not often you find a girl who goes to Carnegie dressed like she doesn't give a fuck.

Most wear pantsuits and pencil skirts. This? This ensemble looks like Little Miss Astor went to a thrift shop and bought the smallest pair of shorts she could find.

Fuck.

Maybe watching this girl won't be as bad as I originally thought. It's better than the other tasks I've been given by my family's patriarch. I always get the shit jobs, the ones in the shadows. The ones no one else is willing to do because they still care about their reputation. I'm not exactly the pride of my family. I don't wear a suit and tie to work every day and fuck people over in business meetings with a smile on my face. I prefer to do that shit out in the open.

I peek at the photo once again, reading Grandfather's writing. The older sister is dead, not that I needed him to confirm that. It's the only thing the news covered when it first happened. The mysterious death turned tragic accident has slowly faded away like it's only a bad memory. Shit like that tends to take place in my world. Pity I'll never get the opportunity to fuck some bad into her. The little sister, though, is a different story. Just from the picture, I can tell she's more my type.

Peering at her in action, I watch as she pulls a piece of luggage out of the backseat and sets it on the pavement next to her. Her thin tank top flirts with the high waist of her shorts as she spins toward her new residence hall—*my* residence hall. Finally. Move-in day was yesterday, and because she didn't show, I had to find a place to shack up last night. One of her roommates was more than happy to let me stay. Kerry.... No, Kasey. Whatever. Doesn't fucking matter. I got what I wanted and was close enough in case little Miss Astor showed up late. Which never happened.

I snuck out at dawn so my temporary fuck didn't get any ideas. After grabbing a coffee down the street, I returned to this spot and haven't moved since. I may not like these jobs, but Grandfather has made it clear what it's going to take to get back in his good graces.

Speaking of.... I grab my phone and send him a text before he accuses me of slacking off. **She just got here.**

I don't exactly know why I'm watching her, other than the fact that her sister, who was a fledgling Knight, died at one of their gatherings. Bad press and all that. I've mused that at the very least, they want to make sure little sis doesn't cause a scene. Worst case, the Knights did something and want to make sure this girl doesn't squeal about it. Which is perfectly fine. I have plenty of other fun things she can do with her mouth.

She starts to walk toward the building, and I push my car door open silently to follow. Now is as good a time as any to introduce myself. I rearrange my semi-hard cock as I stretch from the car. The wheels of her luggage bounce across the cobblestone walkway. Closing the car door silently, I'm already picturing the fear in her eyes when I sneak up on her. I get off on their looks of alarm, their horrified reactions. After they relax, I watch for the moment when they *really* look at me. The twinkle of interest in their eyes. The way their gazes sweep my tattoos. It's always the same with rich girls like her. They fear me, but they're also aroused by the fact that I'm trouble. That their daddies would freak if they found them in bed with someone like me. My balls swell in anticipation.

A soundless step forward later, I stop. The wheels have ceased their grinding, and she's peering up at the three-story building, her long blonde hair dangling past her shoulder blades. A second later, her shoulders stiffen, and she immediately tilts her head. Before I know it, I lose sight of her as she darts in front of her Jeep and takes the walkway that leads around the side of the building.

"Shit," I grumble.

Slowly, I walk after her, hiding behind high-priced vehicles in the parking lot until I reach hers. Moisture dots the exterior from the cool night air and catches the light off the lampposts, almost making her vehicle shine out of the corner of my eye. It takes me a moment to spot Eden again. She's crouched next to the wall of Jarvis Hall, staring toward a single figure moving along the cobblestone walkway toward the building that houses the Knights.

A fiery ball of anger forms in my stomach as I peer past her toward the looming structure. The Knights of Arcadia and I have a spotty history. Emotions so mixed it's as if barbed wire threads through my very thoughts. Can you both want something and hate it at the same time?

I narrow my gaze as she keeps to the shadows, almost like she's spying. Her free hand turns into a fist at her side and stays that way as she watches the lone figure disappear around the building toward the forest. The figure was clearly masculine but too far away to recognize. I lick my lips, watching after her. Could she see who it was? Was she interested because of the guy or because of the Knights in general?

Maybe I misinterpreted the fist clenching for anger when it's really sadness. Her sister did go here, after all. And since she was a Knight, this girl would obviously be curious about the building and the people.

Eden jumps, and I hunker down closer to the side of the Jeep so I'm not spied. Eden squeals and throws herself at a figure that emerges from the shadows. She wraps her arms around him tightly, and for the first time, I can see the tormented sadness clinging to her face. But it slowly fades to fondness as the guy holds her to him.

Grandfather certainly didn't say anything about Eden having a boyfriend. And who the fuck does this guy think he is hanging around Jarvis Hall? It's my territory.

"Edie...."

Edie?

Red hot jealousy rips through me as she clings tighter. She's like a delicate flower seeking nourishment, and he's giving her all she needs. My lip curls in disgust. I don't know why I covet sad, pretty things when all I want to do is tear their petals off one by one. But that's okay. This just became a better game, one a lot more rewarding than my grandfather pulling at my puppet strings. I can certainly fuck with *and* watch this girl at the same time. He didn't say hands off, not that I'm known for doing things one hundred percent by the book, anyway.

I casually walk back to my midnight black sports car that's purposefully lost within the recesses of the parking lot. My body thrums with electricity as I pull the door closed and watch while the couple starts to move.

Reaching for my phone, I send my grandfather another text. **There's a guy with her now.**

He responds immediately, apparently feeling the

need to keep me informed now, at least on this aspect.

Prince Oliver IX. He'll be staying there.

What kind of douche is a ninth? Fucking royalty. I crack my knuckles, calming myself before I break the screen typing out a response. **Staying with her? In a girls' dorm?**

He's fucking royalty. He can stay wherever he goddamn wants. And he wanted Jarvis.

The familiar, territorial anger pushes through the surface. **Another dick? In MY hall?**

In MY hall. Do I also need to remind you that you aren't matriculated at Carnegie anymore? You're to watch from afar. Share with me anything that sticks out.

I think the fuck not. If the old man wasn't feeble and responsible for my entire well-being, I'd shake the shit out of him. *No* men are allowed to stay at Jarvis but me. *Especially* with her.

My gaze tracks to her picture still lying on the passenger seat and then moves to the same figure walking next to a goddamn, real life prince. Seeing her in the flesh makes this all the more real and interesting. A pull tugs in my stomach. She's my next conquest. Only my body will tell me how far I'm willing to go and in whatever ways I want her. For some, just a good fuck is enough. For others, I let my imagination run wild.

My overpaid therapist tells me I have abandonment issues. In reality, I'm just the family miscreant who likes to fuck.

Welcome to Carnegie University, Eden Astor. I'm not sure how pleasant your stay here will be.

2

Eden

I've been waiting for this moment. Biding my time, planning in the background. The first step out of my car and onto the freshly paved blacktop at Carnegie University is the first step in the direction I've been dying to pursue since Dee died ten long months ago.

I'm finally here, amongst the huge maples blanketing campus. If you're into old buildings, manicured lawns, and forests, this place would be your sanctuary. Everywhere you look could be a postcard image. Turquoise blue ocean and powder sand are more my style, but it's not up to me anymore. Standing here, gazing at the gothic-style building that houses my new digs, a pang of sadness for the life I gave up echoes through me. I dropped out of my California state school immediately after Dee died. Following her funeral, I helped pick up the pieces back home. Currently, we're still moving around with robot-like precision, but at least we're not shattered remnants anymore.

Matriculating into CU was about as easy as could be. I have a feeling Admin just whited out Delilah from everything and typed *Eden* in its place. I have her old room. I'm in the same year as she was when she passed. Hell, they'll probably give me her old dining card, too.

Replacing her in real life won't be as easy. In fact, it's impossible. I'm nothing like her. Every time my parents look at me, I must remind them of that very fact. The only aspect I can replace her in is joining the Knights...maybe.

It's the biggest hurdle in my plan, but if I want to find out any information, I have to do what she did. I have to get the Knights to trust me. I have to seep into their rotten core and unveil their dirty secrets.

Infiltrate.

Expose.

Escape.

All in the name of my sister. If I'm wrong about them, I'm fucked. But I don't think I am.

I reach into the back of my Wrangler and pull out my bag. When my parents discussed emptying out her room here, I told them not to bother—my plan had already been forming. They didn't take the news as well as I'd hoped. They'd always wanted me to attend Carnegie with Dee, but apparently after one child dies, they don't want the next to follow in the other's footsteps.

The wheels of my luggage roll noisily over the cobblestones. I've been here a hundred times before but I still can't resist peeking at the building that I'll be all too acquainted with this year. It's far more sinister in the dark, the surrounding lights accentuating the horror movie feel.

Like I'm being drawn, I circle around the side of my new digs and peer across campus toward the stone building that's so far away it's practically in the forest. The Knights of Arcadia headquarters. In the distance, I spy a tall figure striding that way. I'm a day late getting to campus, so the telltale signs of move in day are long gone. There's no game of touch football or frisbee in the quad like there would've been at my last school. Everyone must be inside with the nice air conditioning and posh surroundings with the odd heatwave we're having. Everyone except this guy.

The figure moves with authority, his long strides eating up the walkway. I pull my bag up next to the exterior wall and crouch, spying. From this far away, I can't tell if it's a student Knight or an Elder. They're all the same to me, anyway. Suspects. In my bag, I have a list of Knights that I stole from my father's home office. I'll be crossing off names one by one until I get to the bottom of how the hell my sister died at their Devil's Night festivities. Every Knight was in attendance, which makes them all potential culprits. Except for my father, of course.

"What are we doing?" a voice whispers.

I jump to my feet, spinning. The intruder takes a quick step backward, avoiding my flailing limbs. It takes a minute for his face to come into view, but I spy his cheeky smile first. Recognition jolts through me. "Oliver?" I gasp.

His perfect grin spreads, and he tilts his head to the side, brown hair falling over his forehead, as he inspects me from head to toe and then back up again. "You weren't going to follow that guy, were you? As your best friend, I'd advise against that."

I fling myself at him, and he easily catches me. A sob lodges in my throat, and I attempt to breathe through it. "What are you doing here, asshole? I can tell you've been in England too long. You're all British-y."

He chuckles, his chest rumbling against mine. "That's my Eden, making up nonsensical words."

I pull away. "British-y is totally a word. It means your accent is stronger than it usually is."

He sets me on my feet, tugging the ends of my hair playfully. His grin flatlines shortly after. "How are you, Edie?"

My chest is seconds away from exploding, but I say, "fine," anyway.

He peers from me to the building I'd been scoping out. "Please tell me you weren't going all Nancy Drew already. Your first night here. With no backup."

I shrug, impatience swirling inside me. Even now I want to whirl back around to see if the figure is still there. Oliver showing up could have caught his attention. "I was just...looking." He frowns, a face that tells me he doesn't believe a word I'm saying. After grabbing my luggage, he turns toward the main door, leading the way to my new residence hall. Hurrying to catch up with him, I call out, "Why didn't you tell me you were coming?"

"It's called a surprise," he deadpans.

I roll my eyes. He knows I despise surprises, but that doesn't keep him from throwing them at me every chance he gets.

We turn the corner of the building, and I stop in my tracks. In front of us is a line of Mini Coopers with men in black suits in various stages of unloading boxes from them. "What the...."

He peers over his shoulder. "You didn't really think I was going to let you search for your sister's killer alone, did you?" My mouth unhinges, but Oliver continues as if he didn't just drop a bomb on me. His gaze darts toward one of his servants with silver hair. "Be careful with that," he orders. "My grandmother's tea set is in that box."

"Actually, sir," another voice eloquently starts, "I have the tea set."

Oliver's sharp reply pulls me out of my surprise. He doesn't care if they're holding a gift from his grandmother—the queen—or not. He wants them all to be careful or he'll shove his foot up their arses, *the insipid fools.*

Sounds like Oliver.

Despite the presence of his servants, Oliver keeps my bag. When he gets to the door, he glances back and frowns when I'm not right behind him. After finally spotting me still standing by the corner of the building, he relaxes a little. "Well, come on. We have to get settled in."

I blink, hardly believing the scene surrounding me. "Oliver, are you going to Carnegie, too?"

His eyes flash with a fondness I often see when he

and I are together. "They've been hounding me forever, so I figured it's time to shut their arses up."

I hold back a squeal and race to his side. Reaching up on my tiptoes, I give him a quick peck on the cheek. Oliver and I have been through everything together, and even though he was far away physically when Dee died, he was with me in every way that mattered. In fact, he's the only person in my life who I trust to know the full extent of why I'm here.

His cheeks bloom red, but he immediately trudges forward. "This way," he demands over his shoulder at the bevy of servants holding boxes and garment bags.

I watch him walk in, confusion spreading through me. "Oliver, this is a female dorm."

He laughs, the sound pure amusement. "It's cute that you think I care."

A servant sneaks in first and pushes the door wider. In front of us, a line of girls await. They're all dressed to the nines with their makeup and hair impeccable despite the late hour. I look like the poor stepchild in comparison. My shorts have trendy rips in them, and my tank top shows off my shoulders, which is a major faux pas in certain social situations. I just didn't know unpacking at Carnegie was one of them.

One of the girls starts to curtsy, "Prince—"

I hold back a barely restrained laugh. Oliver, however, practically rolls his eyes. "Oliver is fine."

"Are you sure?" she asks.

"Am I sure my name is Oliver? Quite," he answers without giving her a second glance.

I poke him in the side when the girl looks like she could cry. Sure, Oliver is technically a prince by birth and all that jazz, but he's not. Not *really*. His grandmother can't even publicly claim him because he's the product of a scandal everyone knows about but won't discuss. If you ask me, he's got the best of both worlds.

I step forward, and the line of four girls all move their gazes to me, their expressions paling as they take me in. "Wow. You must be Eden. You look just like—"

"I know," I interrupt, squelching the bitter pain that blooms inside my chest.

The first girl apologizes. "You probably get that a lot. We're so glad you decided to stay with us. We boxed up Delilah's stuff yesterday, and we just want you to know we miss her so much. She was an amazing—"

I turn my gaze toward the area where the girl's stare has wandered and find a dozen or so boxes taped and labeled *Delilah*. My stomach plummets. "You boxed up her stuff?"

"Yes," she says brightly. "We—"

My jaw clamps together as irritation spreads through me. A growl rips up my throat, "You touched her stuff without—"

"And that's our cue," Oliver speaks up, interrupting my verbal assault. He entwines our fingers and tugs me up the wooden stairs past my gobsmacked roommates, my luggage thumping behind us. "You certainly know how to make a first impression," he says as we approach Delilah's old room.

He swings the door open, and the complete barrenness of it slaps me in the face. I'd been looking forward to seeing Dee's room decorated how she had it. Not to mention I'd been hoping to find something to go on. A clue. A piece of evidence. "Fucking bitches," I seethe.

"They were trying to be nice."

"That's rich, coming from you." I turn around in a circle. This could be anyone's room. Actually, it's no one's room. It's deserted. Not one single thing of Delilah's is left in here. "No one asked them to do this."

Oliver sets my luggage down and closes the door behind us. Before he does, I spy his hired servants turning the corner to climb up the next set of steps.

Here we are, the two of us, enclosed in white walls and expensive-looking furniture. The hardwoods need a good sweep and dust has accumulated around the windowsills, except for the areas where Dee must have had something sitting. But I'll never know what, will I?

I run my hands through my hair, tears threatening at the corners of my eyes. It's like I'm losing Dee all over again. She was here, at least the remnants of who she was were all sitting right here as if she never left.

The complete emptiness of this room hits me right in the gut.

"Do you want me to go kick their arses?" Oliver asks. When I don't respond, he sighs. "It's probably for the best, Eden. You don't want to live with her ghost."

I snap my gaze toward him. Just because he's my best friend doesn't mean we see eye to eye *all* the time. "It's not about that," I fume. "Whatever information we could've gathered is fucking packed away in a box because those dumb, rich bitches don't understand anything. What if they threw shit out?"

Oliver blows out a breath, watching me. Turning, he yanks the door open and stops the first servant he sees. "Bring the other boxes from the foyer into this room...now." The servant hesitates as a few of his colleagues pass with more boxes. "I said now," Oliver grinds out.

"Right away, Sir."

My best friend turns, his previous harsh tone now subdued. "Happy?"

"Ecstatic," I deadpan.

"Hey," he says, moving forward, and I suddenly feel like a bitch for not being cheery during our reunion. I missed him, I really did. It just feels like there's so much on my shoulders right now. He slips a strand of my hair behind my ear. "We're going to figure this out. I promise. I'll be the Watson to your Sherlock Holmes. I'll single-handedly go through all the boxes myself if that's what you want."

I take a deep breath and let it out. "I'm glad you're here."

"I know," he grins.

He puts his arm around me and squeezes as his hired staff bring in all of Dee's boxes one after the other. Who knows what we'll find in them. Hopefully something useful, but if we don't, at least Oliver is here to help put together the puzzle pieces.

Relief floods through me. I've been alone for practically the last year, so this feels welcome. Like I have a partner again. Someone to lean on.

3

Oliver

*E*den Astor is like the family jewels I can't bear to lock away out of sight.

If I could, I'd wear her all day like exquisite gemstones dripping from my body. Being this close to her again makes my chest flutter with feelings I once wished I could suppress. She's made it extremely clear that she doesn't think of me like I think of her. A flash of anger springs through me, but it's quickly quelled when she sighs in her sleep.

Fucking beautiful.

Even when I was eight, I understood the figure I

was looking at was perfect for me in all the right ways. Her stubbornness, her smirk, and her refusal to play by the rules. Eden Astor has had my heart for as long as I can remember. Now if only I could steal hers, I'd consider it the conquest of a lifetime.

I trace my fingertips down her bare shoulder, skirting the loose strap of her tank top. Her eyelids flutter, and my cock hardens for her. I shove my free hand down my joggers, gripping myself fiercely. Restraint isn't my specialty. If I had it my way, I'd be flipping her around and burying my cock so deep in that tight cunt of hers that I'd probably embarrass myself immediately. Instead, I stroke the hard flesh in my fist, feeling heat pool in my balls.

As soon as Delilah died, I was on the next flight. I'd landed in California. I was out of the hired car and on my way to greet her like I had last night when she told me she wanted to be alone. From that moment forward, I stayed close, waiting until she gave me the go-ahead to see her. I followed her back home; I watched her every move while talking to her nearly every day, pretending I was still on another continent.

I drank myself into daily stupors because I could hear the life slowly draining from Eden's voice...and yet, she still refused to ask for me. The first hint of her turning around was when she confessed her plan. In that instant, I knew exactly what I was going to do. I'd follow her to Carnegie. I'd stay by her side. I'd go along with this ridiculous plan because it was what she needed.

Then she'd see. I'd make her.

She begged me to sleep next to her tonight, telling me she didn't want to be alone in Dee's hollow shell of a room. I watched as her face became peaceful and then cursed myself up and down for finding my way so close to something I can't have.

It's the greatest torture.

Her lips part, gaining my attention. Her tongue slowly caresses the seam of her mouth, then her breath catches. *Oh, shit.* I know that sound. I've replayed it in my head a million times while doing this very same thing.

Obeying my frustrated tugs, my cock lengthens. My movements are powered by an irrational anger simply because this in no way compares to pumping inside her. I should know.

Eden's a free spirit. Our friendship is a sturdy foundation, but that doesn't mean we haven't fallen into one another's arms for pleasure. Not sex. Not since I took her ripe little cherry when we were experimenting, young teens. And not a day goes by that I don't think about it.

I push the sheets over her hips and trace my fingers

along the edge of her midnight blue lace panties. In her dream-like state, she shifts to give me better access, squeezing her thighs together as if she's subconsciously trying to ease the desire inside her.

God, she's so fucking perfect.

My heart pounds as her shirt rides up, giving me a sliver of a view. Her taut skin moves with her breaths, belly button pushing upward ever so slightly with her inhale. I lower my gaze, tracing the dip that leads to her panties. My skin is charged, fingertips buzzing at being so close to her. I stroke myself harder, envisioning her bouncing on my cock like a porn star, her cunt squeezing the life out of me.

Moving my head, I groan into the pillow, tugging faster. Doing this right next to her is dangerous, but I don't care. If she wakes up, finding me next to her like this will ruin our relationship forever.

A small sigh parts her lips again, and I can't control myself. My balls pucker, and my hips careen forward with short thrusts into my palm until I erupt, my cum shooting onto the bed between our bodies. The milky white pool grows until I grunt into the pillow, finishing myself off.

But that's not enough for me. I need a taste. I need her.

My movements haven't woken her, but she's still flushed, as if her sleeping body and my awake one have shared a dirty secret. I sneak my fingers under the band of her panties, feel the brush of her coarse hair against my palm before settling over her clit. "Edie, baby, open up."

Her legs fall open as I swirl my fingers. I track my gaze up over her flat stomach to the peaks of her breasts. Her thin sleep shirt doesn't hide her pebbled nipples. "Oliver," she whispers, purposefully opening her legs wider now. Peering up, I meet her dream-like stare. "How did you know I needed this?"

I squelch my real response. The truth is, I can read her like a book. I know her better than myself. All the pent-up energy inside her needs to be released in a healthy way. Knowing my Edie, she'd turn to some degenerate, but if I'm right here, willing and ready, my hands will give her the freedom she desperately wants. "I'm smart," I tease, rubbing her right.

She drops her head back, an unrestrained moan filling the room. If there's anything Eden hates more, it's being kept in a cage. Her last name has been like cell bars her entire life.

"Ollie.... Do that thing I like," she breathes before reaching under her tank to play with her nipples. Her movements tug her collar down, showcasing a beautiful amount of cleavage.

Fuck. Me.

My heart pounds in my balls as I watch her lids

flutter closed in ecstasy. She arches her back, and I roll into place, gently easing her legs over my shoulders while moving her panties to the side. I breathe her in, salivating at her altar like a starving man. She lets out an unsteady pant when I settle. The same need swells in my balls, but I want more. I want to mark her, even if she doesn't know. I want her to be mine.

Swiping at my deposit on the sheets, I gather some of my cum on the tip of my finger before running it up and down her pussy, making her glisten with my spunk. She cries out, and I'm hard as fuck again imagining my cum is making her all the more turned on. While pushing her knees open, I scoop up some more. I place my cum above her hole, then push inside, filling her with *me*. She groans, lifting her hips, taking it all. Like she wants it. Like she can't wait to have more of me inside her.

"Oliver...."

I'm in a frenzy now that I've started. Like her pussy is a canvas, I paint her with my seed. An Oliver original. Branding her to prove she belongs to me. As if the next guy to come along will still be able to see me here. Taste me here.

Her thighs close around my head, telling me to get on with it. What I wouldn't give to take my time, to fuck her into oblivion. To announce what I've just done and wait for her reaction.

You're mine, Eden Astor. You don't know it, but you are.

I drag the tip of my tongue across her pussy in the shape of an *L*. She shudders, and so do I. I taste me on her. The combination of our juices is intoxicating. *O* is next. Her breath quickens as I finish, and when I glance up, she's squeezed her tits so tight, I spot a hard nipple spilling over the top of her tank top. *N* and *D* I do in quick succession while my cock strains in my boxers. My lids flutter closed at her taste, but I attempt to rein myself in, finishing off the word London in slow, steady strokes that have her moaning.

London Bridge. It's our game. We see how many times I can write those words across her pussy before she climaxes on my tongue. She tastes like sweet noth-ingness, a reprieve from the darkness my mind holds sometimes. I slip my hands under her ass and squeeze, bringing her closer like she's a savory platter only for me. I finish off the *E* in Bridge, then flick the tip of my tongue across her clit furiously, thinking about my cum marinating inside her.

Her moans escalate to a fever pitch. She's damn close. "Cheater," she calls out as she locks gazes with me. I nearly nut again at the lost look of passion in her eyes. But then she closes them, shielding me from view before throwing her head back and climaxing.

When she finishes, she eases the hold of her thighs

around my head and drops her knees to the mattress. Her fists that held onto the sheets during release now relax. For a moment, she breathes out in pure contentedness, then pulls herself up on her forearms, arranging her tank back into place. "How about you, number five?" She waggles her brows and peeks at the clear tent in my boxers.

Easing off the bed, I plot my escape. That's not part of the plan. "That's what I have hands for," I tell her, pointing to the attached bathroom.

"You sure?" she asks. Sliding her hand along the bed, she just barely misses my remaining spunk darkening the sheets. "This isn't a one-way street, you know."

I cock my head at her, trying to focus on the conversation instead of the fact that she now has my cum on her hands. "Take advantage of my depressed best friend? I don't think so."

She frowns, sticking her chin in the air in that Astor way. I swear in some instances, her family acts more superior than mine. "I'm a big girl, Oliver."

I give her a placating smile to smooth things over. All the things I want to say get stuck in my throat, and I over analyze until I retreat into the bathroom without having said anything. I cum quick—again. The pure white tile of a dead girl's shower now tainted by my splooge. It was especially easy when picturing Eden glistening with my cum, moaning for it, taking it inside her unknowingly. I've rubbed myself raw with thoughts of her in my head before, but not like this. This was like I was a preteen again, and I was glad for the shower to drown out the sound of my own ragged release.

I'm a filthy bastard.

Afterward, I clean up, then grab a towel from a small cubby. Nothing of Eden's is unpacked yet, so this must have been left behind. The bare countertop in front of me is crowned with an ornate mirror. Steam distorts my view as I run my hands through my hair to tame it before opening the bathroom door and reappearing with the towel wrapped around my waist.

Eden's back is turned to me, and she's pulling on a tie-dye shirt with rips across the midsection over a pair of shorts. I swallow my desire. I don't know how I'm going to go through the day with the knowledge that a part of me is inside her. When she turns, I replace my look of lust with a smirk. "What are you doing?"

She reaches down to close her luggage without even glancing at me and zips it back up. "What does it look like?"

"It looks like you're dressing like a homeless person."

She stops to glare at me, her gaze pausing on my

bare chest briefly. "You've never cared how I dressed before."

"That's because you weren't planning on infiltrating a secret society that prides itself on breeding. In fact, you were content with doing the exact opposite."

She frowns down at her clothes then peers at the boxes that are stacked in the corner.

Before she can crack open her sister's things, I announce, "We're going shopping, Edie."

She huffs. "I'm not buying stuffy clothes."

"I guess you really don't care to make it into the Knights, then," I say as I saunter toward the door.

I don't even get that far before she sighs. "Fine. I'll buy some new things. I guess. Though I don't know if it really matters."

She sure as hell does know it matters. She's just fighting against it because that's what Eden does. It's impossible for her not to be herself, but if she really wants to get into the Knights and try to unveil their secrets, she can't be herself. I take a deep breath, hating that I can see her struggling, but not knowing how to comfort her in any real way other than orgasms disguised as friendly relations. "Just stick with me," I tell her, reaching for the handle of her door.

"Going somewhere, number five?" she asks. I peer over my shoulder to find her holding my discarded clothes in her grip. "You better put something on before one of our new roommates has a royal heart attack." She winks at me and chuckles at her own joke.

"I can see the tabloids now."

She throws the clothes at me as she passes. "Meet in a half hour?" she asks before slipping into the bathroom, not waiting for my answer.

Part of me wants to sneak up to my room with just the towel, but I know Eden's right. For some reason, girls seem to lose their minds about the royalty thing. I probably couldn't even make it up the next flight of steps without sneaky pictures being taken that will somehow make their way to my family and the gossip magazines. *Bad Boy Royal* isn't my moniker for nothing. They started to run with it when I was a teenager, so I lived up to their expectations. No one actually sees me as a royal, anyway. At least no one important.

Huffing, I pull on last night's clothes and dart up to my room. I don't spy anyone on the way, but that never means anything.

The servants were busy last night. I peer around, noting all of my boxes are unpacked and put away. My directions were followed to the T. Just like I expect. Surveying the space further, I admire its cleanliness, though it's small. Cramped, even.

Right now, those same servants I brought with me are shacking up in a house I rented a mile away. The plan is to convince Eden to move off campus eventually, but that'll take time.

It'll be safer there. The Knights are dangerous. I may not be fully sold on the fact that they had anything to do with Dee's sad death, but they do prey on girls.

And I'll be damned if I let that happen to Edie.

4

Eden

I open the door to Oliver casually leaning against the doorjamb. He looks like he just stepped off a polo field with a collared shirt and khaki shorts. He's even wearing loafers with a pair of dark sunglasses perched on top of his head. I asked him once if he ever got tired of dressing like such a spoiled rich kid. He told me to bugger off...and I love him for it.

I see his point about needing different clothes to fit in, I just wish I didn't. Shedding this one last layer will be the only remnant of who I was.

"Chin up, Astor. It's not the end of the world."

"Says you. You love this shit."

He scoffs as he steps back, gesturing for me to lead the way down the stairs. "You act as if we didn't have the same upbringing. Quit being a snob toward elitists."

"Said no one ever," I complain. I escaped to the West Coast to get away from all this. I don't want rich friends who would rather stab you in the back than fight at your side. I don't want my money—or lack thereof—to matter more than who I am. And I certainly don't want to be farmed out to another rich family like Delilah is.

Was.

My stomach clenches, but I breathe through it. I have a sneaking suspicion Mom and Dad tried that shit with me, but they didn't get any takers. No one wants the black sheep of the family, and I'm perfectly fine with that. It pays to be the wild child sometimes.

The rooms downstairs are empty. With the impression I made on my new roommates last night, they're probably avoiding me. Maybe Oliver was right. I could've tried to be nice, but really, who touches a dead girl's things? I can't even see a scenario where that would be okay.

This is the level of privilege I'm dealing with here.

Oliver skirts in front of me to pull open the main door. The line of Mini Coopers is now gone. Among the luxury sedans, SUVs, and sports cars in the parking lot, my Jeep sticks out like a thorn among roses.

"Want me to call my driver?" Oliver asks, reaching for his phone. Ever since he got into a car accident that made international news, he's had a thing about driving in America. Now, he brings a driver with him everywhere.

"Don't be afraid," I tease. "Hop in. Point me in the right direction."

He peers over at me before lowering his sunglasses. "You don't know where to go?"

"I know where to go for *my* clothes. Shouldn't you know where to go for *your* clothes?"

He heaves a sigh and pulls out his phone. "Sure thing. I'll look up 'stores for normal people'."

I crack a smile. "Let's just get this over with, Pretty Boy."

A few touches to the screen later, and the robotic GPS voice filters through the phone speaker. Oliver leans back in the seat as I reverse out of the space. With the windows down, the wind tangles my hair as we take the main road into the closest town. It's not large by any means, and I'm pretty sure it only survives because it's a place for all the CU students to get away from campus. I'm honestly surprised it didn't take us to the bigger tourist town nearby, but who knows, that stop might be next if Oliver has anything to say about it.

As the mechanical voice directs me to park, Oliver sits up to stare out the windshield. He spies the small shop called Trendz, his raised brows barely skimming the tops of his sunglasses. I love him to death, but he is the definition of a snob. Despite his scandalous lineage, he doesn't want for anything. A fact that is solidified by the generous account the queen secretly filters money into. "Come on, this was your idea," I remind him.

He pushes the passenger door open with a disgruntled look and steps out. We meet at the front of the Jeep where he holds the crook of his elbow out for me. I snake my hand through, and we walk arm in arm to the main door. A clanky bell that sounds as if it retired after a few hundred Christmases rings overhead when we enter. The browsing patrons don't pay us any mind while we scour the place. Immediately, Oliver leads me to a section that looks like my mother single-handedly designed every piece.

My stomach pulls tight with memories of her dressing me up like Dee's clone—putting bows in our hair, matching outfits...fucking frilly dresses. I never minded regular dresses, but dear God, don't put me in anything with ruffles.

Oliver spies the frown on my face and gives me a heartfelt smile. "It's the only way, Eden. Dressing like everyone else is the lowest rung on the fucked up ladder compared to what you're here to do."

I finger a blue, silk blouse...with frills. "I guess it just feels the most personal."

"Because you identify with being the Astor who doesn't conform. I get it."

I peek at him, finding my best friend thin-lipped, his brown hair falling over his forehead in a cute curl. Growing up, I often thought of Oliver as my opposite. He did everything he was supposed to, despite what everyone thought of him, just for the sliver of a chance to fit in with his family. But they never actually accepted him, no matter how hard he tried. They just gave him scraps of their attention, and he ate it up despite the big game he talked. It's a different story now. He may look like the perfect royal, but he's the perfect royal stain. At least, they dubbed him that in a tabloid headline once.

I give him a small smile and pretend to search through one of the hideous racks. "I'm going to need your help."

"Obviously," he deadpans as he moves to another rack and starts throwing clothes over his arm.

When he keeps going, amounting a fair number of outfits over his shoulder, I gasp. "Hey, how do you even know that's my size?" I stride toward him and peek at the tags. Oddly, he's pretty much nailed it. I shrug, and he gives me a smug smile in response.

After he has way more garments than I've ever wanted to try on in a lifetime, we search for the dressing rooms and find a small seating area in front of two rooms with velvet curtains pushed back, revealing an oversized mirror and a low bench pushed to one side. He walks right in and sets up the clothes on the hooks provided before ducking out again. Instead of sitting and waiting, he takes my arm, walks me in, and then pulls the ivory velvet curtain closed behind him as he exits. Almost as if he thought I might try to escape.

Huh. Maybe he does know me.

I start to undress, my angry movements a staccato of frustration. "I don't know why I have to try these on. I—" When I spot the tired eyes staring back at me in the mirror, I stop complaining. The red veins are practically permanent now. For a girl who wants to find out what happened to her sister, I seem to be bitching an awful lot.

"Eden? You were saying?" Oliver prompts.

"Nothing," I tell him, trying to keep the sadness out of my voice. I'm being ungrateful and prissy. I'll wear a meat suit if that's what it takes to find out what happened to Dee.

After pulling on the first outfit that Oliver's help-fully laid out for me, I stare at myself in the mirror. The soft ivory sweater would've complimented my California tan. Now, though, it just washes me out. The skinny belt paired with fancy leggings are nice, though. I freeze when I stare at the big picture. The blonde hair coupled with these clothes means I look like Delilah. I pull the collar of the sweater up and breathe in deeply, expecting to find her signature scent, but instead, I just get a huge lungful of...nothing.

Before I can think too much, I push aside the curtain and step out. Oliver is sitting on the couch, one leg over his opposite knee. He breaks into a grin, his hair a burnt honey color under the fluorescents. "Little Edie Astor, you're so grown up."

I flip him off, which only makes him laugh. "What do you think? Is it a yes or a no?"

"I think you finally fit in," he muses.

Despite myself, my heart squeezes a little. It hasn't been easy to be the one who thinks outside the box. The one my parents were always worried about, and the one who always got all the complaints. Once I told them I was going to Carnegie, a small part of me thought they would be enamored with the fact that I would be taking Dee's spot, but instead—again—all I got were worried stares. Deep down, I understood that they were for completely different reasons, but I still couldn't shake the feeling that I was letting them down once again.

I try on outfit after outfit, getting Oliver's thumbs up or down. He even pulled a couple of dresses from an area in the back that I modeled for him like the good little high-society girl. I have a closet full of dresses like this back home for when I'm made to play the part of dutiful Astor daughter—and I'm sure Dee has a whole slew of them in one of the boxes the roommates packed up—but we end up deciding to get three, anyway. Because in the elite world, you never know when you're going to need a nice dress.

The whole process is freaking exhausting.

I'm sitting on the bench inside the dressing room, deciding which one of my new outfits to wear out, when Oliver pulls the curtain back a little. "Can I come in?"

I scoot over, allowing him space to sit. He leans his head against the wall, narrowly avoiding a garment hook. When he doesn't talk, I take that as a cue that he came in here so I could. "Dee liked clothes," I start, which sounds so dumb if you pick the sentence apart. Who doesn't like clothes? They're necessary. Everyone has them. But Dee took pride in what she wore. She understood there was a statement that could be made with the right outfit. She understood that about a lot of things. She spoke up when she needed to. She didn't fight at the wrong times, she waited for her moment. Her favorite advice was to tell me I was being so obnoxious fighting about everything all the time when I should pick my fight *and* the time, then really dig down.

The Knights were her digging down. It wasn't just about the prestige that came with being a Knight or making Dad happy, she wanted to make a difference. She wanted to push the envelope of our male-driven society to allow space for women like us.

Her voice rings in my head, and I smile. *It's the twenty-first century, after all. It's about damn time.*

Oliver reaches over, enveloping my hand with his. "You did good, Edie. I know it's hard to lose yourself."

"Just temporary, right?" I ask, trying to shrug it off.

"Exactly. They're just clothes. It doesn't mean you'll lose what's on the inside. The Eden Astor I know would never do that."

"Bullheaded?"

"Terribly. Astronomically," he adds. "Never met anyone like you."

His humor fades while he finishes the sentence, his voice dropping a few octaves as he takes me in. He's been doing that the last few times I've seen him.

I immediately get to my feet and gather the thumbs down outfits. Sometimes I hate that we crossed a line we probably shouldn't have. Sometimes, I'm certain he thinks we're more than we are. Before I'd orgasmed this morning, he'd held my gaze. He *looked*. Like we were lovers.

It's fucking scary. I've already lost Delilah, I can't lose Oliver, too. And if I break his heart, I will.

"I'll get these," he says, voice lost in thought as he gathers up the approved clothes.

After he leaves, I take a minute to breathe. I can't deal with anything new right now. I don't want to break down and talk to Oliver about whatever these looks mean. My hands are full with everything else.

Taking in a slow, ragged breath, I center myself and then walk from the changing room. I spy an empty rack against the wall, so I hang the rejects up to await restocking. Oliver's cheery voice floats through the room, and I follow it until I find him making small talk with a beautiful cashier. I try to hang back so she doesn't think we're together, but when she looks over his shoulder and spots me, she goes pale. "Y-you...."

I close my eyes, feeling the familiar crack in my chest.

"You're—"

"No," Oliver interrupts. "This is Eden, you're probably mistaking her for—"

"Dee," the girl finally finishes. She peers from Oliver to me and back again, questions written all over her face. "Sisters?"

Now I'm curious, too. I walk toward the counter

and notice her hands are shaking. Why would Dee be on a first-name basis with this girl? "Delilah was my sister," I confirm. "I go to Carnegie now."

She blanches, blinking rapidly. "I'm sorry," she says eventually. "It's just—" She pauses to swallow, and then her eyes fade as if she's reliving a memory. "I was there the night she died. Me and my friends were the last to see her, you know?" She finally looks back at me and frowns. "I'm so sorry. I really liked your sister."

My mind whirls. This girl was *there*? At a Knight party? She certainly wasn't invited as a guest, so she had to have been invited for another reason. Even though Dad never confirmed, I knew it was a Knights of Arcadia event. Dee had sent me one final text, a picture of a castle with the message saying, **Don't ask.** That was always code for secret society stuff, and I hadn't cared to ask either. I remember thinking the castle was beautiful, though, right before I put my phone down without responding.

Pressing my lips together, I can feel my body buzz with anticipation. Who would've thought a terrible trip to get clothes would result in finding someone who was actually there—and *not* a Knight? I clear my throat. "So, you were there when it happened?" I ask.

The girl across from me nods solemnly. "We didn't know what was going on at first. She never came back to lead us upstairs to the party. Eventually, we walked out to find people gathering by the docks. It was awful."

My stomach tightens so hard it feels as if I might expel everything roiling around inside. Instead, I take a steadying breath, trying not to let the emotion show. "Tell me everything?" I ask, giving her a small, hopeful smile. "I only know what they told me, which isn't much."

She peers around the shop as if she'd rather do anything else but what I'm asking.

"Tell you what," Oliver interferes. "Eden and I are going to a coffee shop around the corner. No pressure, but we'd love to buy you a drink and you can talk about what happened."

The cashier nibbles on her lip. "Maybe...." She takes a peek at me, then closes her eyes. "Yeah—yes. I'll be there. I get a break in an hour."

5

Eden

*H*olly sits across from us, eyes darting around the small, eclectic coffee shop with owners who must love the color teal more than anything else in life because it's everywhere. Despite the unique interior, it's a popular place. Oliver and I had to wait to get a spot with chairs facing each other. Luckily, we got it just before the Trendz cashier walked in.

The knots in my stomach tighten. Fate is either funny or an outright bastard. Who would've thought that an outing to buy me clothes I don't want turned into an opportunity to talk to someone who was actually at the party Dee died at? Dad stayed silent on how and where she was found, which isn't at all out of character. He never says much about the Knights. They're supposed to be a secret, after all.

I anxiously pull at the new clothes I'm wearing. Oliver sits in the black velvet armchair next to me, relaxing back. Despite his outward appearance, his eyes are sharp as we both take Holly in. If it was a Knights party, why was this girl there? It's the only question that runs through my mind over and over again, but my throat is too thick to ask it. Instead, we both just wait for our new friend to sip her coffee a few times to get comfortable.

"Holly," Oliver eventually prompts.

She nearly jumps. Her gaze darts to me again, and for the second time, she looks as if she's seen a ghost. "Sorry," she whispers. "I'm just trying to come up with the right words."

I lean forward, placing my elbows on my thighs. Somehow, this would be easier if I were wearing the clothes from this morning. I feel like an imposter in this. "Nothing you say is going to make this worse for me, I promise. I want to know what happened that night." Inside, my body feels as if it's one big heartbeat of anticipation. Nerves thrum through me as I watch the girl struggle.

"Start with why you were at a Knights party," Oliver suggests.

Her mouth drops, crimson staining her cheeks. "I'm not supposed to talk about them. NDAs and all that."

My fingertips tingle. "NDA before or after Delilah died?"

"Before. Dee told us we couldn't talk about the party, and if we did, everything we got would be forfeit."

Oliver puts on his disarming smile. Leaning forward, he traces his fingertips over the girl's wrist and thickens his accent. I swear he's like a succubus that switches on the charm, turning everyone to putty in his wake. "We obviously know about the Knights, Holly." Oliver continues to tell the girl everything we already know about that night, including why my sister was there—and it works.

She relaxes, gripping the coffee mug in her hand again as Oliver sits back. She giggles awkwardly. "Right. Okay. My friends and I were Angels for the party. You know, the *entertainment*," she says, widening her eyes as if to convey the message without actually saying it. "Dee organized everything. She told us when to show up, she arranged our gift bags, she was a part of the judges panel, everything. It was awkward at first, but seeing a girl there made everything better, you know? We were all less afraid."

Entertainment? Delilah *hired* these girls? My brain buzzes with questions. That doesn't seem like something my sister would do. She hated the misogyny aspect of the Knights. And hired them to do...what exactly? I can't even wrap my head around it.

"Everything was fine," Holly rushes out, and I try to school my face into something impassive. "Oh, well, she did get into an argument with someone on the dock when we got there. He was tall, muscular, had a nice ass." A second later, crimson stains her cheeks and she stutters, "Forget I said that. It's not important. Um, I couldn't hear what they were arguing about, but then we were given a tour of the castle and shown to the dressing room. She said she had a meeting and would be back, but she never returned."

My ears perk up. "A meeting? Do you know with who?"

Holly shakes her head, frowning. "She didn't say. She was running around like a crazy woman trying to get everything done. The party seemed really important to her. She organized all of our generous gift bags. I was worried we were going to have to give them back since we didn't really do anything, but no one said anything. It was such a shock to watch everything unfold." Her voice breaks, and her eyes glaze over. "I've never been around a dead body before. When they pulled her out of the river—" She cuts herself off and looks over apologetically. "They broke everyone up, then organized boats to take everyone off the island that didn't have to be there. We had just enough time to return to the dressing room to get our things before we were whisked away with threats reminding us of the NDAs we'd all signed."

A creepy-crawly sensation skitters up my spine. "Were the police there when you left?" I wait for her answer, even though I already know what it's going to be. The rich men in my world operate under different rules than the rest of the world. Dilute the scandal before it begins is one of their mantras.

She shakes her head. "No. The next morning, my friends and I saw it on the news, so we think they just wanted to spare us the nightmare of all of that. Hours of questioning and...." She shivers.

"Not fucking likely," I breathe out, keeping my voice low. They weren't caring about anything but themselves.

"So, the police never questioned you?" Oliver asks. "Not even after a few days?"

"No. To my knowledge, they don't even know we were there. Which is fine. I couldn't tell them anything new, anyway. The poor girl drowned. It was tragic."

Her gaze flicks to me. "I'm so sorry that happened to her...and you. They said she couldn't swim."

A dazed feeling takes over as I remember the newsreels, the anchor announcing the tragic death of the Astor heiress who couldn't swim. They made her sound like an idiot for being in the fast-moving river at night without a personal flotation device. Before I can reply, Oliver puts on the schmooze again and miraculously convinces her that she should get back to work. Afterward, he leads her out of the café while I digest everything she's said.

When he returns, he sits and turns toward me. "You've got that cute wrinkle between your eyes."

"I'm thinking," I tell him. He lets me do just that, and after a couple of minutes, I finally speak up. "A few things. One, why the hell was Dee hiring women for the Knights' entertainment? That sounds like the last thing she would do. Two, who did she get into a fight with? Three, who did she have a meeting with? Four, if one more fucking person tries to tell me Dee drowned because she couldn't swim, I'm going to scream."

"Well, she couldn't swim," Oliver offers.

I glare at him. I've never slapped him before, but there's a first time for everything. "There's a difference between wouldn't and couldn't. Everyone acts like she got in the water and then couldn't swim to save herself.

The problem with that is, she wouldn't have gotten in the water at all, Oliver," I grind out, my voice rising. "She didn't do it. She wouldn't have. If she was going to do it at all, she would've waded into the Mediterranean off a sandy beach, not jump into cold river water with retaining walls that no one can just climb out of. For fuck's sake."

"Okay, okay," Oliver comforts, reaching out his hand to place it on my knee.

"I know my sister," I growl.

"I know," he says. "I'm sorry." Sighing, he picks up his drink and takes a sip. After giving it a disparaging look, he peers back at me. "Have you spoken to Keegan? He had to have been there, *and* he's a Knight. If anyone would know exactly what was going on that day, it would be him."

Hearing my sister's forced fiancé's name makes me cringe. I am not Keegan Forbes' biggest fan. He treated my sister like shit, and after she died, he never came around. Some fiancé he was. He couldn't care less that she's even gone, I bet.

"I know that look says fuck Keegan Forbes, but he's important in all of this. If you want, we could try to talk to another Knight, but—"

"No, I know," I groan. "I'm putting it off. We don't exactly see eye to eye, and I've heard fuck all about him. He's supposed to be a senior this year, but apparently follow through isn't his biggest asset."

"He'll be here," Oliver says confidently. "The Forbeses won't accept anything less."

He's right. Even if Keegan doesn't want to be, his dad would never let him get away with not showing up. "I can't promise I won't kick his ass the first time I see him."

"I'll get my mobile ready."

I smile at Oliver's wink and then run my hands through my hair. Keegan's been a glaring blind spot when it comes to Dee. Last I knew, they were fighting, but she always had a propensity to forgive him that I never understood. To me, Keegan is the epitome of what I hate in this society. The words privileged, rich, and monster come to mind. His silence after the fact says a lot, too. Not even a phone call. Not even a drop-in visit.

He was suspiciously absent at the funeral, too. His parents were there, standing off the right shoulder of my father, but Keegan wasn't.

I'm not going to lie that the thought hadn't crossed my mind that he did it. Maybe he didn't want to be tied down to her and saw no other way out. Maybe she pissed him off, and he just overreacted. And this mystery guy she had a fight with? Maybe a boyfriend? I can't even list the number of times I told her to forget about Keegan and get herself someone else. Maybe she finally took my advice and it meant the end for her.

"I know it's going to suck, but I think the next thing we do is track Keegan down and ask him questions."

"We'll have to be strategic," I offer. "If he didn't care for Dee at all, he won't help us."

Oliver turns his head, his gaze narrowing. "What are you thinking?"

"Nothing."

"No, you think he might have done it, don't you?"

I shrug. Like Dee, I remember the Keegan Forbes from when we were kids. He was nothing like the guy he is now. I don't know what the fuck happened, but for whatever reason, Delilah thought she could find the guy he used to be. In my opinion, people don't change. They only grow into their true colors. "Or he might know who did. If it's either of those possibilities, he won't be forthcoming with answers. The Knights are tight-knit...." Which is why they've never been dragged out into the open. Shit doesn't stick to them, even though I'm almost certain of a few times when they should've been exposed.

"If you ask me, Keegan doesn't seem like the type to get his hands dirty."

He's got a point. If I were a Knight and wanted to take someone out, I'd hire a professional. "Unless it was a crime of passion...."

"Okay, come on," Oliver says, trying to reel me in. "Let's not get stuck on one person. It could've been anyone."

"Which is why it's horseshit that they got rid of all the outside witnesses before they even called the police."

"That's typical, though," Oliver hedges. "Minimize the scandal. If the cops came and there were all these women there ready to entertain old men, that would've been the focus of the news. Currently, it sounds like a tragic death, but news of a scandalous party with half-naked college girls hired as entertainment for a secret society of men mostly three times their age would be a whole different story to contain. Absolute rubbish," he spits.

His frustration is well-founded. He's always being dragged into royal drama, and everything he does is dissected and spun until it makes him look like the ultimate bad boy. If the paparazzi were to get a photo of us together, the headline would read something like Bad Boy Royal Stalking American. "No one knows you're here, right?" I ask hopefully.

"No, I pulled some cloak and dagger shit. I figure the best place to hide is in a private yuppie school where everyone else is as self-absorbed as I am, so no one will care about me."

"Except you got that greeting last night," I remind him, smirking.

"Yeah, I'll pass," he grunts, turning away.

"Are you kidding? Don't say that. I'm the best wing woman you've ever had. Actually, you could've totally gotten into Holly's pants if you wanted."

He flicks his gaze to me and the same feelings from this morning pop up again. Immediately, my stomach clenches and I peer away.

"Whatever you say, Edie," he responds solemnly.

"Don't let me kill your vibe this year," I tell him nonchalantly after picking up my drink to take a sip. "You know how the Americans just love your accent. You'll be the hottest thing on campus."

"I'm only here for one reason."

His words punch a hole in my chest, and as he stares, I make a vow not to fall into old patterns when it comes to my best friend. For both of our sakes.

6

Leo

Thinly veiled anger threads through me as I approach the gate to my grandfather's estate, pandering to the emergency summons I received from him a half hour ago.

After inputting the code, the iron bars swing free, and I coast up the driveway while the replica of the White House comes into view. When I was little, he told me to dress for the way I wanted people to treat me, for the job I wanted, and for the life I deserved. He took that to the extreme when he built this place. It's a joke amongst he and his friends, but in reality, his superiority complex knows no bounds. If someone as devious as my grandfather ever made it that high up the political ladder, America would have a lot more problems than they think they do.

I twist the key in the car's ignition and the growling engine cuts out abruptly. Whenever he requests my presence, I never enjoy it. Coupled with the fact that I'm tired as fuck from watching the Astor girl stroll around town with her boyfriend most of the day, I have serious doubts that I'll walk back out of here calm and collected. I'll be surprised if I can keep myself in check enough to avoid a confrontation with him.

After letting myself in the front door, I stride toward Grandfather's office. Despite it being just him, every light in the house is on. My grandmother died a couple years ago of cancer, which allowed my grandfather to focus even more on his business and desires. He lives with his power and greed openly now.

"In here, Leonardo," my grandfather's steady voice beckons.

No doubt he's tracked my approach on the dozens of cameras he has set up around the property. When I appear in the doorway, he peers at me over the rims of his glasses before waving me inside. "Come in."

The patriarch of the Jarvis family, though long past middle-aged, is surprisingly well-kept. Striking silver hair styled across the crown of his head makes him less elderly looking and more distinguished. There's not one thing about his looks that suggests he's frail or weak. It's the opposite, actually. When I was a kid, he told me he drank the blood of his enemies to stay in good shape, and I believed him for the longest time. The few creases currently marring his forehead have only recently embedded his flawless skin, only pointing to the fact that he's too busy with business matters that he's flaked on his Botox appointments. "You wanted to see me?"

His lips thin at my greeting. Franklin Jarvis is nothing if not old school. He frowns at my appearance, but it doesn't get to me like it used to. My grandfather and I have a sordid history. I've never been smart enough, savvy enough, or good enough for my family name. My own father almost drank himself into an early grave because of this man, so I should be happy I haven't succumbed yet. "Still obstinate, I see."

"Same as the last time we spoke."

He mutters under his breath something that sounds suspiciously like rotten egg. The truth is, my grandfather hates most things about me. My tattoos, my disdain for tradition, my lack of respect. But there's one thing we'll always have in common that I can't stand when it's reflected back in his eyes: the crave for power. I don't want to sit in an office chair all day, but I sure as fuck love the high of having people scurry around me like they don't want to even breathe in my direction for fear of my reaction. Louder, my grandfather says, "I'm going to regret this, but something has come up."

The way his gaze drags across the tattoos skirting up my arms makes me smirk. I don't bother hiding it, and we end up glaring at one another. Anytime I can make the old man unhappy is a win in my book, especially since he takes so much pleasure in making my life a living hell.

I don't break first, though I know I should. I'm fucking tired from following a girl around that makes my dick hard. That is...*used* to make my dick hard. She went shopping and came out looking exactly like every other rich bitch I grew up with. After that, I was done for the day. I skipped out early when she and her boyfriend left the café in town. She's boring as fuck—a sheep. If Grandfather's worried about her, he's getting fucking senile.

Instead of going to my place to take a nap, I ended up calling an old friend to fuck out some of my pent-up frustration. I was balls deep inside her when Grandfather called and requested this meeting. I fucked her real slow, her red hair wrapped in my hand, as I confirmed I would be here. Right before I hung up, I slammed inside her so hard her scream would've been the last noise he heard before the line disconnected.

I drop into the chair opposite him, over this

meeting before it's even officially started. "If it's about the girl, she's nothing. Looks like a mouse to me." My lip curls when I replay her walking from the dress shop in those clothes. And I thought she'd be interesting to play with too, but I should've known better. Carnegie girls are all the same.

Franklin Jarvis shakes his head, disappointment darkening his features. "I was hoping I wouldn't have to do this." Standing from his seat, he buttons his suit jacket while he walks around the desk. He comes up behind me, and my shoulders instantly straighten as I wait for the ball to drop.

His presence is looming and sinister, like always. I know the things he's done, and I know how he could just as easily make those things happen to me. When he finally speaks, he's so close that I have to dig my fingernails into the chair to keep from reacting. "You do know how much I have your balls in a vise, don't you, Leonardo? You can keep pontificating that you don't care about this family, but I don't see you out there doing anything about it. It's a lot of talk for a small-minded man. I'll pull the plug on everything you've got coming to you, son. You know I will."

I grit my teeth. When you're a Jarvis, there are stipulations to your inheritance, and yes, my grandfather does have me by the fucking nuts. I wish I'd stayed gone. But there's that little piece of me that wants nothing more than to rightfully take my father's money and do whatever the fuck I want with it. And I can't do that until I'm twenty-five. Dear old Grandfather knows he has me until then, so he gives me the shittiest jobs ever—nothing he would ever ask of my cousins, that's for damn sure. "Yes," I force out.

"Yes, sir," he corrects.

It kills me to do it, but I repeat his words back to him anyway, retreating inside myself at the helplessness that wafts over me. I was witness to so many instances between my father and grandfather that went the same as this. My father was never his favorite. According to my grandfather, my whole branch of his family line is cursed with defiance.

I just call it not wanting the past to repeat itself.

"There," he says. "Was that so hard?"

I swallow to keep my response at bay. I've thought about just murdering the old prick, but there are consequences to that too. Even if I could get away with it, there are always stipulations upon stipulations for family screw-ups like me. In order for me to receive my father's inheritance when I turn twenty-five, my grandfather has to be alive and well—or passed from *natural* causes beyond any reasonable doubt. So, yes, indulging this man is getting harder by the day, but I do my best not to let it show. "Not at all," I tell him, forcing myself to calm.

"Excellent."

He walks back around the side of the desk and slips a shiny object into his pocket. My jaw clenches. In my world, you worry about things like the patriarch of your family taking you out. If I died, he'd take my father's money and add it to his ever-growing stash. There is no next of kin. Just me. That's why I fought so hard to get my father on the right track, but it never worked.

The old man killed him.

I force a smile on my face that likely looks about as fake as it feels with the whipping current of trepidation roaring through me. He wanted me to see the gun for the threat it is. If he hadn't, I never would've caught a glimpse. "What can I help with...Sir?"

His answering smile is telling. He loves breaking me down and making me conform. "The Knights are worried about the new class of pledges and the precedent the Astor girl started."

"The dead girl?" I muse, wondering where this is going. She's dead. She didn't achieve anything but prove women shouldn't be in the Knights.

He rolls his eyes and shakes his head. "We must always look for our weak spots and counteract before a play has been made, Leonardo. Have I taught you nothing?"

My jaw tenses at his reprimand. "What's the concern, then? The sister's a waste of time. Trust me."

He lifts a gray-haired brow before sitting. "Astor is requesting the youngest daughter have the opportunity to pledge."

I run my hands down my thighs. I despise talking about the Knights. The lot of them can go fuck themselves for all I'm concerned, but it's about the part I'm playing now. Pacify the old man, that's it. "She wants to follow in her sister's footsteps?"

"Or is she attempting to drum up trouble? She's probably a meddling little bitch, just like her sister."

"Which is why I'm following her," I remind him. The older he gets, the more paranoid he becomes. I still think she's a dead end, but whatever. Arguing with him will get me nowhere.

"The Elders have had to field questions about our membership," he spits, gaze darkening as he picks up a pen from his desk. "Unfortunately, a brash yet obvious decision has been made to quell the whispers coming from all sides. It pains me greatly, but the Knights are now opening admission to both fine young men *and* women. We're no longer a fraternal organization. At least on paper."

My eyes widen. When I heard Delilah Astor was pledging the Knights as a favor to Astor, I thought it was a big joke. One thing the Knights hate more than simplicity is females fucking up their play time. They're objects, plain and simple. To hold the rank of

Knight would've been impossible even before she started. The Elders wouldn't have let her get that far. I was surprised she made it past Pledge to Fledgling even. "I don't understand. Why?"

"Because the whispers are that Delilah Astor was killed *because* she was a girl."

"Is it true?"

Franklin Jarvis smirks. "Well, that would've been too simple." He sets the pen back down. "Her death was an accident. This, however, is why we don't let women in our ranks. They only make things more difficult. If they just knew their place..."

"Okay," I interrupt. Not that I don't enjoy Grandfather's tirades when they're not aimed at me, but I'm confused. "You're letting females into the Knights, at least to pledge. What does that have to do with me?"

"I'm reinstating your membership to Fledgling."

My chest constricts. My body locks up in a wash of power that thrums through my veins. There was a lot about the Knights that I didn't care for, but the advantages far outweighed the boring bits. In the next instant, reality crashes around me. "The Elders won't agree to this."

"I'm the Elder," he growls. "It's arranged. For now...but I warn you," he says sharply, "one more fuck up and you're out again. However, you'll be far more useful to me on the inside right now."

I swallow, wondering what Franklin Jarvis is planning. It must be something big if he's putting me back into the Knights after the black stain I left on our name. "So, I'm still following her?"

"Don't just follow her. Fuck her. Own her. Do what you have to do. Understand?"

Utter amusement pulses through me. "Completely."

"I'll give you further instructions once you're on the inside again. I still expect continuous updates as that might change my course of action."

Trying to figure out where he's going with this is like decoding a cipher with no starting point or reference. But I need to do what I have to until I'm of age.

A knock sounds on the door behind me, and my grandfather peers up. His butler announces that he has a guest. "Excellent. Do tell her to come in."

That's my cue to get the fuck out. I stand from the chair but freeze when a familiar head of red hair bounces into view. She looks straight past me, those beautiful baby blues zeroed in on the old man.

I turn my head to follow her, and nearly grind my teeth to dust when she happily falls to her knees, smiling up at my grandfather. He's not looking at her, though, he's looking at me. "Leonardo, you really should be careful who you let into your life."

The sound of his zipper lowering makes my

stomach clench. He pulls her head toward his crotch, and I can only count myself lucky that the edge of the desk is in the way. The last thing in the world I want to see is his old cock getting a blowjob by the same lips that were recently on mine.

He drops his head back as she goes to town on him. I turn on my heel, my veins running cold the more the scene plays behind my eyelids. She's either a pawn of my grandfather's, or this is payback for her scream at the end of our phone call. I'm not sure which, but I do know I'll be deleting her name from my contacts. Fucking whore.

Women are all the fucking same. They can sniff money out, and it doesn't matter whether it's attached to a wrinkly old cock or a young one, they'll hop on it in a heartbeat if they think it means they're set for life.

Well, I've got news for dear old Grandfather—I couldn't give a shit about that lousy fuck, anyway.

7

Eden

My sister's boxes are staring me in the face when I wake up. I'm procrastinating. I'm not ready for the memories they'll bring, but I am ready for any clues that could surface. There might be top secret Knight shit in there. If only there was a signed affidavit saying, *If I die, it's the Knights. Blame them.* That might be the only thing that will hold up in court. I'm well aware I'm up against a Goliath. But with everything in me, I believe that the Knights had something to do with Dee's death. There is no other answer.

I pull the covers off and swing my legs to the floor.

Today's the day. First day of classes. First day being thrown to the wolves. I'll have to be smarter and fiercer than them if I'm going to play in their arena.

After getting ready, I stand in front of the bathroom mirror, eyebrows hitched practically into my perfectly styled hair as I stare at the new me. This is definitely going to take some getting used to.

A knock on my door sounds, and I take a deep breath. It'll be Oliver, but I'm oddly nervous about his reaction. The handle jiggles, and I hear a stifled curse coming from the other side.

I smile to myself and walk toward the door to unlock it, my skirt pulling tight over my ass. "Coming," I grind out, trying to shift everything into place.

After turning the lock, the door immediately opens, and Oliver pushes inside. "Edie, love," he greets, not even glancing my way, "look." He holds out his hand.

I blink at the object placed there, stomach clenching. This is proof that whatever my father said to the Elders worked. I wasn't sure if they'd let me pledge considering what happened to Dee, but I had to try. Dad took some convincing, but eventually, he said he would do what he could.

He must've come up with a pretty damn good argument.

"I got one, too," Oliver murmurs as he hands the metal box over. The shield-shaped object is heavy, spanning past the length of my hand. My fingers shake a little as I run them over the crossing keys adorning the middle in aged bronze. I press on a raised section on the side and the lid flips open. Engraved in the bottom of the case is the Knight's motto. *Vivere triumpho.* To live in triumph.

I grind my teeth, the magic of the moment suddenly disappearing. Their sacred saying is like a slap in the face, as if they're laughing at me from all sides. "Bastards," I growl.

Oliver lifts his brows. "Isn't this a good thing? You wanted in. This is your invitation."

"Vivere triumpho," I mock, turning to place the metal case on the bare dresser. They can kiss my ass.

"Yeah, well, that's the Knights."

"No shit."

"Alright, grumpy pants," he retorts, pinning me with his blue-eyed stare.

I grip the side of the dresser until my knuckles turn white. I'm furious with the Knights, but I'm mad at myself for getting caught up in that moment. For a few seconds, I forgot what I was truly here for. Getting in is only a means to an end.

Oliver comes up behind me, placing his gentle hands on my shoulders, and I instantly relax. "I know this sucks. Do you want to go to Tahiti instead? I'll book the private jet."

Of course he would offer up something extravagant and über expensive. I grin and shake my head. "No. I'm fine."

He squeezes me, fingers pressing into my collarbone as he dips his hands lower to massage my tense muscles. "You need to become the best actress of your life. Hate these people if you want, Edie, but you need to pretend that you don't. Smile instead of scowl. Laugh instead of growl. Take the bite out of you a little."

He's right. They'll see right through me if I don't. "What happens when we prove they hurt Dee?"

"*If* we find that out, we call the authorities."

Shock pings through me. I swallow before turning in his grip. Why would he come here if he didn't think they did it? He studies me when I don't say anything, and I can't decide if I'm mad that he doesn't believe me or if I should just be glad he's here anyway, despite *not* believing me. Then again, he's already said he's only here for one reason. I guess I have to add him to the list of people I need to convince.

I know one thing for sure: the Knights are untouchable. The authorities won't be able to do anything to them, so I'll have to get creative in their punishment. I haven't figured that part out yet, but that's just as high up there in the plan as finding out what happened to Delilah.

"You look good, by the way."

"Of course you would think so," I tease, though my cheeks heat a little at his words. "Ready?"

"Ready," he confirms, holding his elbow out to me. I slip my arm through his, grab my bag on the way out, and start toward the stairs.

My roommates are already gone or still in bed when we get down to the main floor. We escape without a flurry of fanfare and start toward our first class. Oliver's arranged for us to have the same schedule since apparently no one in admin at Carnegie can turn true royalty down. Knowing Oliver, I'm sure he put on the charm, too.

Walking through campus is like attending one of my parents' posh parties. It's a who's who of rich families. My presence doesn't seem to be a surprise to them. Their discerning stares watch the two of us, though I can't tell if it's me they're interested in or the royal.

We see nothing of Keegan the first half of the day, but my eyes stay peeled, searching for him in between boring classes. Multiple people attempt to talk to me, and Oliver has to elbow me every single time so I can make nice. Dee was so much better at this socializing shit than I am. Whatever I'm thinking is usually plastered all over my face, but I have to grin and bear it for the foreseeable future.

I walk out of the cafeteria after lunch, dejected.

The classes suck. My friends—bar Oliver—aren't here. And I haven't seen Keegan all fucking day. I'm ready to scream when the crowd parts in front of me and the face I've been looking for miraculously comes into view.

"No fucking way," I murmur.

Oliver's head snaps up. His lips part when he recognizes him. "Okay, alright. What we're going to do is—"

I march forward. Oliver sighs behind me, but I ignore him. I've been waiting to confront Keegan for too long. The gaze of the Forbes' heir settles on me. He stops, shoulders slumping while his already sallow face pales.

His demeanor doesn't deter me. I wouldn't care if he was dying, I'd still approach him. "You motherf—"

"Okay," Oliver says cheerily, coming up to take his place beside me. He places an arm around my shoulder and tries to steer me away. "Let's go somewhere private."

Around us, people stop to stare. "What do you want, Edie?" Keegan asks. He hasn't moved from his spot, so I shake Oliver off and face him again. He barely meets my eyes, acting nothing like the Keegan Forbes I know. The last time I saw him, he was being a dick to my sister, telling her maybe he'd fuck me if she wouldn't give it up—not that I'd ever let him put his dick inside me, regardless of his relationship with my sister.

"Seriously?" I laugh, wondering if he's completely lost it. He must know what I'm pissed about. He didn't even show up to his fiancée's funeral. That's fucked up.

He lifts his bloodshot eyes to mine. "Yes, seriously."

"You look like shit," I seethe. "How dare you look like you care." I step forward again.

Instead of him moving to face me like he would have in the past, he retreats. "I'm not doing this with you right now."

My jaw unhinges. Irritation straightens my spine. Everything he's responding with isn't what I expect. The fucker looks as if he lost his fiancée, even though he doesn't care. He never cared for Dee as much as she cared for him. He wanted the Astor trophy wife, and she wanted anything but. They clashed over everything.

Oliver tries to tug on my arm, but it's a commanding voice that makes me pay attention. "Let's not do this here." It's so sultry and dark that I immediately peer up at its origin. A handsome man in a suit stares us down then switches his gaze to glare at the growing crowd.

I can't place him right away despite his looks, so he's nothing but an annoyance. I've been waiting to pepper Keegan with questions, so I turn my attention back to him. "You have nothing to say?"

"Not here," the man demands once more, his tone deepening.

Anger lashes through me, and I face the brazen man again. "Who the fuck are you?"

"Mr. Barclay. Your Economics professor." He glances at his watch. "A class you're going to be late for if you don't leave right this instant."

I scan him up and down. He certainly doesn't look like a professor. Sure, he's dressed in a button-up and dressy pants, but that's not what has my attention while his green gaze locks me in place. He has carved cheekbones, highlighted by a shadow of deep brown stubble. His eyelashes are impossibly long, and damn if it doesn't look as if he walked straight out of my spank bank dreams. Who knew CU had professors like this? Based on my morning classes, I'd thought only my little California college had the kind of instructors that made you want to actually attend class.

Oliver quickly grabs my hand, tugging me away from the situation and the rampant audience. I'd almost completely forgotten what I was doing while checking out my new professor. We're only a few steps away when Keegan's unintelligible voice rises up behind me. I pull Oliver to a stop again, but this time he's more insistent. "Not here," he grinds out. "It won't win you any points." He leans closer to whisper. "You don't think the Knights are watching you? You got your invite, but you can't go around starting fights with current members, Edie. Come on, you have to be smart about this."

I know he's right, but I want to argue, anyway. I have to remind myself of the long game. Sure, I could blow up in Keegan's face and tell him what a deplorable asshole he is for shitting on my sister all these years. I could make a scene, ask him what he was doing when his fiancée drowned, but all that would do is draw attention to me.

My neck heats. Confronting Keegan in public was stupid. The Knights won't let me in if they think I'm looking into Dee's death. It's best they think I'm just taking over her role in the family. I'm now the only Astor heir. It's my duty to become the polished, educated woman that will someday work for my family now that Dee's gone.

The thought closes my throat, and I follow Oliver willingly afterward. I'll have my time with Keegan, eventually. He's not going to get away without me asking him a hundred different questions.

"He looked fucked," Oliver murmurs.

I scoff. "Maybe he's a better actor than me."

"Maybe he's a class A dick who realized what he lost as soon as it went away."

My heart clenches. I suppose that's possible. But he should've realized what he had in the first place. Delilah Astor was the best person I knew. She didn't deserve the treatment he gave her. She deserved someone to love her like she loved him.

"Miss Astor?"

I turn on the sidewalk in front of the building that houses my next class. Mr. Barclay is striding toward me, and I certainly wasn't hallucinating before. I could do without his stuffy clothes, but the man is sexy as fuck. I'd let him take me into his classroom and bend me over his desk any day.

"May I speak with you?"

I shrug. "I'm in your next class, right? You can do whatever you want with me for the next ninety minutes." Wait, that sounded dirty. I clear my throat, my cheeks heating. "I am in your next class, right? You said so before."

His lips form a thin line as he stares at me. Without answering, he turns his gaze to Oliver. "I'd like to speak to her alone, please."

I squeeze Oliver, letting him know I'm okay. Afterward, I feel him leave rather than see it. Immediately, Mr. Barclay moves to the side of the building so we're not blocking the doors. He looks me up and down, and I squirm in these clothes. I'm much more comfortable when I look like myself. I own that shit. In this, I'm just an imposter.

Instead of showing it any further, I pull my shoulders back. "Is there something I can help you with, professor?"

He smirks, gripping the leather satchel in his hands tighter. "Just wondering if you received something at your door this morning?"

My smile falters. He's a Knight. I should've known. He instantly becomes less hot. Maybe by, like, ten percent, but he's so damn fine, the difference hardly registers. "I did."

"Be there tonight."

"Tonight?"

He blinks, temporarily hiding his distinct green eyes. "Tonight is when we announce more instructions. You will be there, won't you? Or was your father wrong? You're not interested in joining?"

"I am," I blurt. "Yes, I'm interested. I just didn't know there was something tonight. My mistake."

"Be there, Astor," Professor Barclay instructs. "8 p.m." He turns and strides for the doors, his next words spoken over his shoulder. "See you in class."

Great. A Knight for a teacher. Not only that, a *sexy* Knight for a teacher. The only Knights I've ever met were old because they were my father's friends.

Oliver peeks his head around the glass doors as

soon as Professor Barclay disappears inside. "You coming? What the hell was that about?"

I hurry toward the entrance, grateful for Oliver's presence again. "He wanted to make sure I was going to the Knights meeting tonight. I didn't even know there was one." What the hell? Am I supposed to be a mind reader or something?

"Oh," Oliver says quietly. "That's weird."

I eye him suspiciously, but he ignores my gaze. He's my best friend, so I'll give him the benefit of the doubt, but if he's trying to sabotage me, Oliver and I are going to have words.

8

Oliver

Fuck this bastard.

I glare daggers into the back of Barclay's head. What a simpering idiot.

Actually, *I'm* the simpering idiot. I thought by hiding the Knight's note detailing where to meet tonight that I would be saving Eden from everything. If she didn't show up, she'd be out.

But *this* asshole had to ruin everything.

From where I stand, she can't win. She either finds out the Knights killed her sister and can do fuck all about it or this is all a big waste of time and Delilah really did die an accidental death—no conspiracy, no murder. Either way, she's uprooted her life for nothing.

I peek toward Edie who's raptly watching the professor. Jealousy sinks its nasty claws into me. Eden's an open book and always has been. I can tell she's got a thing for this guy already. Her lips are slightly parted. Lust practically wafts off her. When you've known someone for so long, it's not difficult to tell when they're interested, especially when you wish that look was focused on you.

Throwing her over my shoulder and taking her away from here is sounding better and better. And not just because I'm in love with a girl who doesn't love me. If she finds out I stole that note, she'll— Well, she'll fucking kick my arse. She'll hate me. For a little while anyway. I'd rather that than watch the woman I love join a secret society that may have murdered her sister. If Edie's right, there's no reason to believe she won't be next.

Around me, everyone else starts gathering their things. I missed the entire class. It's a good thing I don't need a certificate from Carnegie University, anyway.

I nod toward her as she stands to wait for me. "I'll catch up with you," I tell her.

She gives me a funny look, but shrugs and heads out.

After everyone files out of the classroom, I stand,

slipping the empty notebook back into my bag. Barclay peers over his shoulder and smirks. "Oliver...Smith is it?"

I curl my lip. I certainly couldn't use my real last name. It's pretty recognizable. "Yeah, that's me." I don't know what the hell I'm doing, but this guy needs to know Eden's my priority. He's a Knight, and Knights can't be trusted. It's suspicious as fuck that he would track Eden down to make sure she would be at the meeting tonight. Isn't part of pledging testing that the Pledges can follow directions? If we don't show up, we're out. There are no second chances.

"What can I help you with?" he asks, finally giving me his full attention. "Surely the content of this class isn't already too much for you? If you want to drop, just head to the registrar."

Pompous asshole.

"Funny," I respond humorlessly. Eden and I hate this world for the same reasons. Everyone thinks they're the smartest, funniest, arsehole there is. "I want to talk about Eden Astor...and the Knights."

Barclay's face hardens, brows lowering over his eyes as he glares at me. He pulls at the bottom of his shirt, then stalks toward the classroom door to close it. "That was unwise, Prince Oliver. Just because you're semi-royalty doesn't mean you won't be held to our standards. Secrecy is everything. I'm sure you're aware."

I match his thin-lipped smile. The rich fucks on this side of the pond don't scare me. They're nothing like the family I grew up in. I care about the Knights because of Eden. That's it. "Very. Which is why I'm curious why you cornered Eden outside the building to discuss Knights business within earshot of other students."

The professor grins before leaning against his desk. "What's the actual problem here, Oliver?"

I shrug. "You're the one calling me out for secrecy when I simply followed your lead."

He steps closer, smirk flatlining. "Pretty ballsy of you to talk back to a full-fledged Knight, Pledge. Helpful advice? The Knights don't care who you're related to. You'll be treated the same as everyone else."

"Wouldn't want it any other way. Neither does Eden." It's the best I can do without telling him directly to back the fuck off or threaten to take down the Knights for good while describing in detail how I will make them all suffer if they fuck with Eden Astor. That would basically destroy any chance Eden or I have in joining the group.

I step around him and head toward the door. Barclay speaks up as soon as I twist the doorknob. "You know what's funny? Eden didn't seem to know about the meeting tonight. Odd considering I personally delivered all of the invitations, so I know it was there when I left it outside her door."

I swallow hard at his insinuation. "I guess you should be more careful next time," I tell him before closing the door behind me and heading back toward the dorm.

Let him try to pit Eden and I against each other. It'll take a lot more than that.

———

THE MOON HANGS HEAVY IN THE SKY. THE DAY'S heat clings to the grass in droplets of dew as the night ushers in the chillier air.

I'm on red alert, searching the shadows as if something's going to jump out at any moment and take Eden away. I don't trust anything about tonight. Even if the Knights didn't kill Delilah, that doesn't make them angels. Corporate servitude to the Knights of Arcadia can be a dangerous game in and of itself. Members asking for favors, rubbing your back just so you can rub theirs.

Since my grandmother is the queen of an entire country, I have to watch what favors I give up. I'm so protective of who I let into my life for that reason. People see me as an easy in to the royal family. My black mark a vulnerability, a chink in my armor. I see it differently, but that doesn't keep people from attempting to use me.

My voice as I speak to Edie hides my concerns, though. "Palm trees. Sand. Frozen drinks that slide down so easily you'll soon forget who you are."

She chuckles. "All of that sounds like heaven, but no. I have a purpose here."

My stomach tightens. I would give anything for her not to have to go through this. Reaching out, I pull her to a stop before we hit the sidewalk that takes us to the oldest building on campus. "I'm worried about you."

She cocks her head to the side. "I know. I could tell since you arrived, but you don't have to be, Oliver. Dee would do the same for me."

She attempts to walk away, but I slide my fingers around her wrist and hold firmly. "Be prepared for what you're getting yourself into. They'll treat you like the dirt underneath their shoes. They'll use you and spit you out." She rolls her eyes, and I groan in frustration. "What if nothing sinister is happening and we join the Knights for nothing? You can't get out, Eden. You'll be stuck. For life."

She presses her lips together. "I understand the consequences, Oliver. What you don't understand is that I'm *already* stuck for life." She shakes her head. "Dee hid me from so much shit. She was the angel I didn't know I had. Well, it's my turn now. I can't keep digging my head into the sand. So yes, although I'd really love to be on a beach with you right now, sipping Mai Tais under an umbrella, it's not happening. You can, though. I didn't drag you into this. Go. Be free."

She doesn't say it maliciously, but it feels like a stab in the gut. "You don't understand. Where you go, I go."

"I love you dearly, Ollie, so I'm going to say this once: From this point forward, there are no more warnings. There's no more treating me with kid gloves. This was my idea, and I'm following through with it. You can do it alongside me or not. Either way, I'm doing it."

My throat locks up. It sucks when you want to be someone's hero and they won't let you. Turning away would be the easiest route, but I'm not doing that to her. "Understood," I confirm, her words still spiraling through me. What Eden doesn't understand is that I can't just turn that part of me off. Whether she ever reciprocates my feelings or not, I will always love the girl standing in front of me. And when you love something, you treat it with the care and attention it deserves.

Even if they don't like it....

My fingers squeeze around the bottle in my hand. I was hoping I wouldn't have to do this. Coming here was about talking some sense into her, not running along beside her like a faithful dog. I swirl the contents inside, mixing the drug-laced water that will make her fall asleep before we even hit the Knights building. I can have the jet on the tarmac waiting for us in twenty minutes. All we have to do is show up.

Will she hate me? Fuck yes. Will I be saving her life? No doubt.

I unscrew the cap on the bottle and hold it out to her. "Do you need a dr—"

A guy with wide shoulders walks between us, knocking us both off balance and sending my bottle of water to the ground. "Is this the way to the devil's club?" He laughs like he's told the joke of the year.

Eden narrows her gaze at his leather jacket and short-cropped hair. "Shit," she whispers. "Was that Leonardo Jarvis? I thought they kicked his ass out."

She picks up the pace while I stare down at my last-ditch effort to save her now emptying out into the grass. Fuck me. My window is completely gone. Once we hit that building, it's over for Edie. I catch up with her as more Knights and potential members show up the nearer we are to the building. My heart bangs a final death knell. Someone would notice if I attempted to drag her away now. Fuck.

That's what I get for trying to talk her out of it instead of just drugging her earlier. Trying to be the nice guy doesn't work. You would think I'd have learned that by now.

Furious, I stride through the crowd with purpose, following the others to the hidden door that faces the forest. Jarvis gets there first, sending a scathing look to the robed Knight standing next to the entrance who eyes us all as we arrive. He makes quick work of entering while I try to memorize the way he got in. Who knows if there'll be a demonstration on this or not.

Eden eagerly falls in line with the rest of them, her head on a swivel as we take in the surroundings. The halls are lit with torches, and it makes me wonder if life imitates art or if art imitates life. Aren't all secret societies housed in hidden away buildings lit with flames licking from wall sconces? It's a bit too cliché if you ask me. I've been in dozens of castles and not one of them doesn't have modern electricity.

Men in dark cloaks stand in intervals through the halls as if they're the trail of M&M's leading us home. Their hoods hide their identities, covering the upper half of their faces. At the end of the hall, we enter a circular chamber that's several stories tall, archways dotted throughout outlining even more men concealing themselves in the shadows.

Several seconds later, a huge door closes. The draft causes the torches to flicker, leaving us in complete darkness for half a second. Eden steps closer to me, and I reach out a comforting hand to her forearm. I don't leave it there for long. She doesn't need my reassurance. At least, she thinks she doesn't.

"Welcome, Knights, Fledglings, and Pledges. We'd like to start off this year's first meeting with a moment of silence for a fallen Fledgling. Please bow your heads and remember the life of Delilah Astor."

Eden's audible gasp squeezes my heart. Through the dimly lit room, I see her fingers curl into fists while the surrounding heads bow as requested. The longer the silence lasts, the more antsy she gets, fidgeting from foot to foot. This time, I really do grab her forearm and keep hold of it. All she needs is to blow up and ruin her chances of getting answers. I can't believe my indecisiveness allowed this to happen, but we're stuck now. Just like the ultimatum she gave me out there, I'm all in. Neither one of us has a choice.

She meets my gaze, and I give her a quick shake of my head.

When the silence ends, the Knight hidden in the darkness resumes his speech about the historic group and its coveted membership.

Mercifully, his speech ends only to be outdone by another Knight in a cloak that tells the Pledges what they're in for this year. I tune most of it out until the fuckers throw an even bigger wrench into my plans.

"Due to the unfortunate accident that took place last year, the Knights are proud to institute a new rule for incoming female Pledges. Their safety is our utmost priority."

My heart beats in my chest. The careless way he's saying this bleeds rich, powerful men who really don't give a fuck. However, he has everyone's full attention with a statement like that.

"Each female Pledge will be assigned a Knight, a Fledgling, and another Pledge to ensure their safety as they progress through the Knights Trials."

Eden's body locks up. Through the flickering light, I spy the utmost horror on her face.

I have to make sure I'm on that team. I don't trust anyone else with her, and she won't trust them either.

With this rule, they haven't ensured a female Pledge's safety, they've locked them into a grouping with men who despise their very existence.

I peer down at my hands and shake my head. Trying to be her best friend may have just cost her life —and mine. Because there's no scenario where she goes down and I don't follow.

9

Eden

*B*abysitters? They want me to have not one but three babysitters? How in the actual fuck am I going to look into Dee's death with three men going through this with me?

They did this on purpose.

I stare up at the Knight announcing the new rule. I can't make him out. His hood falls forward too much, and I don't recognize the voice either. My father is one of the other hooded figures standing throughout the space. I try to find him too, but it's useless. He should've told me what was going on before I got here.

I know it doesn't work like that, but shit, this is big. It fucks up my whole plan.

Plus, it's degrading. *Oh, you cute little girls, you. Don't worry. We know you won't be able to fend for yourselves, so we've devised a plan to take care of you —from us.*

Give me a break. Accepting females is clearly for show. Depending on who works with which girl, the Knights may be using these babysitters to sabotage the Pledge too. Then, when none of the females make it, the Knights can say they just couldn't hack it.

I hear my name, and every face in the room peers my way. Suddenly, my throat is dry. My hands start to tremble as my heart rate speeds up.

"Move forward," the man commands. The crowd makes room for me as I make my way directly in front of him. He's perched on the next level, and I have to arch my neck so I can glare at him while he issues my sentence. "Your assigned Knight has the information you need to move forward with the process. Do you understand?"

I lick my lips. "Yes, Sir."

"Do you comply?"

That word skeeves me out. I most definitely do not comply. *Greater good*, I remind myself. None of this matters if I can find out what happened to Dee. Expose the culprit at the very least and take down the Knights at the very best. "Yes," I say, my voice working around a spiked ball that's currently lodged in my throat. What I really want to say is, "Go fuck yourself." Alas, none of that backtalk works here.

"Barclay, Jarvis—"

A figure comes up behind the Knight talking and sets a hand on his shoulder. Whispered words are exchanged, and I wait with bated breath for the third name. Barclay's my freaking Economics professor—my hot economics professor. Jarvis has a reputation for being a reckless thug, even for a Jarvis. I can't imagine who they're going to add next.

A figure moves to my right, and I peer over to find Oliver staring up at the second story with a tiger's determination.

"Ah, yes. There we go. Barclay, Jarvis, and Prince Oliver. You are released."

Relief floods my veins until another man in a hood walks up to me. When he finally lowers the covering, I recognize him as Professor Barclay. "This way."

Oliver and I follow after. I don't see Leonardo Jarvis until we're almost through the crowd. He's standing at the edge, looking grumpy as fuck. He sneers at me, but I give it right back. His look screams his lack of interest in babysitting me, but I've got news for him, I don't need to be pampered. I hate the idea as much as him.

Silently, we walk from the room. Behind us, other names echo around the chamber before the loud door closes with us on the other side. I'd love to say free, but I'm not.

Leo shakes his head. "Unbelievable."

"Problem, Jarvis?" Barclay shoots back.

"You could say that," the grumpy one answers. Now that we're all standing in a circle, I'm able to get a better look at the guy who barreled through Oliver and I when we were making our way to the Knights headquarters. He has dark, cropped hair, sharp cheekbones, and a look that makes you want to steer clear. If you were walking at night and he started to approach, you'd move to the other side of the street. He's covered in tattoos licking up his neck and down his arms. I haven't seen him since these new additions. They make him that much sexier, if you ask me. A dark, dangerous kind of sexy. Tattoos aren't something you see in our world, which is one reason why he's the black sheep of his family. He goes his own way. Reminds me of someone I know, actually.

"That's rich," Barclay answers. "How'd you get back in, anyway?"

The tattooed-man growls, a sinister sound that seems to originate deep within his belly—or the bowels of hell, I'm not quite sure which.

"Granddaddy had a change of heart?"

I don't know the two of them well—or at all—but something tells me Barclay's got balls. Or he's just as much of a cocky bastard as the rest of these assholes.

Jarvis moves as quick as a whip. Before I know it, my professor's back is slammed against the wall, Leonardo leaning into him with a cruel smirk. They match each other in height, but there's something about the fierceness and overwhelming presence of Leonardo Jarvis that makes him scary. "Why don't you mind your business?"

"This caveman talk is all very scintillating," Oliver callously remarks, "but we should probably get out of here...."

As if on cue, the door to the room swings open and Anne-Marie strides out with a babysitter on each arm and the other following closely behind. She giggles, and they look at her adoringly.

They stride past us, and I think we're all so shocked that we actually move out of the way for them, Jarvis letting go of his hold on the professor.

"Jesus Christ," I mutter. Is Anne-Marie here so she can get fucked by Knights? Or become a Knight? I'm confused. She was one of the last women I suspected to follow in Delilah's footsteps. Everything about her screams she's okay with being the trophy wife these stubborn assholes want.

"Since I'm your professor, should I tell you to

watch your language?" Barclay muses. He's got a devilish grin on his handsome face. This one's going to be trouble. He's a smooth talker. The altercation with Jarvis didn't faze him one bit.

"You can try," I snark back, which only makes his grin widen.

"Come on," Oliver grinds out, motioning toward the main hall.

"First off, I'll never take orders from your princely ass."

Jarvis's dark words don't affect Oliver. He has to deal with worse back home. His family treats him like dirt, as if he doesn't belong.

My hackles rise in his defense, and I take my best friend's arm. "Let's go."

Oliver squeezes reassuringly. It was bad enough that he didn't believe in my mission, but to add two more people into the mix just made everything that much more difficult. I'm glad to have him on my side more than ever.

Jarvis pushes past the two of us. "Follow me."

His demand simultaneously pisses me off and warms the V between my legs. He starts off across campus, making his way toward Jarvis Hall—my hall. "How did you know we're staying there?"

"You don't think I know who stays in my hall?" he asks, picking up the pace.

"How is it yours? Didn't your great, great, whoever-the-fuck build it?"

"You better watch that mouth or I'll put it to use doing something more appropriate."

I snap my jaw shut as Barclay says, "Ahh, Leo. Always crass and never dignified."

Ignoring the barb, Leo strolls right up the steps of Jarvis Hall and enters, bellowing, "Hall meeting! Now!"

His angry shout goes right to my chest, making it thrum. My roommates all appear in their doorways and scamper out into the main room in front of him. My jaw unhinges as they line up like they're members of the von Trapp family called to with a whistle.

"Good to see you back, Leo," says the president of the student body. She's currently wearing a half shirt with her hair in a top knot. I'd respect her more if her eyes weren't glistening while she watches the man in front of her. "What can we do for you?"

"It's time to prove your worth again." Leo unbuttons his pants, and my eyes nearly bulge out of my head. "My new friends and I need to be alone for the rest of the semester. Amongst yourselves, pick one of you who has the best chance to make me nut. If she does, you can stay. If she doesn't, you're all out, and we're in."

Instead of objecting, the girls huddle together. I look on in horror. "Are you serious?"

"I never kid about nutting, Astor girl," Leo grunts as he crosses his arms in front of his chest. He has no qualms about standing there, his pants tenting while he waits for them to abide by his demand.

I open my mouth to say something, but Oliver places his hand on my arm. "Let's just see where this goes."

"See where this goes?" I whisper yell. "He's going to make them—"

I'm interrupted by a bevy of giggles, and Oliver gives me a look. "He's not *making* them."

Excitement sparks in Oliver's eyes, and I watch it for the longest time, trying to get a read on my best friend. I've seen the type of girls he goes for—easy lays, no strings attached, that kind of thing. But I've never seen him get off on this before. Then again, I've never been privy to how he is with other girls.

A cute redhead steps forward. "Looks like it's up to me, Leo." She licks her lips, and it's not unlike the look they all gave Oliver yesterday. I almost call bullshit on all of this, but as she moves forward, the pit in my stomach boils with jealousy.

She lowers to her knees in front of him. His arm muscles flex while his hands turn to fists at his sides, making his tattoos ripple. Reaching out, she lowers his zipper and strokes his cock free. I can't see his package from this angle, however if her eyes have anything to say about what's awaiting her, it's like she just opened the only gift she wanted on Christmas morning.

Curiosity burns through me, but I stay where I am while she fists him and dips her head toward his hips. My body heats. I've never witnessed anything like this wanton show of sex before.

"Well, if this is necessary...." Professor Barclay steps forward. He points at the class president. "Gina, you've got me."

Leo cuts daggers toward him. "Don't fuck this up."

"I have more restraint than you'll ever have."

Gina drops to her knees in front of my professor and tugs his dress pants down. She frees his thick, hard cock from his boxers, making my chest squeeze with envy. My knees weaken from the displays of exhibitionism while lust pools in my belly.

Jarvis's girl starts moaning when he fists her hair. My pussy clenches, imagining her mouth is mine. Fantasizing that I have the ovaries to enjoy such a lewd act in front of everyone. If my body has anything to say about it, I'd fucking love it.

I'm distracted when the last roommate lines up in between the others and drops to her knees. Oliver smirks before striding forward. I gasp, and he turns to peer over his shoulder, locking his bright blue gaze with mine. "There's no reason why I shouldn't, right?"

His burning eyes seize my heart, but I immediately shake my head. He turns his attention back to roommate three, the same one he couldn't have given a shit about yesterday. Bending down, he places a finger under her chin and makes her look him in the eyes. "Be a good girl and suck my cock, love. Yeah?"

She practically melts, and a part of me does too. He's never said that to me. All the times we've turned to each other to take the edge off, he's barely ever spoken. It's just harsh breaths in the silence, but as she takes all of my best friend inside her mouth, he praises her like it's his job. "Good girl. You like that, don't you? Fuck yeah. Your mouth is beautiful, love."

"Remember the plan," Leo barks, taking me out of the scene. I shake myself and remember who we are. My mouth shouldn't be watering for Oliver's cock.

We're best friends. Nothing more.

I'm the seventh wheel. My skin skitters with goosebumps, and I shift from foot to foot as sex noises fill the room. "Yeah, great plan," I deadpan, glaring at the man who started it all.

Leo pins me with his gaze. "You can be next, Astor girl." His hands tangle in the hair of the girl kneeling in front of him, but he watches me as if he's fucking my mouth instead. His glare is cold and calculating, like he knows what he's doing to me. What all of them are doing.

This is the reason why I hate my world. The men are all carefree. They make girls like this go to their knees for them, but then call them hoes. What about women like me? I'd drop to my knees if they treated me like an equal afterward.

I hope one of these girls makes them come. I hope *they* take the power back.

For all the sucking noises and moans, none of the guys look like they're about to budge though.

"What do you think?" Jarvis sniffs. "Should we give them another five minutes?"

"Sounds good to me," Barclay announces. He has his hands on his hips, watching Gina go down on him. Their gazes are locked, and although there's a rippling in his arms, there's no telltale sign that he's going to lose his load. I might cream myself watching it, though. He must have the restraint of a clergyman.

Leonardo's girl is getting desperate. She's pumping his dick like her life depends on it. He's so vile, he probably gets off on it. "I'll let you fuck me bareback after," she promises, her face flush.

Damn. Girl must really like her mattress.

"I can do that any time," he answers, sneering.

She frowns, losing interest.

I turn my attention back to Oliver and the

protruding tendons in his neck. I don't know what drives me forward first—jealousy or the fact that I know he might be the one to break.

Coming up behind him, I settle my left hand on his hip. He slowly turns his head with a smirk, but his face slackens when my other hand wraps around his front. I look up at him through fluttered lashes, sliding my hand around the base of his dick. The girl moves her hand away as I grip it...hard. His hips pitch forward. "What are you doing, Edie?"

"Making you cum in that beautiful mouth. Isn't that what you called it?"

He groans long and deep. "This isn't fair."

"Why?" I ask, making sure to drag my lip over the curve of his neck while I match the girl's tempo.

"One minute," Barclay snaps.

Oliver grunts. I lock gazes with him. "You must want to come in that mouth or you wouldn't have walked up to her. Look at her suck you so—fucking—good." I peer down, watching her take Oliver inside. My hips seek out his thigh, edging toward him while my panties drench.

He follows my gaze and makes a strangled cry. I know I almost have him. Then the girls can claim their bedrooms back, lift the middle finger to the alpha repressors and all that.

"Edie," he grinds out, hips shifting into the V of my legs before thrusting into the girl's mouth.

"Hold it!" Leo bites out.

Ignoring him, I answer Ollie in the most innocent voice I can muster, "Yes?"

He bucks forward, slamming into my hand. I give it back to him, jerking him off harder as the girl sucks his tip.

Oliver's breaths ratchet up. "Fuck yes. Please," he begs, catching my gaze.

"Time!" Leo growls. Somehow, he removes the girl off his cock and flies toward the girl in front of Oliver, pushing her to her ass as rivulets of cum stream from Ollie's tip, landing on the floor between the girl's legs.

Oliver's body trembles with his release, and he places his fist over mine, holding me there as he releases every last drop of cum from his dick.

Leo narrows his gaze at me. "That was cheating. Play by the rules."

I pull my hand from Oliver's grip, my whole body flush with excitement. I spot a drip of cum on my pointer finger and lift it to my lips, licking it off with the tip of my tongue while smiling at Leo. "Your rules or mine?"

"My rules. Always my rules. Now it's time for your punishment."

Alaric

Like the narcissistic asshole Leo is, he grabs our charge by the wrist, forces her upstairs, and throws her in a room, locking it behind her. Afterward, he descends the steps calmly, his face the only thing showing true emotion. He's always been one to go off half-cocked, and this is no exception.

"Did you not hear me correctly?" he bellows to the stunned girls whose mouths were just around our cocks. "You failed. Get the fuck out. You have ten seconds to grab everything you need."

His legendary temper precedes him. The girls jump to their feet, wiping their lips as they run to their rooms. Upstairs, little Eden Astor bangs on her door. "What the fuck are you doing? You sick fuck."

I chuckle to myself, watching Leo pace in front of me. "You still have a master key?"

"Is my name still engraved above the door?"

I shrug, supposing it still is, even though I'm sure there were moments when the Knights and Carnegie administrations wanted to do away with it after Leo swaggered inside its doors. He's always had a chip on his shoulder about everything.

Instead of wasting my time dissecting him, I turn toward the new guy. Prince Oliver—also a spiky thorn in the ass, but with him, it's because he's a member of a royal family. Currently, the tips of his ears are scarlet red, and his body is still trying to recover. He's the only one of us who couldn't hold it. It would've been difficult for any of us to get tag-teamed, but I'm suspecting his reasons are due to his feelings for the Astor girl. There's no other reason why he would've approached me after class if he didn't care for her. She's clearly oblivious or doesn't reciprocate.

"Oliver!" Eden screams. "Get me out of here!"

"Don't," Leo and I say at the same time when he finally rouses from his climax haze. He tucks his cock away and stares in amazement at the women scurrying around the place carrying hairbrushes and toiletry bags.

"Ten!" Leo growls.

A few excited shrieks later, and I zip up before slipping onto the couch in the main room, crossing one leg over my knee to hide the boner I'm still sporting. I wasn't in any danger of coming—I chose her because I've had a BJ from her before and it was lackluster. Enthusiastic but boring. Girls like her think we want to be called the best there is. Not that we aren't, but that shit gets old after a while.

"You're just going to keep her in there?" Oliver asks as he stares up the stairs where Eden is calling for him again.

"Until we talk," I say, patting the seat next to me.

"Until *I* say." Leo's rebuttal makes me roll my eyes, but I can't tell him to calm the fuck down because he's yelling, "Five and a half!" as a warning to the girls still running around our apparent new digs.

Ten seconds later, the girls all exit out the front door as Leo holds it open for them, smacking their asses for being late. When he slams the door behind them, he moves to stand in front of Oliver and myself. "What the fuck is going on?"

"I'd like to know myself." I peer over at the prince. "I know whose name was with ours and it wasn't yours. How did you maneuver your way onto this team?"

"We're not a team," Leo barks.

I wave the thug away and lift an eyebrow at Oliver. "Well?"

He peers up the stairs with all his high and mighty aloofness. "I don't know what you're talking about."

I push my tongue against my teeth, surveying the newcomer up and down. He certainly looks like royalty. With all the rumors that followed him here, I was expecting some sort of badass type with tattoos and piercings. Kind of like Leo over there, still seething. "I'm just curious how you pulled those strings? Who's your in?"

He looks at me as if he's bored out of his mind. "I'm royalty. I know people."

"But the Knights don't give a shit about that."

"Or do they?" Oliver asks. "The situation as it is suggests otherwise."

The bastard definitely grew up like us. He's not giving anything away. The only thing that's plain to see about him is his unrequited love for the Astor girl. Who's definitely more mature than I originally gave her credit for. I was not expecting her to grab the prince's cock like that, trying to finish her friend off in the girl's mouth.

I assumed she would be self-righteous about it all, but I couldn't resist joining. I like to test my restraint every now and then, and what better way than to have a mouth sucking on your cock?

"No one's answering my question," Leo fumes. "Why the fuck are we all paired up like we're in first grade?"

I have my own suspicions about that, but I'm certainly not saying shit to any of these guys. Trust is hard won in my world, and the last person I would trust is Leonardo Jarvis. His family has been at the top of the food chain for years, not that he's ever been able to revel in the spoils. His troublemaker ways are nearly dragging his family name down with him. "Does it matter?" I ask, eyeing him. "You're back in the Knights. This is what they've asked us to do."

"Back in the Knights?" Oliver asks. "So, Eden was right, you were kicked out."

"Stop talking, royalty. I have little patience for people and even less with people I can barely understand."

"It's called speaking proper English, you mongrel."

Leo's nostrils flare, and I know from experience he's about two seconds from blowing up. "Let's not have a royal murder charge on our hands," I say calmly, peering between the two of them. They couldn't have paired me with worse choices.

"Our?" Leo bites, switching his ire to me. "Let one thing be clear to the two of you and little miss prissy pants upstairs," he yells. "There is no *us*." He plops into the armchair behind him. "I'll kill someone if I want to."

I watch him, wondering if he's done something like that for his dear old grandfather, the slippery fuck. Nothing ever sticks to him. Leaning forward, I place my elbows on my knees. "Regardless, we're stuck together. Unless you want me to tell your grandfather you've decided not to take his gift of letting you back in the Knights, Fledgling."

Leo's gaze narrows. Pure heat flashes off him, but I've been under enough hateful stares not to get worked up. The problem with Leo is he thinks he has it the worst and always has.

Eden's pounding stops. All of us look toward the stairs but do nothing about it.

For myself, I find it odd that the Knights of Arcadia are letting in females, especially the sister of the girl who died during their function. I thought they'd give Delilah her opportunity before shooting her down, and that would be the end of that. But something is off now. Not only did the last girl die, but they're bringing in *more*. The Knights have done a lot of crazy shit before, and this seems like just another calm before the storm. They're always being tactical, thinking three, four steps ahead of the rest of us. None of what they do usually gets to me, but I'm completely and utterly in tune to this one.

When I heard Eden Astor was attending Carnegie, I knew something was up. The Knights run Carnegie. They typically wouldn't have allowed her admission because of what happened to Dee. It's called clean up. They want family members as far away as possible... unless they have something else on their minds. Something awful.

After a pregnant pause, Leo switches positions in the chair, sitting more leisurely. "Odd seeing you back at Carnegie. Professor."

I shrug, not deigning him with an answer and instead turn to Oliver. "How pissed is she going to be when we let her out of that room?"

"Royally." Oliver grins.

Despite myself, I smirk. This guy might be alright.

"Listen, I didn't grow up with all you rich assholes like Eden, but I do know her. She's used to fending for herself. Whatever it is that we're doing down here without her is a bad idea. She's not your typical spoiled, rich brat."

"Don't kid yourself," I muse. "They're all spoiled, rich brats."

"Oh, get fucked," Oliver grunts. "And you're not?"

"I did say all, didn't I?"

After a moment, Oliver says, "I don't know why they paired us together, but I'm here to do this with

116

Edie. That's the only fucking reason I'm here, not to get into a pissing contest with the likes of you."

"I'm here for myself," Leo says casually. "What about you, *professor?*" he asks with disdain.

Clearly he's not over the fact that I came back to Carnegie to teach. There are a bunch of things I could say, but I settle for, "I'm here as a Knight. That's all."

Oliver's gaze narrows at me, distrust swimming in his eyes. He should keep that notion. None of us are on the up and up.

"Let's just take this one step at a time," I suggest. "We're grouped together to make sure Eden—and the royal—get through pledging. That's it. Help or not," I add, landing on Leo. "But since your end goal is to end up a Knight, I say you toe the line for now."

A stillness settles over us as we inspect each other. Leo's still not on board, and I didn't expect him to be. I have no idea how he's back within reach of the Knights, but he's not my focus. Why Eden is here is. As if on cue, soft moans permeate the silence. Every last pair of eyes turns toward the stairs as the sounds get louder and louder.

"Is she...."

"Playing with herself?" Oliver asks. "Yes."

I raise my brows, impressed. Not only did she not revolt at the scene, it turned her on. "And we left her hanging."

117

Leo stands. "I'll take care of that."

Oliver rises to his feet, jumping in the big man's way. "I don't think so."

Leo grins wickedly. "Just because you're a lovesick puppy she put in the friend zone doesn't stop me from tapping that fine ass."

Oliver's jaw locks tight. "In case you missed it, it was my dick she grabbed. Not yours."

"We'll see what happens next time, Royal." His lips pull back into a tiger's grin. Poor Eden doesn't know what she's in for.

They're not the only ones who have daydreamed about Eden Astor's sweet cunt wrapped around their hard cock though. I could barely get through my lecture earlier with her stare homed in on mine, almost as if she was undressing me. I might not be able to stop myself next time. Let the whole class watch if they want, but Eden Astor will be mine.

A cut-off scream seeps downstairs, followed by a pleasant hum of contentment. I'm hard as fuck again. As if the rest of us are on the same page, we leave for separate rooms, Leo giving Oliver a warning about not letting her out yet.

Once on the other side of a door, I immediately take my cock out, picturing Eden's pretty, plump lips wrapped around my shaft as she calls me Professor.

11

Eden

The next morning, I'm still holding on to the fury from last night. Dickhead locked me in my room. With a key...that he somehow has. I should be the only one who has a key to this room.

As soon as the doorknob twists in my hand, I don't think. I react. Still in my pajamas, I creep down the stairs. I heard them all disperse last night, walking to their rooms. Oliver even walked on by, ascending the steps to the third floor without bothering to check on me or opening the damn door. So much for being my best friend.

Though, I suppose best friends don't grab the

others private parts and stroke while someone else is sucking them off. Nor do they touch themselves to the memory of the other's cum shooting in rivulets to the floor and the way their body quivered in response to the raw sex noises filling the room.

Shaking myself, I put those thoughts onto the back burner. I need to focus. I'm searching out the fucker who has a key to my room. Leonardo Jarvis. The Jarvises are a well-respected name in my world, even if Leonardo isn't. I'm not going to lie, I've mentally fist pumped the air whenever my mother tells stories of the latest unregal-like thing he's done, knowing full well his grandfather, the patriarch of the Jarvis line, is hating every single second of his existence.

Right now, I am too. What in the world gives him the right to have a key to *my* room?

I haven't even been into the rooms of my real room-mates before, but I find myself twisting the knob of the door to the first room I find. It's pink. Very pink. Feminine to the max. However, there's a very unfeminine body sleeping on his side...shirtless. My professor.

His eyes open just before I turn away, and a small grin quirks his lips. "Watching me, Miss Astor? That's not creepy at all."

"Don't flatter yourself," I snark, hackles rising. But my beef isn't with him. Well, it kind of is. He certainly could've stopped Jarvis from locking me in my damn room last night since he's a full-fledged Knight and all.

He unfolds his body, his taut, muscular chest on full display. I will myself not to look. He gives me a wink. "I'm not sure we should be meeting like this, considering you are my student."

"I'm not sure we should be living in the same dorm then, should we? Don't you have your own place off campus?"

"Of course I do, but what kind of helper would I be if I wasn't watching over you all the time?"

The way he says it sounds so invasive. So demoralizing instead of helpful. Yet, at the same time, it curls my toes into the hardwood at my feet. "I don't need a babysitter."

He chuckles humorously. "I'm definitely not your babysitter, and if you think the Knights meant for us to be one, you're way off base, Miss Astor."

I grind my teeth at the way he addresses me, like I'm still sitting in his class, basically undressing him with my mind. I mean, really, I couldn't help it.

I shake my head. "I don't have time to deal with this right now. I'm looking for the other one."

When I say "other one", he smiles wider. "He always has a way of making friends."

Instead of answering, I turn on my heel and try the next door. It swings open to an empty room. I thought the pink room would've been the worst, but I was so, so wrong. This one has unicorns plastered all over. But not just unicorns. Madonna *riding* unicorns. "What in the...."

"My sentiments exactly." Barclay's warm voice coats my skin, locking my muscles and making a tremble run through me. "I believe the door you're looking for is down the hall. Last one."

Of course he would sequester himself as far away from us as he could. It was clear he was as sullen as I was about the situation. Only, he made it a hundred times worse for me.

I stomp down the hall and try the door. It's locked. Of course.

"He has a master key."

Peering over my shoulder, I find Professor Barclay leaning against the doorjamb as if he's waiting for the show to begin. "Well, that explains it," I mutter to myself while glaring at the knob. It's one of those old school doors. They all are. At first, I thought it was a fitting decoration for the time period of the dorm, even though the rest of the building is modernized. However, now I'm beginning to realize it's that way because the Jarvises want it that way.

He's obviously got the key with him, so there's no luck there. Fortunately for me, the keyhole is also of the old school variety and should be easy to pick.

Brushing past my professor, I head into the unicorn room and move straight through to the attached bathroom. Sitting on top of the vanity is exactly what I was hoping to find—bobby pins.

I grab two of them and march right back toward the door to the douche's room. These were what I was missing last night from my own room. I even tore open some of Dee's boxes looking through her toiletries and found nothing in the entire room that would help me escape.

"I'm wondering what you should call me," he asks as he watches me work. "Alaric should be fine as long as we're not around any students."

"Yeah, sure," I mutter.

After some finagling, the lock clicks free.

"I'm curious as to how you know how to do that...." Alaric's voice is somewhat surprised with a hint of caution.

"Don't all rich girls know how to work bobby pins?"

"Not in that way."

I shrug. "Guess I'm not like the rest, then."

His response is muted by the door being thrown open.

There stands Leonardo Jarvis, his low-slung jeans hugging his waist. He's also shirtless, but unlike *Alaric*, he doesn't greet me with a wink and a grin.

He glares from me to the lock, brows pulling in, then he shoots out his hand. Before I can move out of the way, his meaty fingers wrap around my wrist and tug. I fall into the room with a surprised shout, the door slamming shut in my wake. Immediately, I'm encased in flesh. Jarvis's front wraps around me like cellophane. My lungs squeeze. It's as if I can't breathe in his presence. "What are you doing, Little One? Don't you know you don't break into the wolf's house?"

"If you're calling me a little pig—"

"If I was, I'd blow your house down, Astor."

"How can you when you're currently living in it?"

His face turns hard, and his nose touches mine as he growls, "Let's get one thing straight, little girl. This is my house. It always has been."

His words dry out my mouth as I try to suck in air. His presence falls over me like a shroud wrapped in nightmares. Maybe it's his reputation, maybe it's the fact that he locked me in my room last night, but something tells me not to poke the bear.

I always did have trouble listening.

"It may be your house in name, but you don't own the people in it."

He gives me a devilish grin, moving a lock of my hair out of the way. "Wrong again. Do you know what I usually do to new girls in my house?"

I can only imagine. Just the way his hips shift into

mine makes him go from something dangerous to something sexual.

"There's a toll for sleeping here. A toll they must pay."

I swallow, the heat between my legs burning with a mind of its own. Suddenly, I'm thrust into the scene from last night, watching my roommate get on her knees in front of him...how everyone else followed suit.

There was that initial disgust—the anger that they would lower themselves to do something like that—but then the heat started. It flickered in my cunt, then spread outward until I was practically sweating. I would've gotten on my knees, too, but not because I'm like the other girls. They did it out of duty. Out of a sick, misplaced need to do whatever the men in our world tell them to.

Not me. I would've done it for the sheer fact that sucking dick makes me hot. Plain and simple. Especially when the guy looks like Leonardo Jarvis.

"I think you'll find that I don't like rules, Jarvis."

"The only rules I like are mine."

He reaches down, fingertips grazing across my thigh. I lean back against the door, willing myself not to move. No matter how much my hips want to search his out, I paste them to the solid surface behind me with willpower I didn't know I possessed.

A knock comes on the door. "You're not breaking

her in there, are you?"

"Move along, Alaric," Leo hums.

"We need to talk. All of us."

"Fuck off," he grinds out.

With his words, he moves his grip higher and higher, slipping his knee between my legs.

He licks his lips, placing his mouth near my ear. "Next time you try to break into my room, wear something that makes you look older than fifteen." He tugs the waistband of my jammies, and I cringe.

I close my eyes briefly in embarrassment, but I'm not one to bow down that quickly. Sure, my jammies have little suns all over them—a gift from my old roommates—but it's not because I have a sunny personality.

I shift my hips forward, finding what I suspected would be there, but also giving me the perfect amount of friction on the part that's practically purring with need. I clamp down on a sigh and say, "Look who's talking. You're getting hard over this girl in cutesy pajamas."

He bites my earlobe. "No, I was getting hard over the memory of hearing you get yourself off last night. Were you thinking of me?"

"You'd like that, wouldn't you?"

"We know it wasn't the boyfriend."

"Ollie? He's not my boyfriend."

"Does he know that?"

"If he didn't, do you really think he'd let you lock me in my room last night?"

"Actually, yes. He seems like a bit of a pussy."

Talking shit about Oliver never ceases to piss me off. I slam my heel down on his foot. "You say pussy like it's a bad thing, when in reality it's the reason women will run the world someday."

He growls and leans into me further. The weight on my chest blocks the air in my lungs again. "Keep dreaming, Astor." He runs his fingers just inside the elastic of my shorts. "I bet you're wet for me right now, which only proves I'm the master of you. Should I check?"

His fingers sneak lower and lower, moving my shorts down with them. I know for a fact I am dripping. All the pent-up tension from last night, the lackluster orgasm when I really wanted something else—anything else than my own fingers—to get me off. It's returned with abandon.

I give myself away by searching for him, letting out a sigh when I meet the hard lines of his cock through the denim material. It's only a tease, though, not enough.

But it is for Leo. He stops his downward exploration and quickly removes his hand, stepping away from me at the same time. I fall forward on a whimper at the loss of him like a besotted schoolgirl.

Leo smirks, placing his hands on his hips. A growl of frustration rips through me as the fog clears. Taking another deep breath, I say, "You locked me in my room last night."

"You bet your ass I did."

"Give me the key," I demand.

He laughs, but it comes out less joking around and more serial killer. "Not a chance."

I turn, peering at all the flat surfaces in the room. It has to be somewhere. I walk toward the dresser and am almost there when I spot it. I'm within reach when a hand comes around behind me, lifts me in the air, and throws me over his shoulder. "Now you're getting annoying." He strides across the room, carrying me easily, then places me on my feet in front of the now open door with little care. I stumble into the hallway.

He gives me a pat on the butt, and red-hot shame courses through me. "Run along, Astor."

I spin just in time to see him shutting the door in my face.

Asshole.

Whatever I do, I'll be getting that key. I also make a promise to myself not to let my libido get in the way when it comes to Jarvis. A guy like him thinks he has all the power if you start getting hot and bothered every time you're around him. He won't see it for what it really is...a healthy sex drive.

12

Oliver

*E*die's shoulder is about as cold as a galactic iceberg. She's refused to look at me throughout breakfast or when I tried to follow her up the stairs when she went to grab her bag.

The four of us are currently walking across campus like a group of posh academy students. Well, three of us are walking in a group. Jarvis is trailing behind, the same moody look on his face as when he told one of my new roommates they were going to get down on their knees for him. Not exactly one of the first impressions I wanted, but I don't regret it either. It felt empowering for Eden to see me as something other than a friend. As something desirable. Yes, she may use my body sexually, but there's no life to it on her side. It's as if my dick is a sex toy to her. You don't catch feelings for a vibrator. I don't want her just to want me, I want to own her love, body, mind, soul. All of it.

Judging by the way she's currently ignoring me, I've got a long way to go.

Alaric glances at his watch. He can't be more than five years older than us—seven tops. But with the way the student body dresses, he fits right in. "I've got to get to my class or I'm going to be late."

None of us respond. Edie's not just icing me out, it's everybody. Not that I can blame her.

He sighs. "I trust you two will keep track of Eden while I'm busy."

I grind my jaw. I was doing a fine job of looking after her before they were added into the mix. If only I'd known they were going to put us into groups.... At least I had the in to get me added to Eden's.

Alaric tries again. "Then we'll meet up after everyone is done for the day? We need to talk."

More silence. I'm just following Edie's lead. Otherwise, I don't have a dog in this fight.

Alaric huffs out a curse as he walks away. Eden and I continue on. Peering over my shoulder, I find Leo still hovering behind. I don't know why he's even bothering. It's clear he hates this—being here, being assigned to Eden as if we're her bodyguards or some shit. They should've just come right out and said they were doing all of this because of Delilah, instead of hiding it behind words of compassion for the female pledges.

The Knights are legendary, even in my country. They're known for being ruthless and unyielding. It's almost laughable that they're making this ruse be about anything other than giving a good show. It's something I'd love to talk to my best friend about if she'd even look at me.

"I got it from here," I tell Leo, dismissing him.

"I—" He breaks off after a pretty girl walks past us. "You know what? I don't fucking care." He sneaks after the woman, staying two steps behind. He doesn't look like a guy that's about to hit on her, he's stalking her, choosing the perfect time to pounce. The guy gives me the fucking creeps.

I wait several more steps after it's just the two of us, seeing if she'll make the first attempt at talking. When she doesn't, I say, "How much longer is this ice-out going to last?"

"Depends," she ponders. "Did you even try to get me out of my room?"

"I don't know if you noticed, but that dude's scary."

She gives me a withering look, which tells me I'm not about to charm my way out of this. "I'm sorry, okay? I was a little out of sorts because my best friend had just wrapped her fist around my cock."

I watch her intently. The tips of her ears turn red as she runs her fingers through her long blonde hair. I'm still trying to decipher the momentary embarrassment when she says, "Not like I haven't done it before."

"Well, it was a little different this time when I happened to have another girl's mouth on my cock too."

"Shh," she hisses. "The fuck, Oliver?" She waits as a group passes us before slowing down so she no longer looks like she's trying to run away from me. She seems flustered all of a sudden. "Okay, listen, last night was fucked up. Let's forget...*that* happened."

Not exactly the response I was hoping for. I want to remember that moment with her forever because it was different from the others. This time was without discussion, without weighing pros and cons, without clarifying what we were doing ahead of time. This seemed as if it was out of passion, something I've desperately wanted from her for a long time. "Whatever you say, Edie."

Anne-Marie strolls out of the café with two guys

on either side of her. Unlike our ragtag little group, they look as if they're taking their job seriously. From what threat, I'm sure they don't know. They're just following around a sure bet between the sheets.

"She seems to be adjusting well," Edie remarks. "She's probably not smart enough to know how humiliating this all is."

Anne-Marie smirks at us as she walks by. "Where's your entourage, Astor?" Lowering her voice, she whispers, "Wouldn't want the Elders to see that you're not following the rules, would you?"

Edie's lips thin. "It just so happens my—" She cuts off abruptly, obviously not knowing what to call us. "They have very important things to do."

Anne-Marie presses her lips together as she tips her head toward something behind us. "Yeah, if you call Lynette Foley important."

Leaning up against the side of a building is Jarvis with his hand up the girl's skirt that he was stalking. I have to hand it to him, that was fast.

Edie's cheeks burn red while she stares at the two of them.

Anne-Marie's laughter follows after her as she continues on. "I don't like her," I say.

Eden tears her gaze off the scene behind us, and we finally start for our first class. We're already late, but it seems neither one of us cares. Carnegie is just a show for Eden, too. A means to an end.

This time when Edie starts walking toward class again, she's picked up the pace. If I'm not mistaken, anger is driving her. "So, tell me, since you're now besties with the other two, what did you figure out after I was banished to my room like a child?"

"We didn't really talk," I say. "I told them you were going to be pissed you were locked in your room."

This time, her narrowed gaze is aimed at me. Fair enough.

"What did you do? Have a circle jerk?"

I glare at her. "No, pretty sure we all did that when we went to our rooms, considering you"—I loop my arm around hers, slowing her down and pulling her in close—"decided you were going to have a good time in your room...by yourself...loudly."

She smirks proudly, but then shakes her head. "What are we going to do with the other two sniffing around, Oliver? This is serious."

"The Knights did this on purpose."

"Agreed. Bunch of old farts. They're trying to deflect in every way they know how. Putting makeup on a pig." She swallows harshly. "Or in this case, a corpse."

She fumbles her next step, but I'm there for her, making sure she doesn't face plant. "We'll figure something out," I reassure her. "Right now, we just need to make it through the Trials. Those two might even be helpful during this phase. There's some difficult shit to endure. Alaric's survived, right?"

"Jarvis, too," she muses.

"He seems about as useful as a wet paper bag," I grouse. "But they'll be helpful with Trials. We'll play everything by ear after that. Jarvis doesn't seem like he cares about this foursome, anyway. Alaric.... We don't really know much about him, do we?"

"Other than he's a full Knight," Eden states, her brows pulling together.

"He can't be trusted."

She lets out a deep breath but doesn't agree or disagree with me. If I know her, she's still trying to work him out in her head. Alaric certainly appears to be nicer than Leo—well, if you can call any guy nice who lets girls go down on them for a challenge. Then again, I'm in that same boat, and I'd call myself nice.

Barely.

"So, I guess we're stuck with this, then?" Eden questions, even though we both know what the answer is.

If the Knights want it this way, this is the way it has to be.

Something tells me the new guys will be a hindrance in more ways than one. In searching for

Dee's killer *and* getting Eden to realize that I'm the guy for her. I'm not naïve enough to think that she pleasured herself only thinking of me last night. It was the whole scenario.

It was them too.

13

Leo

A fucking group text? That's where we're at now?

I scowl at the screen even with my grandfather's words ringing in my ear. He doesn't care that I don't want to babysit Eden Astor. This is just part of his plan to make sure she's not snooping around. In fact, he made this plan so I could be up her ass—they're just playing it off as if they're Good Samaritans worried about their new pledges. It'd be so terrible if another female pledge drowned on their watch, wouldn't it?

I have no idea what the Elders plan for Eden, but I'm sure it isn't good.

Whatever it is, it's not my problem. I'm stuck doing Grandfather's dirty work, so that's what I'm doing. He told me to "do what you have to do," and I'm taking full advantage of that statement. Locking her in her room last night was fun. Her cute attempt to take my key this morning made it all the more worthwhile. Watching her squirm when I touched her was icing on the cake. She might prove to be more entertaining than I thought.

If they think I'm going to respond to their group text, though? They're fucking insane.

The engine roars underneath me as I head back toward campus. Remembering last night and this morning makes my dick thicken in my pants. I have to give it to her, she has more fight than the average Carnegie girl.

My phone dings again, and I peer over at the screen, rolling my eyes when I see Barclay's name pop up. "For fuck's sake, quit riding my dick," I grumble.

Let them stew about whether or not I'm going to show up to their stupid meeting. I don't need another person in my life dictating what I do.

The familiar curve of the blacktopped roads blur as I make my way back to Carnegie. I could make this trip with my eyes closed. One thing I can't believe is how I made it back into the Knights.

Sure, I'm not a full Knight, but I wonder if this is

all for show or if I have a real shot of making it. My grandfather is an Elder. My father was a full-fledged Knight. Me? I only made it to Fledgling before I got kicked out. I left Carnegie after that. Left my entire family altogether until I came back on my hands and knees at my grandfather's feet. It was the hardest thing I've ever had to do, but it was unavoidable.

Even if I ended up dead, sometimes I wish I'd never made that drive back.

I pull into the parking lot in front of Jarvis Hall and then stride toward the campus café where they asked to meet. The door rings overhead as I make my way in. A few people spot me, eyes rounding. My reputation precedes me, I guess. I smirk as I make my way through the restaurant, searching for the girl.

Eden sees me first, but she turns her gaze away as soon as our eyes meet.

So it's like that? She's going to pretend she doesn't get all hot and bothered for me?

Oliver's next, and he gives me a disgusted glance that tells me he's worried about his chances with his princess now. He should be. She's more of a freak than he is. He'll never satisfy her.

"Oh, Leo. Thank you for joining us."

"Fuck off, Barclay."

He gives me a pleased stare, but it's more of a fuck you than the words I graced him with. He just has this way of looking at you like you're nothing. It's no surprise he thinks of me like that, and I fucking hate him for it.

"Well?" I question as I plop down in the armchair that was obviously saved for me.

Before they can fill me in, a figure steps between Barclay and me. "Okay, I got a latte and—" He cuts off, and I peer up at him, annoyed as fuck. He isn't looking at me, though. He's staring at Eden. My hackles rise, and I have the sudden urge to grab this fucker by the throat.

"You—"

I get to my feet, about to remove his ass, when Eden's salty voice perks up behind me. "Yeah, I look like her. One difference, though, she had way more patience than I'll ever fucking possess so move along."

The dude's cheeks blush, and I smirk at the way her response cuts him.

He swallows, and the tray trembles as he moves to set it on the table between all of us. "Sorry. I knew your sister. That's all."

Eden glares at him.

"She was nice."

"And I'm not," I reply after checking on Eden. Her shoulders are stiff, and it's obvious she doesn't want to think about her sister right now, only he's not taking the hint.

"We've got it from here, thanks," Barclay interrupts before I show this guy how fucking rude it is to stare. He looks like he's seen a ghost, and for a brief moment, my black heart twitches for Eden. To be constantly reminded of your dead sister, that's gotta suck.

Good thing I don't actually care.

The guy glances at all of us before stalking away, disappearing behind the counter and through an employee only area. My body stays alert after he's gone, watching for anyone who may approach.

"Sorry," Barclay states, staring at Eden. His tone is infected with feeling. I've seen this fucker at work. He must be playing some sort of angle with her, and whatever it is, I don't like it.

Turning my attention back to Eden, I find her reaching for a cup on the tray. She's dressed in a frilly top that cinches around the waist. Lace and satin. If you ask me, it's begging for cum stains. "It's no wonder he thought you were her."

Her gaze darts up to meet mine. It's filled with venom, but I'm used to being glared at like that. I want to know where the girl is who showed up late to unpack with ripped shorts so tiny I could almost see her ass and a tank top that screamed fuck the patri-archy. The girl in front of me right now is too demure.

"Look at the way you're dressed." Her face sours, but I trudge on. "You look like half the girls here." I'm seconds away from asking her about those shorts, but that would give away the fact that I spied on her.

"You mean fashionable?" the prince asks.

"No, I mean like the female version of your stuck-up ass."

Oliver peers toward Barclay. "He really is this way all the time, isn't he?"

Eden stays oddly quiet on the subject, which doesn't go unnoticed by me.

"Can we get back to the problem at hand?" Alaric takes a mouthful of his coffee before setting it back on the table in front of him. "The first Trial is tonight. We have to prepare Eden."

"And Oliver," Eden adds.

"I'm here to watch you," I snap. "Not his royal pain in the ass."

"I'm sorry, is there a gnat nearby?" the prince questions. "I'm constantly being pestered and irritated, but I can't see anything."

Barclay sighs like we're insufferable. "You all have one common goal, right?" He even glares at me. "You want to be Knights? You help each other. That's it. That means you two get through the Trials with flying colors, and you... You make sure you don't fuck up again. You've been tasked with helping her, you help her."

His tirade silences us.

Grinning, he continues, "The Trials are meant to test you in every way possible. Your mental toughness. Your physical toughness. Cleverness, aptitude, and even the ability to push through your fears."

I swallow as memories of my own Trials bombard me. Not going to lie, they were killer. Some of the guys I started out with didn't hack it. And they were a lot bigger and stronger than Eden.

It's all a big test, and if you fail, you're out. There are no second chances.

Eden pulls her shoulders back. "Okay, what's the first thing?"

"They start with a big one," I say. "It's meant to weed out the weak early."

To her credit, she doesn't balk. She just waits for us to give her the answer.

"They point out your greatest vulnerability...then torture you with it."

14

Eden

*B*iggest vulnerability? That could be anything.

Alaric and Jarvis are oddly quiet. Alaric especially seems to have retreated from his egotistical, if good-natured façade—his brows pulling together in contemplation.

The Knights can do with me whatever they want. They want to break me? Fine. Try. I'm already broken.

Oliver, however, looks worried.

Never in a million years did I believe I'd find myself at Carnegie, let alone surrounded by my best friend and two guys from the richest, most powerful families in the US. This was always supposed to be Dee's life, not mine. She knew how to maneuver inside it while I didn't have the fucking patience for playing games upon games. It's like constantly walking through a house of mirrors. Nothing is as it seems.

The sad part is, I didn't give Dee enough credit when she was alive. If I could have her back for one second, I'd tell her how proud I am for all that she did.

"When's all this stuff going to happen?" I ask. Hell, if they're assigned to me like I'm some sort of celebrity, I may as well take advantage of it.

"They switch it up every year," Barclay remarks. "Knights are usually in the know, but since I'm part of your group, they haven't told me anything. Afraid I'll pass it on to you, I suppose, giving you an unfair advantage."

"What are some of the other obstacles I have to get through?"

The guy who came up to our table before passes behind Barclay and Jarvis, shooting looks over at me. I try to make myself smaller. I never anticipated all the looks I would get by being here. Back in California, I was just a part of the crowd—somewhere I would rather be.

"In years past, they've made Pledges follow through on a favor for a Knight," Leo answers as if he doesn't think I'll be able to do that. "They're never the fun kind either. It's to prove loyalty."

I squirm in my seat on that one. I don't want to do any of these assholes a favor. Who knows what kind of atrocious things they could dream up.

Alaric leans in and lowers his voice. "Listen, I have a sneaking suspicion about something." He licks his lips, and I have to kick myself to listen to him instead of drooling over the smooth, plump lines of his mouth. "When you progress through the ranks, you usually buddy off with a Knight who's similar to you. Loyalty like that is tested all the time, and I'm wondering if they're going to do the same with this...unit," he finishes. "I said it before, but we really need to work as a team. If anyone here is unwilling to do that, speak up now so the Elders can be made aware."

All of our gazes land on Leonardo Jarvis. The dark shadows I find there don't help convince me that he'll be on my side. He seems more intent on his own needs and wants, like when he strolled off with that other girl this morning.

He smirks, but it's more menacing than anything else. "I don't like you guys, but I'm in this for the long haul. Don't expect birthday cards in the mail, but I'm here. That's all the reassurance you'll get from me."

"For the record, I don't like you guys either," Oliver grunts. "Except Eden, of course."

Well, this is some alliance. I don't trust any of them except Oliver. And the other two absolutely cannot know the real reason I'm here. Barclay would run to the Elders for sure, and the jury is out on Jarvis. I think I'm more like him than the others—a comparison I'm sure he'd hate.

"Wonderful," Barclay muses in his unamused tone. "Just the show of unity I wanted."

He seems slippery, this one. Like insults and grievances don't stick to him. It's intoxicating but also unnerving. I don't think I'm seeing the real Alaric Barclay. I'm not sure anyone actually has.

When none of us answer like petulant little kids, he calls us out on it. "Well, children, I have a class to teach." He stands, his half-finished drink still on the table in front of us. "I assume we're all staying at Jarvis Hall?" He peers at the only Jarvis at the table for the answer, who simply shrugs.

"Just remember: my hall, my rules."

"I'll be needing that key," I growl, remembering the complete embarrassment of last night.

"Not a fucking chance."

"Just don't kill each other until I get back," Barclay grinds out before leaving. The entire female student body—and some of the males—watches as he picks his way through the crowd toward the front entrance.

Without a word, Leo stands too. He strides through the room, and people practically jump out of his way.

"Come on," Oliver says. "Since you're making me go to college, I have homework to finish. Can't have the headlines also say how stupid I am." He takes out his wallet and throws down a few bills.

People stare at me, too, as I follow after him, but not because I'm a gorgeous professor like Barclay or a scary motherfucker like Jarvis. It's because I look like a dead girl.

There's a hint of chill in the air as we turn the corner toward Jarvis Hall. We step off the sidewalk to cut through the quad at the corner of the café when a hand shoots out to grab me.

It never makes it.

I hear a thump, and when I whirl, Leo Jarvis has the barista pushed against the brick building, an arm over his throat. He snarls in his face. "Didn't we tell you to get lost? She's not a sideshow."

My eyes nearly bug out of my head, but the clue-less barista snaps back. "Go ahead. Hurt me, asshole. You're all the same." Leo leans in further, and the barista's face pales. He peers over at me. "You shouldn't be here. They'll get to you too."

My heart skips a beat, landing like a thud in my chest. Before I can say anything, Leo yanks him off the wall and throws him to the ground. The guy's too stunned to move as Leo unbuttons his pants. He pulls his cock out right there for the growing crowd to see.

"What the fuck are you doing?" I hiss, my mind reverting back to last night. Just what the fuck is he going to do?

"Putting this guy in his place."

He closes his eyes and takes a deep breath like he's about to piss...on the guy.

The barista tries to scramble away, but Leo places a boot-clad foot on his shoulder. "Don't move. It'll be over in a second."

A few cheers erupt from the crowd, as if this is how we're supposed to act in the everyday world. No, I didn't particularly like getting gawked at by this guy, but he doesn't deserve to be pissed on.

"The fuck is wrong with you?" I aim for his hip but end up slapping Leo's dick out of the way as I reach for the other guy to help him up.

"Not a smart move," a voice growls in my ear. Before I know it, I'm thrown over the big guy's shoulder again.

Humiliation thrums through me. I grip his hair and pull, kicking wildly. I can't have the entire student body see Leo manhandle me like this. I bite down on his curved shoulder blade, and his grip loosens enough for me to push off him and land ungraciously on my feet. A stunned silence follows as Leo glares a hole into me. His pants are still undone, his impressive cock still out...becoming more and more prominent by the moment. "If you wanted to touch my dick, you just had to ask."

The smirk tells me all I need to know. Leo Jarvis gets off on this shit. He also apparently has no qualms about standing around with his dick on full display.

"What's this?" an authoritative voice calls out.

I don't look, hoping it's Barclay come back to smoothly put this to rest in front of everyone. I don't have the finesse he has, and Jarvis clearly isn't going to stand down. Nor will I. I'll fight him all the way back to my locked room if I have to. Weakness in this world is like chum in the water.

"Miss Astor, come with me."

Blinking, I finally look over at the newcomer. It's not Barclay. It's the head administrator, and somehow, he's calling on me instead of Leo making a public exhibition on his campus. Unless this guy is short-sighted and missing the growing bulge protruding from Jarvis. Fuck, is that a...piercing? A piece of metal glints in the light, and I nearly forget where I am with the need to inspect what he has going on down there.

"Miss Astor. Now."

His sharp voice brings me back to my senses, and I peer at the crowd who's obviously looking for a show.

I'm no match for Leo's caveman personality, so I do what I must to save grace and follow the old fart.

No one parts for him as we make our way through the crowd. "Move!" he bellows.

That shocks some into giving us space, and I keep my head held high as I walk with him through campus toward the administration building. After a while, the two of us just become other bodies moving amongst the flow of students and professors, leaving behind everyone who witnessed what happened near the café.

When we enter through the doors of the building, my heart rate has self-regulated. I have a hate hard-on for Leo Jarvis the size of a fucking elephant, but that's normal amongst people like this. They worm under your skin like parasites until they devour you from the inside out. I have to find a way to keep myself from being eaten alive.

We walk straight through the building, passing other administrators working happily in their offices, their secretaries typing away. Somewhere, classical music is being played, and I almost roll my eyes. Everything is too picture perfect. Passing off refinement like some of these guys aren't getting down to the new Cardi B track after work.

Just when I think this guy's office must be at the end of the hall, he opens a metal door with a red *Exit* sign overhead. I stop in my tracks, suddenly wary. I barely get out my next breath before I'm grabbed again. This time, fingernails dig into the skin at my wrists, and a bag is tugged over my head, plunging me into darkness while a scream gets stuck in my throat.

I'm thrown forward. Instead of landing on the hard ground, my knees hit something semi-soft. Two hands lift my legs and shove me forward seconds before a car door slams.

"Silence, Miss Astor," a calm voice sounds from what must be the front seat. "Knights Trial number one, and you're failing."

15

Oliver

When Eden doesn't return within a half hour, worry clenches my gut. I've stared down at the homework I'm supposed to be focusing on, seated by a window in the café so I can keep an eye out for her, ready and waiting to bitch about the whole fucked-up scenario that wasn't her fault. But she doesn't show.

Another fifteen minutes go by. Then another half hour. I eventually go search the admin building, but no sign of her anywhere.

Dread makes me shiver to the core. Maybe it's Eden's voice in my head too much, but I'm suddenly worried she'll get the same fate as her sister. I never actually thought...

I type out a text to the group thread Barclay started as I jog toward Jarvis Hall. **Anyone seen Eden?**

I get a response a few moments later. **Been in class. What do you mean has anyone seen her?**

I don't get a chance to respond because Barclay and I make it to Jarvis Hall at the same time. "What's going on?" he asks.

Worry-spawned fury envelops me. This never would've happened if Jarvis wasn't such a fucking arsehole. "Jarvis," I grind out.

"What about him?"

I burst through the doors and straight for Leo's room. The door swings furiously on its hinges and slams against the opposite wall. Leo is lying casually on a bed, any remnants of the girl who lived here before completely gone. He probably threw her things out into the parking lot like the dick he is. "Where is she?"

"Leave," he deadpans, not even sparing me a glance.

"Where is she?"

"How the fuck would I know?" he growls.

"Oliver, what is it?" Barclay asks, annoyance threading through his words as if I'm making a big deal out of nothing.

I point at Jarvis. "This fucker decided he was going to piss on someone. Fucking literally. Eden stopped him and wound up being escorted away by an administrator."

Barclay's eyes round. "Escorted away? Neither of you went with her?"

"Calm the fuck down," Leo grunts. "It was Cummings. I'm sure she's still dodging spittle from his lisp."

Ignoring him, Barclay asks, "When was this?"

"A couple of hours ago."

The doorbell rings, interrupting his response. He drops his bag and strides toward the front of the hall with me hot on his heels. Something is wrong. Eden would've texted me if she were doing something else. Or going somewhere. Or basically anything.

Then again, she would've if I didn't let Leo fucking Jarvis lock her in her room all night like a barbarian.

Doubt creeps in, but it's squashed when I spot the bouquet of black roses sitting on the front step.

"Fuck." Barclay grabs the roses, looks both ways, then slams the door. "Jarvis!"

At the end of the hall, Jarvis rolls his eyes like he's sick of our shit, but when he spots the black roses, his face clouds over like the storm of the century's rolled in. "Fucking mind games."

I pluck the note from inside the flowers and tear

the envelope open. In red ink are the words "To the death of your partnership...unless you can find her."

Jarvis's face darkens in shadow tenfold as he reads the note in my hands. He grabs it, fingertips turning white at his fierce hold. The blood devoid skin highlights the note just above it: "Knights—1 , You—0."

"I can't believe this," Barclay spits. "I leave to go to class and our charge gets abducted."

I swallow my anxiety. What if this isn't about the Trials? What if it's about Delilah?

It's possible the Knights could have figured out the real reason why Eden's here—why I'm here. I wouldn't put anything past them.

It's clear the other two are coming at this as strictly a Trials problem though, and I'm fucked because I can't say anything.

"I knew they were going to do something like this. I knew it."

Barclay's simmering anger triggers Leo. "If you knew, you shouldn't have gone to class at all."

"Because you two are apparently inadequate to do a simple thing like make sure the Elders don't get a hold of her?"

Leo's unfazed, but my fury ripples through me. "No, he was too busy trying to piss the world off."

"I grabbed that guy off her. What would you have

done? Ordered him not to take her arm in a gracious tone?"

I get in his face. "You don't think I would've protected her? I'd protect that girl with my life." I push against his chest. "Stay fucking clear of her. You're the reason why she was even walked off."

Leo growls back, recovering from my shove easier than I would've liked. "Careful, Royal. Wouldn't want you to break a nail."

"Focus, please," Barclay interrupts. "Tell me exactly what happened."

I peer at Leo, but his lips are in a defiant, thin line. "The barista? You know, the one who mistook Edie for Delilah? He wanted to talk to her after we got out of the café."

"Talk to her? He grabbed for her."

"Anyway, this guy," I say, hiking a thumb toward Jarvis, and then continue to fill Alaric in on what he missed while he was in class.

"So, Daniel took her?" He glares at Leo. "You know he's a Knight."

Leo's face morphs into one devoid of emotion, which is somehow scarier than his normal, ever-present scowl. He grabs his phone from his pocket and prods his screen a few times. When someone picks up, Leo growls, "Where is she?"

Unperturbed, the man answers, "The question is,

where are you? I'm wholly disappointed in the situation you find yourselves in."

"What's new?" Leo grinds out, and I'm not exactly sure of the nuances of the conversation, but he's clearly called someone he thinks knows where Eden is. He probably shouldn't be giving him shit. "I got your message."

The man on the line laughs, and I'm struck by the comparison of how close it sounds to Jarvis's own dangerous laughter. "Is Barclay there?"

"Here," the professor says.

"And the prince?"

I'm not even going to balk about the name. "Here."

"See how easily things can be taken from you?"

My hands turn to fists. This guy must be a Knight with some power. He lets his words fall on our shoulders, and I don't know if the others are feeling it as heavily as I do, but I'm raging inside. Eden's tough. She's not one to go anywhere willingly. I suppose she could be laughing with the other female pledges somewhere, talking about how their watchers failed them, but with the Knights, I seriously doubt that's the case.

Since this was a test, they aren't just putting her up in some posh restaurant while we search for her.

"We won't let this happen again," Barclay promises, and at least with him I feel his conviction. I wish I was getting the same vibes off Leo, but the only thing I get from him is pure hatred. Whatever phone call he's made, it's clear it's taking a lot out of him to make it.

"You're lucky the other teams were as careless as you. Now the race becomes who finds their Pledge first."

With that, he hangs up the phone. I stare at the screen, *Call Ended* blazing like a warning. Leo whirls and throws his phone against the wall. It shatters upon impact, bits and pieces falling to the floor.

"Who the fuck was that?" I ask.

"My grandfather," Leo grinds out, chest heaving. "He's an Elder."

Of course.

Jarvis fingers the note we received with the flowers, eyes darkening. "I might know where she is."

"We have to get to her before the other teams recover theirs," Barclay says, moving toward the front door.

I follow the two of them out of the hall, my pulse still fluttering at my wrists. "We have to find her to make sure she's okay. There, I fixed the sentence for you."

"Play this game like a Knight," Barclay throws over his shoulder as he barges out into the evening air. "Keep showing your hand, and they'll make you regret ever having feelings for her."

I bite the inside of my cheek. I really wish I'd dragged Edie away from here when I had the chance. Even if I had to drug her to tear her away, it would've been worth it. Maybe after this, she'll realize that losing herself isn't worth all this nonsense.

"Mine's closer," Barclay calls out, pointing at an SUV parked in the lot outside the hall.

"Mine's faster," Jarvis says, pointing at a suped-up muscle car. Any other time, I would spend a moment to appreciate the fine machinery in front of me, but I have only one thing on my mind right now.

Before I know it, we're squealing out of the parking lot, scaring the shit out of a group of students walking lazily in our path. They scramble out of the way, the guys yelling obscenities after us. Jarvis gives them the one-finger salute before flying down the road, taking sharp turns at high speeds.

"Why do you think you know where she is?" Barclay asks.

"I just know."

"Not a good enough answer."

Jarvis shrugs, pressing down on the pedal further, and the engine roars in response. "If I'm wrong, you can attempt to berate me then. How 'bout that?"

The angry growl of the muscle car is a lot like its owner. He has the driving skills of someone who thinks they're a professional racecar driver when they're not.

If I had time to feel even remotely scared for someone other than Eden, I may have said a prayer or two, but my mind is consumed with getting to her. Fortunately, the other blokes seem to be on the same page.

We pull into a community with large, semi-modern houses. Barclay gawks. "Are we—"

He's cut off by the squeal of the tires as Jarvis slams on the brakes. The house in front of us mirrors the others on this same street, except it appears to be unoccupied. No light spills from the windows. Children's laughter peals from the neighbor's back garden, but this house boasts overgrown grass and several bounded newspapers littering the stoop.

"Knights one, you zero, huh?" Barclay questions as he reaches for his seatbelt. He peers over at Jarvis. "That's fucked up."

"That's life."

The car doors slam, and I follow Jarvis who seems to be running the show at the moment. After finding the front door locked, I peer around, wondering if we've got the right place. What appears to be leaves from last fall litter the corner of the veranda. It looks as if a family lived here one day and just vanished the next.

Jarvis reaches into his pocket and pulls out a set of keys. He inserts one into the lock and swings the door open.

Well, that's interesting...

A muffled cry comes from within. I push past the two in front of me and hurl myself into the house. "Eden?" Another cry comes, louder now. I follow it into a sitting room, and I sigh in relief when I spot Eden's blonde head over top of a chair facing a fireplace.

Barclay and I reach her at the same time. He goes for her gag while I start untying the knots around her wrists and ankles. As soon as he pulls the cloth free, she growls, "What took you guys so long?"

She doesn't fool me though. Her voice is strained, and when I finally meet her gaze, there's an odd look in her eyes.

Behind us, Leo walks up to the mantle and leans down. As I fumble with the last ankle knot, he grins into a camera. "Found her. What else you got for us?" Casually, he picks up the piece of technology and throws it into the flames.

Eden watches him as I pull her to her feet. He stalks out of the room afterward, and Barclay tells us to leave him be for a moment.

"Jesus, are you okay?" I ask Edie, massaging her wrists where the rope rubbed. It's clear she'd tried to save herself but couldn't manage it.

"Wonderful. I love being tied up for hours. How'd you know where to find me?"

"Jarvis," Barclay admits. "I'm not exactly sure how, and I wouldn't ask him because he probably won't tell you."

"Did they hurt you?" I ask, still looking her over.

"I'm fine," she says tersely, but I think it's just for show in front of Barclay. When we're alone, I'll get her to tell me everything. "What was all that about, though?"

"If I had to guess," Barclay starts. "A few things. One, they're always watching. They knew at that exact moment that you were vulnerable. Two, they can pull us along like puppets on a string. Three, they're testing our relationship already. Four, teamwork. If you know anything about the Knights, you know the whole foundation is built on relationships. You don't have to like each other to help your fellow Knight. The greater good is better than one person."

"I take it we failed?" Eden asks Barclay, fire in her eyes.

If we don't make it into the Knights, it'll be damn near impossible to find out what happened to Delilah. All of that fear is displayed in the fierceness of her gaze.

"Yes, we did. We can only hope others failed worse than us."

16

Eden

I hold the strange sensations clawing at me until we're back at Jarvis Hall. Oliver tried to get close while we were in the backseat, but I cringed away, unable to stand the thought of anyone touching me right now.

Panic flutters in my chest as I remember their rough grips and the nothingness. The horror of those few hours tied up God knows where, the future like a death knell clanging above my head, still tears at my bones like it can break me apart from the inside.

All the while, I held it in. All the fear, the anxiety

spiking every sense I had. I couldn't let it show for fear of them seeing me as weak. In the moments when it was me in the darkness and the faint sound of a clock ticking away the drawn-out seconds, I wondered if this was more than just a Trial. If they'd taken me like Dee, wanting me to suffer like her. Still, I held tight to those emotions, not letting them spill out because I'll die before I ever give them the satisfaction that they've broken me.

As soon as Leo parks the car, I'm the first to exit. I walk as steadily as I can to the big building in front of me. Even though everything else is in a haze, Jarvis Hall stretches like a black abyss toward the sky, surrounded in tangled webs that I didn't realize I was caught in since setting foot on this campus that first night.

Oliver calls my name behind me, but I don't stop. I need to be alone with my thoughts, so I can dissect my reaction to the last few hours. So I can prove to myself I'm safe, even though my body is still on high-alert, searching out a threat.

I guess I am afraid of something after all. Ending up like my poor, murdered sister.

My feet thud up the staircase, and I turn into Dee's old room, locking it from the inside. Sure, that bastard has a key, but I doubt he'll bother me. He never even glanced my way on the way back from that house.

While Oliver and Alaric dug for information, he was a stony, silent bastard.

It was about the Trials. It was a game, I tell myself. But it felt much more real than that. When they threw me in the car; when they tied me up; when they led me into that place blindfolded, leaving the outside world a shroud of mystery...

I didn't know if I was walking into a place to get beheaded or being led off a dock to drown...

It hit too fucking close to home.

I knew they'd do something like this to get to me. There were no doubts.

Distracted, I trip on one of Dee's boxes, landing ungracefully in the middle of the room, the wood floors digging into my knees with a sharp pain. A strangled cry wrestles free from my throat, and I kick out, sending a box with her name on it sliding across the room. Right now, her things aren't a beacon of hope. They're more like a coffin.

Why in the fucking world would she ever want to be part of a group like this? Why would she fucking put herself through their bullshit? What happened to her during Trials? My sweet, innocent sister...

I never asked. Once you're in the Knights' grasp, you're not supposed to talk about it. And to be honest, I didn't fucking care. That was Dee's thing, not mine.

Not mine.

I suck in a ragged breath, almost afraid to let it all out. I haven't let it out, not any. I could've drank myself into a stupor like my father. I could've walked around our enormous house as a zombie like my mother. But no, someone had to keep their shit together. Be strong. Faking the façade. It's what Astors are the best at, right? My heart squeezes, and I fall forward, placing my forehead on the wood floors, my fingernails biting into the wood. I'm going to break.

A knock sounds on my door. "Edie love?"

My head snaps up, panic rising. I don't want Oliver to see me like this. I don't want anyone to see me like this. Taking in a deep breath, I hold it while forcing a smile to my face. "What's up, Number Five?" My hands shake, and I suck in another muted breath to hold myself steady. Oliver sees too much. If I give him any inkling of what I'm going through right now, I'll end up with my door hanging off the hinges.

"You okay?"

Shaking my head, the first tear starts to fall as all of my surroundings press in. I blow out a quick breath and paste the façade on my face again. "Yeah. Just tired, you know? I think I bored myself to sleep back there." The lie makes my stomach clench with the need to purge myself of it.

Oliver tries the doorknob, but it catches on the

lock. "Edie, you know I'm here for you. You can be straight with me."

"I'm fine," I spit too tersely. I grimace, closing my eyes so tightly that stars dance across my vision. "Just jumping into bed," I try again, praying my best friend will just leave it for now.

I know he'd help me. He'd take me into his arms, make sure I'm comfortable on the bed. Hell, he'd probably even bring me hot tea, put in my favorite movie, and hold me all night, because that's what Oliver does. *He loves.*

But love is what brought me to this moment. It's caring too much. It's letting someone crawl under my skin and live there. My sister did all of those things, and I just can't right now. Because of her, I'm having a panic attack in my room after being abducted by a secret society who's playing it off as if it's all just fun and games. A secret society who may have killed my sister.

"If you're sure..."

"Yep," I strangle out. "All good."

The floorboards creak when he walks away, and I let out a *whoosh*. Pretending to be something you're not is draining, like tiny, stinging cuts all over your body. I feel the slices more when I'm lying to Oliver because I know he'd do anything for me. *Anything.*

His footsteps climb to his room, and I'm about to

drag myself to my feet and go after him when a key slides into the lock. It twists, and my door opens with a creak. Glaring over my shoulder, expecting to find the big thug Leo, my mouth parts when it's not him.

It's not Oliver either.

It's Alaric Barclay.

His hair sticks on end, his face strained—something I hadn't noticed in the car. He must be at least six years older than me, but right now, he could pass for even older than that. His gaunt features pass like a shadow over his presence, making me think today's events took their toll on all of us.

After closing the door and relocking, he slips forward, taking in my odd position. His lips thin, and my hackles raise at his look of pity. I crawl away, but that doesn't stop his approach. He catches up to me easily, and I shift to stare straight into his striking green eyes as they assess me. Fear bubbles to the surface again, and I gasp at the near physical blow of anxiety when it punches me in the gut.

My professor bends, stretching an arm around my shoulders, fingertips brushing over my buzzing skin. His other hand slides under my knees, and he lifts me from the floor, cradling me like a child until he moves with ease to the bed. "He's a good friend. You shouldn't shut him out."

Tears gather in the corner of my eyes. "I know."

He sets me on the bed, staring for a few tortured seconds before sliding in beside me with a sigh. Moving my pillow against the headboard, he rests against it then holds his arm out. I bite my lip, staring at the invitation. We're crossing all sorts of lines if I do this. "Don't tell the class."

His joke—if that was what it was supposed to be— falls flat. It was more like a threat, a nod to our current circumstances.

What a scandal. Teacher and student. The watcher and the watched.

He smells good—like old, expensive cologne. The distinct aroma you would imagine his grandfather's grandfather also wore. It's too enticing to pass up, so I move in, settling my head on his firm chest. "Are you Alaric right now? Or my professor?"

"Neither. I'm dumb," he says immediately, his fingertips gripping my upper arm. "Call me fucking stupid." My body locks up at his tone, but he pulls me even closer, his chest moving up and down in a steady rhythm. His expelled breath tickles my hair. "I'm not your professor right now, but the next time you have a fucking panic attack and shut yourself in your room, you're going to get punished. Understand?"

I'm not quite sure how he's taken my innocent question and turned it into something so dirty. My body flushes as the images of him getting his cock sucked flood my addled brain. Whether he meant it as a sexy taunt or not, my body went there because his allure is just too much. If only he wasn't a Knight...

Fuck. Why the hell am I lying in bed with one of them? He's probably taking notes to give to the Elders. He can tell them how badly this Trial fucked me up so they can do worse next time.

I try to pull away, but he tugs me right back. "This is your fault. You sent away your friend, so now you only have me." His grip on my forearm is a little too strong to be comforting. It's just this shy of possession. "Relax," he sighs, even though his tone does everything but make me want to do so.

But...he has taken the chaos out of my mind. He's...distracting.

"What was that place?" I ask, my face still plastered into his dress shirt. I peer upward to find the first couple of his buttons undone, giving me a peek of a strong chest. Alaric Barclay might be the finest specimen I've ever seen in my life. And I'm This. Close.

"That house..." Alaric huffs out a breath. "It's the house Leo grew up in."

I gasp at that revelation. I'd imagined it was some creepy, abandoned house that the Knights had randomly chosen. Or perhaps that's always the place they leave their abducted girls.

I lift myself up and peer into his dark green gaze.

"Why?" I ask, wondering if it's possible that this isn't only about me. "Why there?"

Alaric shrugs as if this is all so commonplace. "Leo's grandfather likes to fuck with him. He's a sadistic old bastard. Like the rest of us," he quickly adds, glaring down at me. "Only he's been doing it a lot longer, so he's really fucking good at it." He tightens his grip again, and my skin burns underneath his touch. "Leo's the one who knew how to find you because of the note they sent with the black roses."

"Black roses." That seems a little too on the nose. "You're kidding?"

"We're nothing if not dramatic."

We're... I keep forgetting that he's a Knight, then he does or says something that brings me right back around to the truth. Is it possible that Alaric knew where I was this entire time? He'd deny it, of course, but *we* sounds suspiciously like an admission. It's a reminder that no matter how hot he is, I can't trust him. Or Leo for that matter, whether he deciphered the note that set me free or not.

Alaric and Leo are doing this because they have to. Because the Elders paired us together, and they have some sort of sick loyalty to them—maybe Alaric most of all.

The feelings creep back in again. I try to close my eyes to block them out, but the complete and utter darkness and loneliness of being in that empty room, my hearing the only sense that was working... Every gust of wind across the windows... Every tiny squeak... All of it meant something was about to happen. The entire time I was tied up, I was on full alert, waiting for the hammer to come dropping down.

To be at someone else's mercy is terrifying. If I never feel that way again, I'll count myself very lucky. It's like walking a tightrope with no understanding of where the hard surface that will break you is.

Alaric must feel the panic surge through my body again. He presses in close, his chin resting on the top of my head. I squeeze him tight, not because he's a demigod of good looks, but because he's the most stable thing I can cling to right now—even if he isn't safe at all.

"Shh, you're in your room at your residence hall. You're free. You're safe." He repeats this over and over, and right before my eyes flutter closed in sleep, he grinds out, "And we won't let that shit happen to you again."

If only someone could make a promise like that and keep it.

17

Leo

*I*f you can't beat them, join them.

My heart pounds in my chest. As soon as the last tether to this godforsaken place exits my car, I reverse out of the parking lot, the tires once again sticking to the pavement like glue as I push the engine to its limits, leaving them all—and this night—behind.

My grandfather is a sadistic bastard. He knew what he was doing when he sent me there. It's like I'm undergoing Trials right alongside the Astor girl and the prince. He's fucking with me.

I'm hardly dressed for where I'm going now, but I

really don't give a fuck. The only thought pulsing through my mind is asking my grandfather what he's playing at.

The corner building in the two-stoplight town is a little fancier than the rest of the places in the area. Downstairs, it's a regular old townie bar with grime on the floor and sticky countertops. That's more my scene —drinking beer and watching the game on the big screen, ogling girls in tight clothes that give just as good as they get.

Once you go past the velvet curtain and up the winding staircase in the corner, though, you're in a completely different world. More often than not, you can find Knights drinking whiskey at the posh bar or smoking cigars in designer chairs. Up here, the men are all wearing tailored suits and polished Oxfords. Sure, they may have their ties loose around their necks, but they're never far away from business. This isn't a place to chill. It's a place to make backroom deals and plot someone's downfall.

Grandfather often asks me to meet him here. Only because he wants to show me how respected he is.

Like I could ever forget.

As soon as I step foot in the section that screams money, the walls squeeze in on me. Heads swivel at my entrance then peer away as if I'm nothing but the dirt under their shoe. Part of me has always wanted to make them choke on how much they despise me. It's the only thing that keeps me going sometimes.

I spot the old man in a velvet settee straight out of the Victorian era, puffing on the butt of his cigar. Seconds later, a plume escapes from his lips that reminds me of the atomic bomb detonating. The woman who lit it shakes the match until the flame dies, then climbs onto his lap. The slit in her dress allows her to spread her pussy over my grandfather's thigh.

It's disgusting. The girl is younger than me. Sure, she may be wearing a dress that's as fashionable as it is slutty, but her actions scream *would do anything for a handout*. I suppose if she squints, she wouldn't be able to tell how old he is, but even then, she'd have to be intentionally blind when she reaches for his wrinkly dick.

"Ah, son," Grandfather greets, as if he's just seen me. "Come, sit right here."

He pats the place next to him on the couch. I do as he says but perch myself as far away as possible from the two of them. The woman glances over, but I don't pay her any attention. I'm here for him.

A crystal glass is placed in front of me with a deep brown liquid poured almost to its rim. Picking it up, I swallow three large mouthfuls, knowing I'm grating on my grandfather's nerves by not appreciating whatever the fuck is in the glass.

"If you came here to ask me how you stack up against the others, save your breath," he mutters.

He keeps his words intentionally vague around the girl, even though she's probably signed her life away to be this close to him. NDA upon NDA, blackmail, threats, whatever it takes to make the little people comply.

"Don't care about that," I grind out, feeling the alcohol coat my throat, my voice rasping like Clint Eastwood's for a brief moment. "Why give me a job and then intentionally screw it up?"

He knows what I'm getting at. I'm supposed to be watching Eden. He reiterated the point by making me be on her fucked-up Pledge team, but then whisked her out from under our own damn noses, making us —*making me*—look like a damn fool.

He sighs, taking another puff on his cigar. "If you're not smart enough to understand that you're also being evaluated again, Leonardo, I don't know what to tell you."

Evaluated again? As in a *real* second chance at the Knights? Not just a temporary role he had to plug me into in order to do his bidding? "You're always evaluating me," I counter. It's the truest statement of my life.

From childhood, he watched me. Even then it wasn't difficult to ascertain that I was his least favorite.

My grandfather smirks in response. "And you're always failing."

I flinch before rapidly recovering. The old Leo shows up sometimes. The one who had a conscience. The one who wanted his grandfather to respect and love him instead of being used as a pawn. What my grandfather's just said is his truth. He firmly believes I'm nothing but a failure.

"You shouldn't have left her alone."

His rebuke makes me feel like a kid again. "She wasn't alone. She was with us, but Cummings threw me off."

The head of the Jarvis line glares at me for using names before slipping his free hand up the woman's thigh who's rubbing on him. "Don't let anyone deter you from this task. I mean it. I can't stress the importance enough." From the corner of my eye, I see him pinch her thigh...hard. "Trust is hard to come by, don't you think?"

"I do," I growl, thinking of how he led me right to my nightmare. It's a special kind of torture growing up with a grandfather who does shit like lead you to the setting of the most horrific scene you've ever witnessed in your life.

Memories violently flip through my head, consuming my thoughts.

A pool of bright red blood.

Two legs sticking out from around the couch.

My heart pounding so hard in my ears that I couldn't think.

I tip my head back and down the rest of my drink. Afterward, I glare at him and receive the same cruel face I saw that day. He doesn't turn it away from me when he reaches around to grab the young girl's hip, urging her forward on his thigh.

I stand, my stomach flipping. People say I'm fucked up, but they have no idea how much worse I could be with a role model like him.

He peers up, catching my gaze again. "Don't fail me, Leonardo. I have my suspicions about the girl."

Turning away, I don't say a word. He knows I follow orders because he has me by the balls. If he's so intent on the Astor chick, maybe there's something I'm missing. Right now, all I see is a girl who came to Carnegie and is joining the Knights because that's what's expected of her after her sister died. She's slipped right into the good little rich girl role.

Pathetic.

I stride across the room, and the images keep coming. Setting foot in that house has triggered everything I've tried to forget. Before leaving the building entirely, I stop at the bar downstairs. The bartender flashes fuck-me eyes while I drink four bottles of cheap beer and pretend to pay attention to the game plastered on every screen in the place.

The night draws long. The edges of my vision start to blur, as do the memories I'm desperately trying to forget. Mission fucking accomplished.

Right before I'm tempted to call it a night, the busty brunette behind the bar leans in front of me, squeezing her tits together. "What do you say you take me home tonight?"

Sometimes, it's that easy. I've barely said two words to her as she drank in my tattoos and handed me bottle after bottle. I must mumble something coherent because she flashes a white smile, tells me to meet her outside in thirty minutes and that she's driving. *Probably a good idea*, I think to myself as I stumble toward the bathroom, then head outside.

I'm not sure whether she gets out earlier than expected or if I really did fill the time waiting for her by staring at the canopy of stars above. "Aren't you cold?" she asks as she bounds toward me, wrapping a small jean jacket around her.

I turn, taking in her luscious curves. "Nope." It must've taken as long as she predicted because I'm not slurring anymore. Damnit. Good thing I'm taking this girl home. She'll help keep me out of the abyss.

"Keys, bad boy?"

I love a girl with confidence. However, I must not be entirely sober since I hand over the keys to my baby, threatening her not to damage my baby as they're sailing through the air.

Once she revs the engine and pulls out, I give her directions toward Carnegie. She peers at me with wide eyes. "You go there?" Her gaze drops to my tattoos. The disbelief on her face is definitely warranted.

"Not by choice," I rasp.

She turns back to the road, and I take in her side profile, my cock hardening in my pants. Reaching out, I slip my hand over her thigh, moving higher and higher. Instead of swatting me away or cursing me out, she opens her legs wider, giving me as much access as I want.

Disappointment beats through me with every thump of my heart. The image of a blonde, rich girl back at Jarvis Hall fills my thoughts and drives me forward—whether because I want to fuck her out of my mind or I'm trying to fuck her in my mind, I'm not sure. I hit home, my fingers working over the seam of the bartender's jeans. She throws her head back, and I spit out a warning about crashing my car.

"Don't you worry. I'll do the driving, you do the fingering."

There's not enough time to get that far before we're turning into the parking lot of Jarvis Hall. She stares, mouth wide, as we enter the campus. It's a ghost town at this time of night. Especially with classes tomorrow. It's a good thing I don't give a fuck about those.

"You got roommates?"

"Yes."

"I can be quiet," she says reassuringly.

"Don't bother," I grind out. An image of little miss Edie Astor waking to this girl screaming her orgasm while riding my cock makes me that much harder. Picturing the fire in Astor's eyes, the refusal to believe the heat pooling in her belly is because of me makes this encounter much more satisfying. I didn't push it far enough earlier to check—I didn't trust myself—but she was wet for me. I could tell by the way her hips kept searching me out.

We exit the car, and the girl grabs for my hand after tossing me the keys. Slipping out of her grip is easy. I don't do touchy-feely bullshit. I scare most women in the bedroom before they realize they fucking love someone who's a little dangerous and can talk so dirty it curls their toes.

I push the main door open then close it behind us. I don't give the pretty bartender a moment to take in her surroundings. Instead, I move right in, pinning her against the door, my lengthening cock pressing into her pelvis.

A squeak sneaks past her lips followed by muffled laughter. Her body relaxes minutely as I breathe onto her neck. "I'm going to claim you tonight. I'm going to—"

"Oh, don't let me stop you," a feminine voice calls out from the kitchen.

The girl I'm currently pressed against pushes me off, only succeeding because I'm still unsteady on my feet from the alcohol.

Eden turns on the kitchen light, revealing a sly grin.

"Shit, you're not a girlfriend, are you? If so, he agreed to this."

Eden chuckles, but there's no humor in it. Unconsciously, my gaze moves to her wrists that were tied up not twelve hours ago. There's a pink line slashed across them, and my head practically explodes. "No," I growl, pissed off at the world. Everyone gets hurt here. Everyone. "And unless she wants to watch, she can run back up to her room."

Little Miss Astor forces a smile to her face, striding by in those same silly pajamas she wore this morning. All the blood in my body moves south as I watch her ass walk away. She's almost to the stairs when she turns around again. "Hope he told you about the sores. I mean, I'm not saying it's an STD... It's probably not... You know, forget I said anything."

The girl who was supposed to be my easy fuck whips her head to stare at me, uncertainty flashing in her eyes. It's clear her desire is gone, and this whole foreplay to climax was ruined by one smart little mouth.

The girl's gaze darts to the door. "Just go," I spit, fists flexing.

She doesn't waste any time, scampering for the door like she's being chased by a chlamydia-laden dick.

When the door slams, Eden's smile beams like it's powered by the sun. Here is the rough-around-the-edges girl I saw that first night. Physically, it's not hard to tell the hell she went through today, yet here she is, giving me lip and motherfucking cock-blocking me.

"You enjoy that, did you?"

"Probably a little too much," she says honestly.

I take her in. She's never seemed stronger—a fire-cracker with welts around her wrists, unbrushed hair, but her chin raised in the air, smirking at me. I can't figure her out. The way she flounces around, dressing like all the other girls, but then has the nerve to join my little fucked-up goodbye party for her old roommates. She didn't get down on her knees like the others. In her own way, she fought back, trying to force the one guy in the room she knew would come easily for her.

And she almost won.

Almost.

Maybe Grandfather's right to be worried about her. There's definitely more under the surface when it comes to Eden Astor.

She moves toward me with a curious expression. "Where were you?" As she nears, it's clear I don't need to tell her. Her little nose scrunches. "You okay?"

Her question takes me aback. The fuck would she ask me that for? She was the one who was abducted by the sickest secret society around and bound to a chair for hours until we found her. I narrow my gaze, taking in her sallow skin and bloodshot eyes. Still, she stares at me as if *I'm* the one who's hurting.

Barclay. Barclay, that motherfucker. I wasn't sure he'd noticed where we were, but obviously he did. He did, and he felt the need to share.

I can't have her feeling sorry for me. No one better fucking feel sorry for me.

"I'm about to be," I grin. My hands find the button on my jeans. After slipping it through the hole, I lower my zipper. Her stare drops to my fingers and then straight to my face again, clearly trying to keep focused on me, but I spot the subtle shift in her. The tips of her ears turn pink; a blush starts across her chest, barricaded by the spaghetti straps of her tank top.

"What are you doing?"

"Since you're so goddamn interested in my cock, you're about to inspect it...you know, for STDs."

Her tongue darts past her lips, and I wonder if she even realizes she's giving off the subtle cues that she's clearly getting turned on. Mine is much more obvious as I pull out my cock, stroking down its firm length.

Though she must know I've taken it out, she doesn't take her muted blue eyes off mine. "Don't you want to look so you can better educate the girls I bring home?"

"How many girls do you plan on bringing home?"

Ah, jealousy. The way my balls cinch up surprises me. I *like* that she's jealous. "If I have another day like today, plenty. And I foresee shit like that happening a lot."

Her gaze burns into me. "You plan on letting me get kidnapped again?"

I reach out, my free hand working its way around her throat. "No," I growl. "That won't happen again."

Her skin is soft and warm under my palm. The muscles in her neck tighten as I stroke the curve of her neck with the pad of my thumb. She lifts her chin defiantly as I continue to jack off in slow, steady pumps.

"Now, be a good girl and inspect my cock."

She swallows, the movement apparent with the grip I have on her. She tries to turn her head, but I hold her still. Worry flashes in her eyes, along with a spark. "What if someone sees?"

I see. She likes that. Maybe she won't admit it to herself yet, but the electricity in her blue eyes paints a different picture. "Let them. You asked for this."

"It was a joke."

My fingers tighten over her throat as I lean in close. "Don't pretend you don't want to be eye to eye with my cock, Astor. I saw you sneaking glances when your fist was pumping away on your boyfriend. I bet your pussy is so fucking wet for me right now. I bet as soon as you go upstairs, you're going to rub one out at the sight of me."

She swallows again. "You're pretty full of yourself."

"For good reason." With added pressure on her neck, I guide her down. She puts up a bit of a fight—just enough to show me she doesn't know if she's okay with this but her curiosity wins out. As soon as she hits her knees, I straighten, working my hand through her hair and gripping hard. My dick juts in her face. She has no choice but to inspect it now. Blood pumps south under her stare, and the tiniest bit of precum filters through my tip. Her gaze moves to my piercing first, her tongue gliding out of her mouth once again in a short sweep of her lips.

I stroke it for her, my finger teasing the edge of the barbell on the underside of my cock. The desire to surge forward and press my dick between her lips is almost inescapable as she watches me. My movements become more pronounced, and with it, I elicit a low groan from deep inside her throat.

"You like that?" I urge, yanking on her blonde strands. "You're so curious you could self-combust." She starts to squirm while still attempting to keep her shoulders straight. "Have you ever been with a guy who has a piercing before?"

She shakes her head, her hair falling over her shoulders. The movement draws my attention to her nipples coming to a point under the thin fabric of her pajama top.

If I let this go on for much longer, I'll be doing whatever I want with her. I'll take her ripe little ass, her mouth, anything and everything. Already, I feel the telltale sign of an imminent climax, and there's no fucking way I'm going to give her the satisfaction that I jerked off in front of her, blowing my load *for her*.

A little part of me tells me it isn't right either. Not with what she went through today.

That little voice makes me want to do it anyway, but I don't. "That's too bad," I say, tucking my cock away and pulling my pants back up around my hips. "You probably never will, either. You wouldn't satisfy my appetite."

Then, I leave an open-mouthed Eden Astor still on her knees in the foyer. Because I'm an asshole like that.

Kicking a girl while she's down. Clearly, my grandfather should be more proud of me than he is.

18

Eden

I procrastinate upstairs in my room—even though I'm sure everyone is downstairs, waiting to leave for today's classes—my mind too filled with recent events to face the world just yet. The clear goal I had coming into Carnegie is getting blurry. My sheets smell like my professor. I've confirmed the glint of hardware on Leo's dick, considering it was right in my face last night.

They're Knights. I should despise them, but what scares me the most is how badly I wanted to reach out with my tongue to play with Leo's cock piercing. How intoxicating the moment was. Right up until he said I'd never satisfy him. Honestly, that sounds like a challenge I'm willing to take on, but with all the other things piling on my plate, I'm not sure I can—or should —tackle Leonardo Jarvis right now. The grumpy, moody-as-fuck asshole. I don't care if he's the reason they found me.

After one last check in the mirror, I pull my big girl panties on and head downstairs. Before I hit the last step, I glance toward the foyer where I was down on my knees in front of Leo less than eight hours ago.

"Here she is," Oliver greets when he sees me. He holds a mug of something steaming out to me, and I grin at him. "My lady."

I take it from him gratefully, still guilty that I turned him away last night. He's another one where it seems like the lines are fraying. There's a strict friendship line drawn with Oliver, even with the agreement in place that we might sometimes use each other to feel good. Friends with benefits, that's it. We're scuffing the line, though, and I'm not sure that should happen.

"Good. We need to sit down and discuss things," Alaric notes, pulling out his professor voice. I try not to let it show how much I like that demanding tenor. Instead, when I peer over at him, I'm reminded of last night. How he came into my room without permission because he knew I would need someone. He carried me to the bed and hugged me to his body.

I just can't fucking figure out why.

The small kitchenette in Jarvis Hall isn't that big. It's enough for a bit of countertop space, a fridge, microwave, cupboards, and a peninsula with bar stools on the other side of it. Oliver and Leo are inside the kitchen while Alaric and I sit on the stools sipping our drinks.

Neither Leo nor Alaric has met my gaze, so I concentrate on Oliver, who's inspecting me as if I'll break. He's leaning across the peninsula, so I reach out to grab his hand and squeeze. Oliver's my partner in crime, always will be. The other two, we'll just deal with until I get into the Knights of Arcadia. Then, Oliver and I can do what we came here to do. I keep my hand in his, drawing on his strength. When Leo turns, he gives our entwined hands a cruel smirk, then leans against the wall, separate from the rest of us. "Let's get this over with."

Alaric doesn't pay his attitude any mind. He launches into a plan. "It's obvious the Elders will try to fuck with the groupings they made. They were successful once, which means they'll likely try it again."

Oliver clasps my hand more firmly in his grip.

"I've got an alarm company coming in to set up a security system."

Leo snorts. "You think I leave *my* hall unprotected?" We all turn to look at him, but he's glaring at me. "There are exterior and interior cameras, and I can set the window and door alarms to alert."

"You have cameras in here?" Surprise colors my tone as I blink at him.

"Of course I do. I protect what's my family's. Want to see what the foyer camera caught yesterday?" He pulls out his phone and starts pressing on the screen. I think he's only trying to scare me, but when I hear my voice come through the speaker, my stomach plummets.

Reaching out, I snatch the device away from him as he's turning it around to show everyone. I throw it, not aiming at anything in particular, but it sails all the way into the living room and hits the opposite wall.

Leo's face turns ruddy. "If that's broken, you'll pay. And not in money, sweetheart."

Alaric sighs at the two of us. "Do you have feeds anywhere else besides your phone?"

"The basement," Leo states, still fixing me with a hard stare. I can't take my eyes off him. I want to scratch his eyes out. One, for playing games, and two, attempting to show the others.

"Can I trust you to arrange all that? I'll cancel the guys I have coming."

Leo only shifts his death glare to Alaric, so I guess we're all just assuming that's a yes from him.

"Someone needs to be with Eden every second of every day. If we get caught again, it could mean she and Oliver don't make it to Fledglings—and who knows what might happen to us."

This would usually be the time I give my two cents about being smothered, but instead, I stew inside at the Knights for putting me in this situation. The truth is, Alaric is right. The Knights will keep trying to ruin us, and the only thing that matters is that I make it to Fledgling. If that means I have to spend time with my hot professor and the dickhead, then so be it. This particular torture is temporary. Not knowing what happened to Dee is a life sentence I don't want to serve.

Leo seems like he'd be the last person to agree to this, though. I lift my stare to inspect him. Day-old stubble moves with the tightening of his jaw. He locks eyes with me, and my heart makes a solid thump in my chest at the dangerous look I find there. I'm simultaneously afraid *and* drawn to him, a treacherous combo. "I can babysit the princess. No problem."

Oliver breaks his silence. "That's what I'm here for," he simply states. When I peer over, I realize I'm no longer squeezing his hand. He's backed up all the way to the refrigerator with his arms crossed over his chest.

He avoids my gaze, and after we finish our drinks,

Alaric gives us tasks. The main priority is to watch out for any Knight and steer clear until the next Trial. I'm too tired to ask what that could be.

Afterward, Oliver and I leave for class. Alaric and Leo stay behind, probably discussing security measures, like they think the Knights could sneak into my room and grab me. And who knows, maybe they would.

Around campus, I spot the other female Pledges being closely followed by at least one or two of the men they're grouped with. Anne-Marie is eating the attention up, strutting to class as if she's a celebrity being followed by paparazzi. She turns straight toward us where the sidewalks cross, and I brace for her bitchiness. She's always disliked Delilah and I, even though we were often forced together at parties. Her bright red lips pull apart into a grin. "Heard we beat you the other night. Looks like my guys are better at taking care of me than yours."

I walk right past because I don't have time for her Barbie bullshit. Determination threads through me, though. I've always had a competitive nature and beating her at the Knights' game would be both satisfying and rewarding.

"Wouldn't it be something if I got in and you didn't?" she calls out, still trying to bait me.

I keep my voice low. "God, I hate her."

Oliver says nothing. A quick check-in with him, and I find his cheeks pinched like he's about to explode, so I know we're on the same page. Anne-Marie is a cunt. That's all there is to it.

Only, when we get inside the building that houses our first class for the day, Oliver immediately grips my hand and pulls, dragging me under the first stairwell. The area is steeped in shadow, which only highlights the dark look on his face when he peers down at me.

"What are you doing?" I hiss, wondering if he's taking this watch thing too far. Did he see a Knight? He probably didn't need to barricade me in here with all these people still around.

The noise in the nearby halls is still loud with foot traffic—people talking about their upcoming classes or what they did last night. When Oliver presses in on me, though, my world is reduced to the area surrounding us, as if we're in a bubble. "You like the bad boys, huh? You want to get down on your knees for them?"

It takes me a moment to understand what he's talking about. Fuck. He'd seen more of the video than I'd thought.

"Oliver..."

"No, don't," he growls, his rough voice intoxicating. His hand moves to my hip, pressing into the indentation there and forcing me flat against the wall. "You're mine. You always have been. Open your eyes, your ears, your senses…" He leans in, his hot breath hitting my neck. He drags his lips down my sensitive skin and bites the soft curve that leads to my shoulder.

I gasp, not expecting that from Oliver, my best friend.

"I fight for the things I want," he grinds out, forcing his hips into mine so I can feel his erection. "When I'm through, you'll be begging to drop to your knees for me."

My mouth suddenly dry, I swallow. My heart beats an erratic rhythm in my chest, like it doesn't know whether it should be excited, angry, or turned off. But my core knows exactly what it wants. My body went straight past the smoldering phase and into a rushing inferno.

He licks across the bite he just made, and a groan passes my lips that I can't hold back.

"That's right," he praises, breathing me in. His chest scrapes against my sensitive nipples.

"The difference between him and me is that he's a taker, and I'm a giver."

Oliver grips my skirt in his hand and hikes it up. The rush of cold air feels even more frosty as it collides with the heat of my skin. Splaying his hand across my thigh and dragging it upward, he brings goosebumps along with him. He maneuvers his fingers between my legs and directly to my nub, using the friction from my panties to drive me crazy.

"I know your body. I know how much you love clit play and how wet you must be right now, wondering what I'll do next. Will I drop to my knees and play London Bridge?" My own limbs start to shake, and he chuckles. "Will I just take you right here where anyone can watch?"

"Oliver," I plead. Part of me knows I should be telling him to stop, but I can't. It feels too good.

He shifts his knee between my legs and forces me to ride it with a quick tug. I rock into him as he swirls over my clit, my body taking over as I use Oliver's thigh. I just can't get enough. A whimper escapes my throat at the need barreling through me. I need more.

"I'm right here. I got you," he says, untucking my shirt. He sneaks his hand under my bra and lifts. A flash of cold air hits my skin before his hot mouth takes in my nipple.

"Fuck, Ollie. More."

"You're so wet," he says around a mouthful of my flesh. "You're gushing for me. Relax. I never leave you hanging."

I take a deep breath, calming myself as much as I can, even though it feels as if I'll never fall over the edge. It's complete torture.

I shouldn't doubt Oliver, though. He presses on my

bundle of nerves, moving in tune with the attention he laves on my breast. "These are so fucking beautiful," he coos. "Watch how you respond to me. Tight, perky bud straining for my mouth. Mine."

I start to shake uncontrollably. Oliver's hips join in on the action, working together with mine. He pinches my breast as he kisses a trail up my neck before biting down on my ear. "One day," he promises. "You're going to let me fuck you properly."

My mind obliterates. Stars dance across my vision when my climax hits until I'm clinging onto my best friend, fingers sinking into his upper arms as I ride out my pleasure. My short gasps fill the area around us until I shudder one final time. I drop my head to his shoulder, breathing in his heady scent.

"Now tell me that didn't feel good," he prompts. "Next time you want to feel like that, you come to me." He covers me back up, making sure my panties are in place and my bra is on correctly. He flares out my shirt and skirt, then tucks the hem of my shirt in like I had it.

It's easier when we do this in the dark. Then, I can just roll away in a blissful haze to fall asleep. Here, when we still have to go to class together, I don't know what to say. However, I do know my knees feel like jelly, and there's a heightened sense of awareness still clinging to my skin.

"I take it you're mad about the Leo video?"

"Not mad," he says huskily. "Only trying to make you see what's been in front of you this whole time."

Nerves tighten my stomach. I could fall into an abyss with Oliver. Besides Dee, he's my person. He's everything to me and changing that scares the shit out of me. With Leo? It's just about playing games and sex. Even ogling Alaric is pure fun. With Oliver, though, it's not like we can go back to where we were. Once you cross a line, there's no returning to blissful ignorance.

He presses a soft kiss on my cheek. "It's always been you, Eden. Always."

19

Eden

*D*istraction. That's what all of these moments are. I'm almost blindsided by the realization as I make my way through the day pissed and angry at myself. Ollie is always there, but he doesn't say anything about what happened. He just continues on as if nothing out of the ordinary occurred between us.

I see what he's doing, though. He's making me curious. I keep looking at him. Keep remembering. Keep wondering...

Obviously, he's fucking hot, but I'd placed him

firmly in the friendship zone years ago. We've been friends since before crushes and feelings—way back before I even knew sex existed. His heart of gold has nearly always gotten him in trouble. Like me, he doesn't want to be pinned down or put into a category. He wants to live freely and without regret. A part of him yearns for his family's approval, which has led to that giant chip on his shoulder. I *know* him. Or at least I thought I did...

"Eden..."

Alaric's voice threads through my thoughts, unraveling my current mindset. He peers at me with a look that squeezes my heart. Sometimes, he's just too beautiful. He has a way of putting on a face for whoever needs it. He's got the professor thing down. He's got the trying to be my helper thing down too.

I get caught up in looking at him, and he raises his brows. Slowly, I come to my senses. Right. We're heading back into the Knights' lair. There's a Trial tonight.

Based on the postcard that Leo revealed to all of us after classes, we think the next Trial will be designed to test us physically. All I can think is an arm-wrestling competition, which is ludicrous. It'll be far more sinister than that.

I blow out a breath, and Leo glances over his shoulder at me. He's dressed in ripped jeans, a hoodie pulled low over his brows, making him look more dangerous than normal. It doesn't help that it's pitch black out as we walk across the quad toward the Knights' building.

"Stay strong, the both of you," Alaric orders, moving his gaze to Oliver too. "All you have to do is endure it. Whatever they ask, don't refuse. Don't give up. Do everything they tell you to."

My head hurts already and I'm not even inside the building yet. Going through the Knights' Trials sounded easier in my head. Maybe I was thinking about the *Skulls* movie where they stole their competitor's weathervane. I'm up for a little breaking and entering, but all this mind game shit is beating away at my already deteriorated mental health.

"Any words of wisdom?" Alaric asks Leo.

Leo turns, stopping our group abruptly. "Yeah. Don't let them see that you're scared. Understood? There're no places in the Knights for pussies."

O-kay, then. That was such a Leo pep talk.

A chorus of laughter makes us all turn. To my right, another group joins us. They walk under the intersecting streetlamp, and I see Anne-Marie perched on two of her guys' shoulders, Cleopatra style. She's beaming as if she's on a Miss America float in the Thanksgiving Day Parade.

I roll my eyes—hard. I'm pretty sure the Knights

don't want princesses. In fact, I'm pretty sure the Knights don't want girls at all. This is nothing but a show for them. The fact that Anne-Marie can't see that is disturbing. She doesn't seem to be treating this as seriously as she should. My sister died while in their grasp. It doesn't matter if all the Knights perch Anne-Marie on their shoulders, she'll just fall the furthest.

Idiot...

A figure standing at the Knights' entrance lets their group inside. I don't see who it is at first because Leo's broad body is in the way, but then my gaze collides with Keegan Forbes'. He's not nearly as put together as he usually is. He's just wearing a t-shirt and jeans, his hair all over the place, and if I'm not mistaken, he needs a shower....bad.

When recognition hits him, his jaw drops. "Eden? No." He starts forward. "What the fuck are you doing here?"

He doesn't get very far. Leo puts a strong hand on Keegan's chest and pushes him back against the building. "Did I say you could talk to our girl?"

Our girl? A thrill shoots down my spine at that description.

"Eden..." Keegan says again, finding me over Leo's shoulder. It's as if he hasn't registered that Leo's holding him away from me.

"What?" I spit, ignoring his bewildered look. "You think Dee was the only Astor who could hack it? It can't be that hard. You got in."

"Edie..."

He tries pushing through again, but Leo continues to hold him back. "It doesn't sound like she likes you very much. I'd keep my distance. Girl's got bite when she wants to."

Keegan finally peers at his captor. His scared look turns disgustingly conniving. "Jarvis? You've got to be kidding me." His gaze darts to mine. "You're fucked, Eden. No one survives being close to this asshole." He ducks under Leo's arm and grabs my shoulders, placing his lips near my ear. "They don't want you if they paired you with him. Don't trust anyone. Don't—"

In the next second, Keegan flails wildly as he falls to the ground, but he doesn't stay down for long. Blood-shot eyes turn stormy as he stands. Alaric moves in now, putting his hands up as if to diffuse the situation. "You, too?" Keegan asks, eyes rounding. "Run, Eden. Don't walk. Run the fuck away from here or you're going to end up like her. You will. I fucking promise you that."

Leo pushes Alaric out of the way and lunges again, his meaty fist connecting with Keegan's perfect chin. I flinch at the brutality of it. I'm used to hearing about fucking people over financially and in business games. Physicality isn't really the thing of the elites. There are plenty of ways to ruin someone's life with only a few presses of a keyboard. Sending an incriminating photo. Email someone's boss. Laying bare a rival's secrets.

Not this.

Keegan's head snaps back, and a part of me celebrates Leo's actions. The other remembers the boy my sister fell in love with. The same boy I think I recognize now. How did they leave things? He wasn't at her funeral, but he looks like he's...

Maybe he's not sad. Maybe he's guilty.

I press my lips into a thin line as Leo gets in another punch. Crossing my arms, I watch as the guy who tormented my sister gets what's coming to him. I know he fucked around on her. I know he made her miserable. I know he—

Alaric and Oliver pull an enraged Leo off of Keegan who has fallen to a knee, shaking fingers coming up to wipe blood away from his nose.

Leo breathes rigidly, his whole body moving with the mechanics of it. Still taut with tension, he looks as if he could go at him again.

He shakes the other two off and turns. His hard gaze collides with mine, and the world stands still. Everything that's reeling in his eyes is currently embedded into me.

Anger.

Fear.

Sadness.

The whole slew of negative emotions swirls there like he feeds off them. If that's his appetite, I understand why he has the reputation he does.

But it moves something inside me. A slight shift that...makes me feel sorry for him.

"Astor, get your ass in the building."

And there it goes. As quick as it came, the feeling left. Gone. Vanished. I brush past him, rolling my eyes until I feel a smack on my ass.

Hard. So hard, it still stings when I glare over my shoulder at him.

He smirks at me while shifting his hair back into place as if beating up rich heirs is something he does daily for fun. "You're a caveman."

"And you like it," he says, gaze dropping to my breasts.

I don't need to look down to know that I'm nipping. I can't remember if I was nipping before he punched someone or after, but it's not like I'm going to tell him, anyway. "It's cold out, asshole."

He whips off his hoodie, displaying his white wifebeater underneath, and throws the clothing at my face, along with a whole lungful of his essence.

He smells damn good.

This push and pull with Leo is fun, but what if Keegan is right? I already know I shouldn't trust these two, but he acted as if there was something else. Like I got the Knight knockoffs when it came to my grouping. If they gave me the team that should be riding the bench, there could only be one reason—and Keegan called it. They really *don't* want me here.

"Eden!" Keegan growls, but a hand on the small of my back pushes me through the entrance.

I already know who it is before I look. Oliver doesn't touch me like that, and it's too soft to be Leo. He'd drag me in kicking and screaming rather than put a gentle hand at my back. "We have to get you inside on time," Alaric relays as if he has to give a reason for hurrying me.

I begin to pull Leo's hoodie on, but Alaric stops me.

"Not a good idea." His face colors as I look at him for an explanation. "You have to use everything you've got to get in. If I were you, I wouldn't cover up. They don't want people who walk around in hoodies. They want members who command boardrooms. If you're cold, next time wear a blazer."

His focus drops to my chest, and I'm fully aware my professor's stare is on my tits. It's hard not to flush and react.

Slowly, he drags his gaze away. "They were going to get married, right?"

I nod, my throat closing up. "They had a strained relationship, but yes. It was Astor and Forbes approved."

"She didn't like him?"

"It was the other way around. Delilah thought she could save everybody. In my opinion, Keegan isn't worth saving."

"He seems broken up."

"Or is he—" I stop myself. I don't know what I was going to say. Allude to the fact that he may have helped kill my sister? I can't lay my cards down like that.

"Maybe he realized what he had after she was gone."

"Or maybe he's just a dick. Guys like Keegan Forbes don't feel anything past their cocks. He's more apt to feel grief over one of his side pieces."

"That's a cynical view of this world," Alaric responds quietly while we make our way into the main chamber where everyone else is. Luckily, you can't hear what's going on outside from in here. I don't know what kind of trouble Leo would get in for fighting —if any.

"It's the only one I know," I say.

"Not everyone in this world is like that," he replies, guiding me closer to where the Knights are congregating, and I can't help but think he's doing the exact opposite of what his words imply.

The Knights are the enemy, and he's leading me right to them like a lamb for slaughter.

20

Eden

Oliver arrives just in time for us Pledges to be blindfolded. Leo follows him in like he didn't just have an altercation with someone out front. I don't see Keegan enter, but the complete and total darkness I'm suddenly plunged under might have something to do with it.

My breathing picks up, memories from just a few days ago closing in, but then a strong hand grips my forearm, centering me.

I'm not sure whose grip it is, but it helps alleviate the helpless feeling. They're here, and for the time being, they've promised to protect me, even if it is for the sake of their own Knight standings.

I'm led down a corridor with only the footsteps of those around me reverberating off the walls. A blast of cold air snaps at my face, and I realize we're being led outside again. Panic starts to hit home. I move in closer, sure it's Alaric who has me now. He's already aware how well I handled the last challenge. Instead, it's Leo's voice that rings out. "I've got you, Little Astor."

I immediately pull back, but he doesn't let me get away with that. "Oh, you thought it was the professor? Too bad. You're stuck with me." He's silent for a moment as we walk down the sidewalk. Distrust rings through me. He might lead me right into a brick wall. Instead, he says, "There's a bus up ahead. We're all loading. I'll be right here."

I do as he says as he directs me up a set of steps and to a seat, scooting me all the way to the inside where the cold steel of the bus brushes my arm. It's freezing tonight, as if Mother Nature has finally decided it's truly fall. And I can't even wear the hoodie he threw at me earlier.

When the bus's engine roars to life and starts to pull away, voices rise up around me, chatting happily. I don't know if it's just the people who aren't blindfolded or if it's everyone. I turn in Leo's direction. "Where's Oliver?"

"Across the aisle from us with Alaric."

I nod, grateful that he's here. What kind of best friend would start going to college and attempt to join a secret society for you?

Apparently someone who wants to be more than a friend.

"Talk to me about Forbes," Leo grunts.

"What about him?" I sigh, annoyed he's taken me out of my thoughts by talking about someone I despise.

"He seemed pretty adamant in protecting you."

I roll my eyes. "Your guess is as good as mine. He's loathed me since... Well, since I grew a backbone and told him to fuck off when it came to my sister."

After a moment, Leo says, "Never liked him."

"Welcome to the club. He's a cocky, overindulgent bastard who thinks women should get on their knees for him just because of his last name."

Leo makes an amused grunt. "And your sister wouldn't do that?"

I press my lips together. It was well known that Keegan and Delilah had an agreement. It was also well known that Keegan went ahead and did exactly what he wanted, anyway. Just like my father, the understanding in this world is that if the guy wants to fuck around, he can. After all, the women get all the positives, right? The money, the parties, the distinguished pleasure of being on their arms.

Fucking gag me.

"It was different for Dee. She actually loved him." I shake my head while the sadness threatens to take me under. "No idea why. She deserved so much more."

Leo sighs beside me, and the seat dips as he moves closer. "I wish I'd hit him harder now."

"Ha," I practically snort. "Next time."

"He's right about one thing, though," he murmurs, lowering his voice. His breath hits my hair, making goosebumps spread over my scalp. "Don't trust anybody."

I shiver. "Even you?"

"Especially me, Little Astor." His overwhelming presence looms larger. "The only thing you can trust me to do is ruin you." He moves in closer, his lips brushing against the fabric of the blindfold just over my ear. "Understand?"

I swallow, a heat burning between my legs with just those few words. What I understand is that he thinks I'm a toy to be played with. "Maybe you and Keegan are a lot alike."

He chuckles, the low sound making my belly flip. "Because I'm a bastard who thinks you should get on your knees for me?"

"Do you?" I ask, voice wavering.

"You know the answer to that, and you like it. You

may have a blindfold on, but I see the heat in your cheeks, your clenched jaw." He draws his finger down the line of my chin to my throat. My pulse jumps underneath his touch. In a bus full of other people, it feels like it's just us. "I bet you're thinking of me." His guttural tone makes me swallow. "How I forced you to your knees. My dick piercing..."

Fuck, that did it. My pussy constricts like it's dying of thirst. I can't help that I'm innately curious about what that might feel like.

A piece of fabric plops onto my lap. I tense for a brief moment, but Leo's in my ear again. "It's just my sweatshirt. Unless you want the whole bus to see me check if you're wet for me?"

My jaw slacks. My heart feels like it's going to explode out of my chest as his hand sneaks under the makeshift cover. "What if I don't want you to?" I ask, trying to keep some semblance of control. Right now, I couldn't stop him if I wanted to. My knees fall apart as he drags his palm up my thigh.

"Don't lie to yourself. It's unflattering."

I reach out, finding his leg and moving my hand up to cup his very thick, hard cock, right through his jeans. "As long as you don't lie to yourself either." He immediately switches positions, angling his hips toward me.

"The difference between us is that I'd let you jerk

me off right here with little care to who watched. You'd be shy about it in the morning, though. Second thoughts. Regrets. But I am who I am, Little Astor. If you want to play, I won't stop you. Hell, I'll make it easier on you." He reaches the apex of my thighs and drags a finger down the seam. "I'll unzip my pants."

My whole body is ablaze. In a way, I'd love to be the girl who would fuck him right here, not caring if people watched. It would be the ultimate freedom of choice.

But it's everyone else's opinions that make it not worth it. I can hear the shaming tomorrow. Slut. Sloppy. Unclassy. Everything someone from my world shouldn't be.

And maybe the biggest reason not to: I can see it being a reason why the Knights wouldn't take me.

Leo traces his thumb up and down my seam again. I freeze, but he's back in my ear. "No one's watching. I promise."

"I can't trust you." Despite my words, I squeeze his cock.

"You'll have to."

He unzips my pants, hand sneaking down to rest the pads of his fingers on the crotch of my panties—my currently soaked panties.

"I knew it," he breathes. "Wet for me."

He leans into my shoulder, rearranging his body so that he can casually circle my clit with the pad of his finger. I doubt the sweatshirt is even moving that much. Now, if I can just keep the moans that want to escape inside. Deep, deep inside. Not just for the sake of my reputation, but so that Leo's head doesn't get bigger than it already is.

My fingers curl into his package with the influx of pleasure. I pull up every restraining cell in my body to keep from moving with him. I just take it, like a puppet on strings.

"Damn, Astor. You make me want to see what you would be like without all the restraints. I bet I can make you scream."

My breasts are so tight with anticipation. They ache like crazy, screaming for attention. I pull the sweatshirt over my chest, hiding my own hands as I squeeze my tits. My jaw drops in pleasure, but I hold back the cry. Rubbing them over the layers of fabric isn't enough, though. I reach my hands under, maneuvering my bra out of the way as I pinch my nipples and stroke.

"Fuck," Leo bites out. "You're always surprising me."

"I need—"

"I know what you need."

The bus comes to a stop. He pauses his movements, but keeps pressure on my clit, pressing down as sparks crackle from the source.

Shuffling ensues while I hold my breath, keeping my own hands still. "Just get off the fucking bus," Leo growls.

"Fuck off, Jarvis," a voice retorts, one I don't recognize.

There are more footsteps, and then silence. "She needs a moment," I hear Alaric call out. Then some more jostling. "What do we have here?" he asks.

"We have a soaking wet woman in our care," Leo answers. "Is taking care of her needs part of the deal?"

"It is when you got her to this place," I groan, angling my hips toward him.

It isn't until I hear Oliver's voice that I remember he's here and the declaration he made earlier. My sudden spike of panic is erased in an instant when he responds, "If my girl is turned on, she loves it when someone goes down on her. Makes her so wet."

"Really?" Leo asks, the tenor in his voice telling me he's turned on too. He lowers the sweatshirt. "Let's see you fondle those tits, Astor."

My shirt pulls up, exposing my thumb while I return to flicking it over my nipple. The cool air gives me another surge of electricity.

Fingers grasp my foot, pulling it around and

yanking so that I'm lying on the bus seat. A firm hand places my knee against the seat in front of me. "We have to do this quickly," Alaric states. "They'll be waiting."

I'm surprised he's not calling this off. The fact that my professor is watching me touch my breasts makes this so much hotter. I yank my shirt higher and arch into my palms, plucking my nipples while waiting for something to happen.

"Who gets the honors?" Oliver asks. I'm assuming he's still blindfolded, but I really don't know. I'm just surprised he seems as into this as Leo.

"I say we don't tell her," Leo suggests seductively. "Keep your hands on your tits. Play with those perfect mounds and just enjoy."

A body moves between my legs. I have no concept of who it is other than the seat depressing with the weight of his body as he moves my ankles around his shoulders. His hot mouth pauses at my center. He doesn't groan. He doesn't speak. He just laps at my seam, and I cry out.

The tongue retreats, and I hear three distinct groans. My mind whirs with the possibilities. Would Leo lick me like that? Or would he just obliterate me with his tongue in quick thrusts?

Is my professor on his knees for me right now? That's so wrong, but oh so fucking hot.

Or my best friend? Who knows exactly how to get me off this way.

How did I fucking get here?

Not that I'm complaining.

Someone pinches my thigh, and I gasp as the pain threads up my leg. The tongue currently devouring me moves away. "Relax," Alaric rasps. "Enjoy this because in a few minutes, you're going to be tested in ways that you'll be glad we gave you something else to focus on."

As soon as the words sound, the tongue is back on my clit, lapping and sucking. I move with him, arching my hips into his mouth, with still no inclination of whose mouth it is.

I try not to guess. I just go with it, reveling in the sensations charging through me and the excitement of one guy's lips on my pussy while two others watch.

"More," I demand on a dark groan. I shift to grab onto the hair, but hands stop me, lifting them back to my breasts.

Once more, the mouth rises from my needy flesh. This time, it's Leo's dark voice. "Say our names. It's not just one of us doing this, and you're so damn turned on you can't stand it."

"Got it, Eden?" Oliver prompts. "Say our names."

Lips latch back onto my heated flash, sucking my clit into his mouth. "Fuck, Alaric," I pant. "Oliver," I groan. "Leo..." He spreads my pussy lips, diving forward with renewed interest. A guttural sound comes from the back of his throat, and I rear into his mouth, pinching my nipples to the point of pain.

"Again," Alaric demands.

I rock into the skilled tongue. Fuck this is all sorts of wrong and so fucking hot. "Leo, yes. More please. Oliver...Alaric..."

His tongue swirls over my clit, moving faster and faster. All mental capabilities float away. My cries heighten when my climax finally hits. I ride it out as my head falls backward. A late scream lodges in my throat, and then threatens to escape when a hand clamps over my mouth. I cup my breasts, my breathing stuttering out of me. My erect nipple brushes across my palm while the greedy mouth stays on me, breathing unsteadily over my cunt.

The body leaves and the hand over my mouth disappears, but I stay where I am, still trying to control my breaths. Agile fingers arrange my clothes, then pull me up by the belt loops. "You should see the look on our faces."

I tilt my head, believing it was Alaric who spoke. It's confirmed when he says, "We have to get out there. Now."

A hand leads me away, but my knees are practically Jell-O. I want to rewind what just happened and do it all over again, leaving me time to lie there and enjoy it afterward. Or for a round two where I get to watch them.

"You were a good girl," Leo's rough voice growls in my ear as I step out onto the hard ground next to him.

Warmth spreads through me. Instead of being repulsed by his words, I bask in them. If that's what being a good girl takes, I proudly volunteer for next time.

21

Leo

I ache for pretty things that hurt. For as tough as Eden tries to be, she doesn't fool me. The tension radiating off her after they blindfolded her brushed against my skin like sandpaper. It made me want to do things. To help her.

I stay back at the last second, forcing Barclay to escort both Eden and Oliver across the torch-lit path. I'm no good at feelings. Every time I've ever felt something for someone, it's wilted and died.

I'm self-aware enough to know why I am the way I am. Why I can't stand the Knights who've fucked me over since I was a kid. Honestly, I'd love to be as far away from here as possible, but I'm also—when you get to the heart of it—weak.

It's the thing I hate most about myself. My pathetic need to come crawling back to my grandfather like a lost puppy.

It's no wonder why people have left me time and time again. I'm unworthy.

She called my name, though. The lilt of her voice, all wrapped up in pleasure as it cried out for Leo, shot straight to my dick. Many girls have done something similar, but with their porn star voice. Like, if they cry out loud enough and perfect enough, they'll cement a husband in no time.

But Eden lost in pleasure? It was so raw, so electric. I wanted to shove Barclay out of the way and ram my cock so far inside her pussy it'd take a pry bar to get me out.

My stomach tightens at the thought. If I'm getting close to her, I need distance. Grandfather hasn't ordered me here just to help her through Trials. If I get too friendly, I won't be able to detach when Grandfather makes his move. It'll be just like my dad all over again.

I pull my hoodie on over my head, hands fisting at my sides while I search for our fucked-up little group. I feel the caged monster inside me come alive, even if I had to force it to the front this time. No friends. No feelings. I work on a primal level, and that's the way I like it.

Soon, Grandfather will have me at his beck and call again. I won't be holing up in the nice warmth of Jarvis Hall. I'll be off on some mission he believes is necessary for the greater good. Which usually just means for the strength of the Jarvis line.

I almost wonder if he made me like this on purpose. As if from birth he knew exactly what was going to happen. I wouldn't put it past him. He's the greatest mastermind I've ever seen.

Today, I'm watching over Eden Astor, but tomorrow? I might be expelling her from this life based on his tactical play.

Maybe he did get rid of Delilah. I never gave it too much thought before. It seemed like an endeavor that was beneath him. She was only a girl.

But so is Eden, and he's had me watching her ass since the moment she got into town.

I don't know what his play is—and it's not my job to know, either.

Following the flames takes me on a rocky path into the woods. I hadn't really been paying attention on the bus ride here, but sniffing the air brings me the fresh, cool scent of the river.

My heart stampedes forward, but I tamp that shit down. It's up to Eden to get through this, and I sure as fuck don't care what happens either way. If she fails, I might be able to get back to some semblance of normalcy. If she passes, I can keep using her as my toy, like my grandfather said. Win-win if you ask me.

The flames from the torches end at the edge of the trees, but in the distance are circles of burning embers littering the ground. Barclay and Eden stand near one. Oliver just adjacent to them near another.

I'm jealous as fuck of the professor, who has Eden's pleasure all over his lips. In the heat of the moment, I wanted to ask him what she tasted like, but she would've figured out who was between her legs then. Most of all, I'm hoping it was picturing me that drove her over the edge.

I start toward Oliver. He must sense me when I walk by because he swivels his head to follow me as I take the place next to him. To my left is the riverbank. The water laps against the barrier wall, illuminated by the soft moonlight. My gaze darts to Eden to see how she's doing, and I spot Barclay zeroing in on me. I shrug. Cool and aloof is easy. Concerned is something I haven't quite mastered in a long time. In fact, it was beaten out of me by the man who now starts talking.

After a brief introduction, my grandfather says, "You may remove the blindfolds."

He leers at me, and I'm certain he thinks I should be beside Eden during this. I've wondered whether

Barclay is a plant too. He's such a Knights enthusiast that I've almost asked him dozens of times who sent him here, but that would be giving myself away.

I untie Oliver's blindfold and clench it in my grip. Immediately, he turns to find Eden, his jaw hard when he spots her behind us. I don't let myself look again. Not yet. He shoots a glance toward the water next, and I can read the thoughts on his face because they're the same as my own. Is it me or is everything we've been putting the Pledges through have something to do with breaking Eden Astor? And not in the fun way.

Why her? She's just another rich girl.

I tilt my head as Grandfather talks, trying to remember if there's beef between the Astors and Jarvises. I'm sure there has been at some point, but none recently that I can recall. No bad business deals as far as I'm aware, but obviously Grandfather doesn't share most Jarvis business with me. I'm just the muscle. The fall guy. He couldn't care less if I was restrained in prison for the rest of my life.

Sometimes, I don't think I would either.

"Through the seasons," my grandfather speaks again, his voice raining down like thunder, "you will be a Knight of Arcadia. There will be periods of pain and pleasure, heaven and hell. And through it all, you will always be a Knight. It is not a choice, it is a privilege, and you must tread with dignity. You cannot only love the Knights when you are riding a high from one of its benefits. You must believe in our kinship to your core. If you choose to move forward, this Trial will test your physical strengths...and pain endurance."

When I pledged like this, we stayed the night in a completely dark room, barren of sight, sound, smell. It was torture to the mind. Sensory deprivation at its cruelest.

"If you are up to the task, you will jump into the cold depths of the river. Then, on our marks, to the fiery coals. Through it all, you must persevere for the greater good."

I swear the greater good is his fucking motto.

This is going to suck. The weather has finally turned, so I can imagine the river is frigid even in the height of day. At night like this, it's probably dropped more than a few degrees.

And for Eden? Her sister drowned in this fucking river, and here she is, about to jump into it. ...If she doesn't back out.

"This is bullshit," Oliver growls under his breath.

"Just fucking listen," I snap, even though we've come up with the same assessment. Eden will be the only one who's directly affected by the water in a different way. Oliver makes to peer over his shoulder again, but I reach out and grab his forearm. "Focus on yourself."

"Easy for you to say, Jarvis." He sneers. "Have you ever cared about another person's well-being more than your own?"

His haughty fucking British accent is pissing me the fuck off. "It's not about that, Prince. It's about making her look weak. Worry about your damn self before you ruin your chance...and hers."

I grind my teeth while he glares daggers at me. I should just let him do whatever the fuck he wants. If he fails, maybe Eden fails, then I'm off the hook. I'm out. Unless this is part of my test too. He told me they were assessing me.

And like that, I'm a little boy again, vying for his attention, and I hate myself for it.

His voice rises again. "You will traverse from river to coals for as many times as we ask. Remember, there is always a great reward after a great ask."

I swallow, sudden memories of the nude woman who met me at my grandfather's house after I survived this Trial assail me. To this day, I don't know who I fucked until we both lay panting on the floor. It was just a body. Just a reward. No emotions involved whatsoever.

"Who is strong enough to weather this storm?"

All the Pledges' hands raise into the air. Oliver doesn't even hesitate, and I almost feel bad for snapping at him.

Grandfather looks around approvingly. "To the riverbank, then... And I suggest you strip down to your skin. Wet clothes are a nuisance, and sometimes a liability."

Oliver's hands turn to fists. He glances at Eden, then at me. "If it's me or her, it's her. You understand me?"

"Relax, Royal. Nothing's going to happen." Inside, though, his words harden my resolve. The same feelings that had me reaching for her on the bus strike again. Pledges have been seriously hurt in the past. I wish I'd paid more attention in health class to know what extreme temperatures do to the body. Polar Bear Dips are a thing, but frostbite is very real. I've also seen people walk over coals as some sort of personal development highlight, but what about standing on them when your feet are chilled to the bone?

My mind rages with every possibility, and I haven't even scratched the surface of Eden's mental health right now. During Trials, the Knights push the boundaries as far as they can because if it wasn't difficult, everyone would make it. Sure, you'll be handsomely rewarded, but Christ. I'm seeing it through a different lens this time.

"Once you begin, every time you hear this horn"—a bullhorn echoes through the air, and even though I'm braced for it, I nearly react—"you'll move from one test to the other. As always, you are being judged."

Finally, I let myself glance at Eden. Barclay is speaking in her ear as she unbuttons her pants. She's not looking at him, though. Nor me. She's staring at Oliver. They seem to be having some sort of silent conversation while we both stand here like twats. Jealousy twists my gut.

I glare at my charge. "You going to get naked or what?"

"I didn't know you were so keen on seeing my junk again, Jarvis."

A few chuckles sound around us, and my face heats. "See that tiny pecker again? No, thank you."

Oliver smirks. I'm far from judging, but he has every right to be confident. He had more than a few inches to spare, even with Eden's fist wrapped around his length and that whore's mouth sucking him down.

Eden unclasps a black, lace bra, handing it off to Barclay. She stands there in nothing but her delectable skin that was so needy for all of us. It's hard not to stare, but I make myself watch her face, looking for any signs of tension. Fear.

She does a good job of putting on a show. When her gaze finally meets mine, I spy the hollowness there. She's putting aside her emotions, and she's smart to do it. Emotions and feelings don't get you anywhere with the Knights. They're just a hindrance.

The bullhorn sounds.

A few cocky fuckers jump right in while the others are too busy staring at the girls in nothing but the skin they were born in. I growl at the asshole next to us who hasn't taken his eyes from Eden. His partner elbows him, and he jumps in, gasping when he emerges at the surface.

After that, my attention is right back on Eden. She and Oliver share a look, then walk to the wall and jump. My heart constricts when she goes under. The Elders are definitely fucking with her. Grandfather must think she's here to shake things up. To ask about her sister, maybe?

Then why not just deny her membership into the Knights? Why go through all this torture?

Oh, I forgot. This is the secret society that not only likes to lord over all things, but to teach people lessons too. *Everything* is a lesson, or so my grandfather tells me.

Eden emerges, treading water to keep herself on the surface. River droplets cling to her lashes. Her body shakes uncontrollably, but she doesn't cry out in shock. Or laugh like some of the others. Or do anything, really. She just keeps herself in the water like a good little Pledge...even though her dead blue eyes say another story.

The bullhorn sounds, and Barclay and I walk to the ledge to help our Pledges out. Oliver is white as fuck, the veins on his wrists a pale blue in stark contrast to the rest of his body. He hugs himself as he strides toward the hot coals. The embers pop and hiss when teardrops of water fall onto the hearth-like circle.

Someone grunts, and the others hesitate briefly until Grandfather yells, "Get on the fucking coals!"

I nudge Oliver forward. They're not going to sound the horn until everyone has their feet in the embers.

Eden closes her eyes, stepping onto the coals with a grimace, her fingers flexing.

I peer around. Everyone else has followed suit, including the prince.

Five seconds go by.

Ten.

Painful, animal-like grunts escape Pledges lungs.

Before I think they're not going to be able to take much more, the horn sounds. Thank fuck.

Both Oliver and Eden jump out of the coals. This time, they don't waste any precious seconds waiting to plummet into the water. They want to.

Barclay steps up beside me. "Is it me, or does this get worse every year?"

"Upping the ante, I guess," I shrug as I keep my gaze peeled on her.

He grunts in agreement.

I check on Oliver briefly before something in the water catches my eye. Long tendrils bubble to the surface. At first, I think it's seaweed, but it's not green and definitely doesn't have a slimy consistency. It's a straw color.

Strands of...pale blonde.

Eden recognizes it a second before I do, and her gasp connects the last remaining piece for me.

It's hair. Her sudden lurch to get away from it makes it shift. The head turns over in the water, and plastic, lifeless eyes peer toward the star-dotted sky.

It's a model head. A model of a very blonde woman with the same pale hair as Eden. The same pale hair her sister had...

Eden's horrified gaze gives way to a desperate scream that curdles my stomach.

On the forehead of the mannequin head are two words: a name.

Delilah Astor.

22

Alaric

*E*den's taste on my tongue had been slowly fading, but her scream will ring through my ears for eternity. I'm not sure I'll ever be rid of it.

She finished the Trial, enduring ten more rounds of jumping into the Saint Lawrence River with the fake head of her sister. Of course, the incident was brushed under the rug as soon as she composed herself, looking anywhere but at the head of the mannequin.

It could've been a coincidence. A tossed mannequin that matched Delilah's hair just happened to emerge at the same moment that Eden was in the river. It could've...except for the block letters spelling out its true purpose.

It could've even been a joke—one the demonic little assholes my world breeds make happen.

Or it could've been a strategic play meant to scare Eden from Trials. And if I had to guess, my money would be on the Kennedy bitch.

Anne-Marie laughed loudest. Her own voice strained by the frigid water, she didn't have any problem asking Eden what the problem was, attempting to provoke her.

"Kennedy needs a lesson in manners," I growl to Leo as soon as we're all corralled back onto the bus. Eden's currently wrapped in Oliver's arms, sitting across from us in her dry clothes but curled against him like he's her teddy bear.

"More than a few of those fucks need a lesson."

I lift my brows at him, and he nods as if to say consider it done. He won't be the only one dishing out punishment though. I don't care if he isn't known for working well on teams, he's going to learn in this case.

I'll have to reel him in, I'm sure. I saw his horror-stricken face when the hair rose to the surface like a perfect sheet of gold-spun tresses.

It looked real. It was real.

The Elders' faces were as placid as can be. They didn't give the stunt any attention, other than to roll their eyes at the scream as if it was just some outburst to the freezing water.

I wouldn't put it past them to put Anne-Marie up to the task of getting into Eden's head. The coincidences are too many now. The Knights don't do coincidences. Eden's being targeted.

Both Leo and I stare straight ahead, though I wonder if he's as attuned as I am to what's happening in the seat beside us as Oliver whispers into Eden's hair. I sure as fuck shouldn't be wishing it was my words she was hearing, considering I'm her professor, but Eden Astor is another breed all together. She's not like the rest of them. She doesn't play games. She doesn't walk around like life is one big courting fiasco. I've often wished I was already at the part where I cheat on my stuck-up wife with the big-breasted secretary so I can skip all this pretentious bullshit, but maybe that was because no one caught my eye like Eden before.

Sweet, young Eden.

Six years isn't a huge age difference, but it's enough to make me feel like a horny old man.

If these Pledges are rewarded the same as in previous years, they'll be getting sex. I might beat the living piss out of any guy who tries to sneak into her bedroom. Her taste is still so decadent on my tongue. I shouldn't have gotten into position. I should've made

Leo do it since he was the one who riled her up right before a Trial, but I was too busy wondering how good it would be and reveling in the wrongness of it.

I'll have a stiff one for the rest of my life. During class, I'll be fantasizing about bending her over my desk and having her call me professor in a sweet purr that will make me blow my load into her tight cunt.

She's seeped under my skin.

This isn't good. I'm only here to observe. To place puzzle pieces together. That's it.

When the bus stops, I pick up her shoes as she walks gingerly down the aisle with the rest of the group. Oliver attempts to pick her up, but he's not a hundred percent himself, so Leo pushes him out of the way and flings her over his shoulder like the brute he is. She doesn't even protest. Her tiny fist grips the back of his shirt and twists.

She can't lock herself in her room this time. She can't hide it away.

Oliver looks at me, and I bend down to grab his shoes. "If you think I'm carrying you, keep thinking."

"What the fuck's going on?" Oliver whisper yells as we watch Leo make a beeline for Jarvis Hall.

I shrug, the back of my neck itching like crazy. "I don't know."

"You're a Knight. You should fucking know."

"I'm not an Elder," I growl, searching around to

238

make sure our conversation isn't being overheard. "I don't have anything to do with Trials. I came back to teach at this school, and I went to the first meeting because I'm on campus so I'm expected to." I tell him, leaving out the important part, but I don't care. No one deserves to know my business. "I didn't know I was being grouped together with you guys. I didn't know how much I'd be involved in any of this."

That part is true. If I'd known, I may have changed my mind when I asked to be instated at Carnegie. Hell, the Knights could be suspicious of me too. I'm supposed to be running my own company right now, not frolicking around with students.

Oliver huffs. "I don't trust you, but I'm going to say this once. If they do something to Eden, I'll make them regret it."

He glares at me as if I'm going to pass this on to the Elders. First of all, threatening them is a death wish. Second of all, notwithstanding the fact that he was just in the position I'd give anything to be in, I'm not going to turn him in. And third of all, they're not afraid of people like Oliver, even if he is a prince. They literally don't care. They believe themselves to be above everyone. The Knights' reach has no limits.

"You're wasting your breath," I tell him, attempting to look as honest as I can despite the Knight brand I've destined myself with.

Oliver charges forward, and we both catch up to Eden and Leo at the front door. I let them in, setting the alarm once we're all inside. Leo tries to let her down, but as soon as her feet touch the floor, she hisses. "Fucking bastards," she grinds out.

"I'll raid the bathrooms," I tell her, hoping one of the past inhabitants left something useful. My cabinets come up empty, but in the room with the unicorns, I find a First Aid Kit under the sink. Bringing it out, I sit next to Eden on the couch. She avoids my gaze as I peek at her feet. They're an angry red. In some places, it looks as if the skin has melted right off, giving way to the virgin skin underneath. I hate to say it, but the river water probably saved them.

She takes one look at my face and grimaces. "Can an injured girl get a drink in this place?" she asks.

Leo moves into the kitchen and finds a couple bottles of liquor along with some shot glasses. He starts pouring the brown liquid and hands one to Oliver and then to Eden. I'm surprised he hasn't holed himself up in his room yet. That seems to be his MO, but not this time.

Oliver and Eden raise their shots toward one another, then drink them down, leaving their glasses out to be filled once again.

"This is going to sting," I say. A doctor I am not, but I know broken skin needs to be cleansed and

240

treated. I dump rubbing alcohol on her foot, and she nearly jumps off the couch. Leo drops the bottle of liquor to hold her shoulders down. "Fuck, sorry." The nearly full alcohol bottle empties out onto the same carpet that saved it from breaking while I search the kit for bandages.

"Jesus Christ," she pants. "That fucking hurt."

Unbelievably, Oliver chuckles.

Eden shoots him a death glare. "Watch it. You're next, Number Five." This reprimand makes his laugh deepen.

"Number Five?" I question as I glance over at Oliver losing it. It's the stress. They need this right now.

"He's fifth in line to the throne," Eden informs us, grinning. "Well, should be fifth in line."

Oliver's still clutching at his stomach, tears clinging to the corners of his eyes. "Sorry," he rasps out. "You just reminded me of that time you fell off your horse. We were—"

"Nine, I know." Eden flinches away from me as I slather some burn ointment on her feet. "Your relatives really didn't like it when I yelled fuck in the middle of the game. British people are so hoity-toity," she says, winking at Oliver.

He shakes his head at her. "You did it in the presence of the queen."

She mock gasps. "The horror."

"I knew then we were going to be best friends for life."

Her smile shifts into fondness. At first, I thought there was nothing between these two, even if it was plain as day how much Oliver cared for her. Then, that one night, she gripped his cock and jerked it like it was hers, making him splooge. Hell, if she'd taken my cock, I'd have probably lost it too.

Then, I could've rationalized it away, but not today. I don't like the hold she has over me.

"So, you guys have known each other for that long?" Leo asks, brows rising as he rights the alcohol bottle and places it on the coffee table.

"We met on a polo field," Oliver explains. "We were super young, untalented little arseholes at the time, but we grew up. Bet you didn't know this girl could've been a professional polo player."

She rolls her eyes. "It's such a rich people sport. Surfing's better."

"You can surf?"

She tilts her head at me as I wrap her feet in bandages. "I love the water," she says, and the glassiness that comes over her eyes is the only thing that brings me back to what just happened. It's a sobering fact over the rest of us too.

Leo swoops down to pick up the liquor bottle

again. He fills their shot glasses and then hands one off to me as well.

I swallow it down, basking in the fiery wake it leaves as I move to Oliver's feet.

"Don't be a bitch," Eden chides when Oliver shies away from me.

I turn toward her, worry clenching my gut. I held her after the last Trial. This one far surpassed that, but she's doing everything she can to cover up her true feelings. "We should talk about what happened earlier."

She clams up, glancing at her feet. "For what reason?"

Without warning, I dump alcohol on Oliver's feet, and he hisses. "You're just going to pretend?" I ask.

"No, I'm just not going to sit here and focus on one thing. We're not idiots. We know someone did that on purpose. But who? How are we going to prove it?" she says. "So, fuck it. I can be mad at the world, or I can move forward in victory." She swallows suddenly, face paling. "My sister used to say that. She probably got it from my dad." She clears her throat. "So, no, I don't want to fucking talk about it. What I want to do is kick all their asses in the Trials. Show them it's going to take a lot more than that to break an Astor."

Her gaze slides to mine, and I press my lips together as I wrap Oliver's feet. I don't mention the panic attack she had before. It's not my place. Besides, just because you break for a few minutes doesn't mean you're broken. It means you can fix yourself up stronger and trudge ahead with purpose.

"Alright, I agree with all that," Leo says, his firm voice threading like ice. "But Anne-Marie needs to pay for her taunts."

"She's always hated me and my sister."

"She's a spoiled little cunt," I agree.

Oliver smirks, holding out his shot glass for another fill. "What did you have in mind?"

Ideas are thrown out, and I shouldn't be shocked that the minds in this room are as devious and twisted as they come. Anne-Marie is going to rue the day she ever crossed paths with the four of us together.

I watch Eden lighten under the talk of bringing her nemesis down. It's sexy how excited she gets about humiliating this girl. Even better is that we're distracting her.

I have no illusion that when she goes to bed, she's going to see those strands of hair in her nightmares, but at least for right now, we may have made her feel a little better. Just enough so she doesn't break.

Not under my watch.

"Alright," Leo barks out, suddenly tightening the cap on the bottle of alcohol. "Eden sleeps with me tonight."

"Wait, what?" The smile on Oliver's face withers.

"We agreed that Eden would never be alone, so she's sleeping with me."

Jealousy mixed with anger raises my hackles. "Don't you think that should be Eden's decision?"

She peers at the three of us, and my anger burns out quickly. We did agree to her never being alone, and I'm sure there's some part of her that probably really doesn't want to be alone tonight. But it should be *her* choice.

She flicks her gaze through all three of us, then straightens her shoulders. "I'm fine with Leo."

Oliver pushes himself to his feet, glaring between the two of them before limping up the stairs as fast as he can. Eden just stares at her hands in front of her.

I don't know what made her decide on Leo, but I said it's her decision, and it is. Standing, I send Leo a warning glance. I've seen what women look like after he's through with them. If he does the same to her, it won't only be Anne-Marie's downfall I'll help plan. It'll be his too.

Eden

I'm still bitterly cold. My insides shiver like they'll never be warm again.

That's not why I picked Leo's room to sleep in, though. I don't suddenly think he'll turn into a teddy bear and use that large body of his to heat me up tonight, melting the ice chips currently freezing to my body's cells.

No, I picked him because... Well, with Oliver, it would've meant something. After what happened under the stairwell, if I'd chosen him tonight, it would've sent a signal to him that I'm ready to be his. Alaric has already seen me vulnerable—something I'd rather not replicate. So, for just one night, even when inside I feel anything but, I want to be the girl who doesn't have to be anything for anybody.

I can just be me.

Since the other two skulked from the room, I flick my gaze toward Leo who's looking pleased as fuck. Like he won the lottery without even playing.

I can't figure this guy out, other than it's evident he doesn't respect women. He uses them. He loves sex and control—loves to dominate. But he's also done some things that surprised me. Not the starting something on the bus part, that was Leo to a T, but after the Trial when he threw me over his shoulder, that was caring. Almost. He still did it like a caveman, but I had him pegged as the type that would let me walk it off.

He saunters toward his room, peering over his shoulder when he reaches the doorway. "You coming? If you need shit from your room, go get it now."

I peek down at my feet, wondering how much transporting my ass there is going to suck. He sighs, returns to where I'm standing, and hoists me over his shoulder again. "I can walk," I feebly protest.

"Just stop talking."

"Wow," I say with some surprise. "I guess you're not sugar coating anything that happened tonight."

"Don't act shocked. That's why you picked me."

He tosses me down on his bed, and I bounce on the mattress.

I gawk at him, flabbergasted that he has that much insight. He clearly sees way more than I thought he did.

"I think you pissed off the prince, though. You better watch it. He won't stick around when he keeps coming in second place all the time. If you like him, you better let him know."

My lips thin, anger spreading through me. "My relationship with Oliver is *our* business."

Leo shrugs. "Just a little friendly advice."

I lie back as he moves into the attached bathroom, noting the way he's taken over the room little by little, like he's feeding it testosterone by the hour.

After a few minutes, he comes back out in nothing but a pair of gym shorts hung low on his hips. His chest looks as if it's carved from stone.

He walks right past the bed, digs through the closet, and then retreats to the couch in the corner of the room with a blanket in his hand. "What...are you doing?" I ask.

Lying back, he spreads the blanket out. It doesn't nearly cover all of him. "What? Did you think I was going to make you swallow my cock? Maybe pin you to the bed while I fuck tonight's events out of you?"

Well, maybe. Kind of, actually. But why the fuck

does my body heat at those thoughts? If Dee were here, I'd probably call her up and ask if something was wrong with me. Is this why she stayed attracted to Keegan, despite how much of an ass he was to her?

I shake that thought off because, ew.

When I don't reply, Leo narrows his gaze at me until I force out an answer. "Sort of..."

"If that's why you're here, pick someone else's bed. Oliver would be down, and I'm pretty sure Barclay would hit that. I mean, he'd feel awful about it afterward, but he still would."

"He'd feel awful about it?"

Leo rolls his eyes, shifting his position on the couch. He looks more than a little uncomfortable. Guys with bodies like Leonardo Jarvis weren't made for furniture like that. "You're his student, he's the teacher. It wouldn't stop him, but he'd probably think of some holier-than-thou reason why it shouldn't happen again."

"You think you know everyone," I grumble.

"I do know everyone. I've seen the worst of people in this world—the very worst. And for the record, I think you'd come all over my cock in two thrusts, which is why I'm not going to waste my time."

I blink at him. Is he fucking serious?

"How long do you last with Oliver?" He scrunches up his forehead like he's going to speculate an answer.

"I don't fuck Oliver," I snarl. "I guess you don't know everything."

"Bullshit," he chuckles. "If you're not now, you have."

He's right, but I don't owe him an explanation. Oliver was my first. We arranged it that way on purpose, and honestly, I'd recommend it to any girl. Who better to go through that first-time experience with than someone who loves you unconditionally? Your best friend is the perfect choice. I should put it on a billboard, a PSA.

We're both silent for a few moments until a light shines from the corner. I turn to find Leo holding his phone with one hand and his cock in the other, the small piece of jewelry he's sporting glinting in the light.

A woman's sultry cry curls my toes, and Leo starts running his fist down his shaft in slow motion.

I ignore the way my pussy clenches, wondering if I should just watch and keep my mouth shut, or say something. Of course, he's doing this for show. There's no way he thinks I'm sleeping already.

When he continues to wonder, I can't stop myself from word vomiting. "Wonderful. You're watching porn."

"Jealous?" he asks, voice strained.

"No."

"Why? This girl is hot. Her pussy's so slick with want."

"Watching people have sex doesn't do it for me," I say, even though the unrestrained cry from his phone's speaker grabs my attention and holds it. I wonder what's happening to her to make her sound like that?

My nipples peak underneath my shirt. Slowly, I pull the covers up around my waist as my core heats with every moan emanating from his phone. Maybe I do get off on it. Or maybe it's just seeing his body tensing as he slowly strokes.

Leo oozes sex, working himself until the veins pop out on his forearm. "Perfect fucking tits," he breathes. "She keeps touching herself, and it's so fucking hot."

I sneak my hand toward my core. I've had my share of encounters—I love sex—but there's just something about Leo that makes me want to hide this.

"Her perfect little rosebuds peek through her fingers. Wanna see?"

He peeks over at me, and I tear my hand away. I'd been almost there, but now he's gazing at me, his stare moving down as if he knew exactly what I was doing.

The girl cries out again, and another voice speaks up. It's familiar, haunting. A chill spreads through my veins. "That's...that's me." He goes back to watching the screen, a smirk on his face. "You recorded me? So, you weren't...you weren't the one..."

"Or did one of the other two record and already send the video to all of us?"

"Who did it?" I ask, flush now. I'd thought it was him. "Who?"

"Who licked you until you came around his tongue?" he taunts. "I'm not telling."

"Leo," I warn, pushing myself up with my hands.

He pins me with a glare. "No, Eden. Stay. I can just as easily delete the video by the time you get here, and you're interrupting my moment."

"You mean *my* moment."

He shrugs, and I grind my teeth together in frustration.

He wants a moment? I'll give him a moment.

Kneeling at the edge of the bed, I peel my shirt off, my breasts spilling over the cups of my bra. Next, I hook my fingers under the waistband of my pants, shifting closer to my zipper. He peers over when he hears the noise. His gaze focuses as I shift the pants down my hips, revealing my lacy panties.

It's difficult to look sexy while slipping pants off, but I manage to escape from them without landing on my face. I skirt my fingertips across the tops of my panties until I dip inside, letting my head drop back as I push toward my clit.

"Take them off," he demands.

I smirk, ignoring him.

"I want to see," he growls.

As soon as I hit my mark, I buck, not taking my eyes off his. He's sitting now, his phone forgotten as he watches me, still fisting the base of his cock.

"What was it that you liked?" I ask. "My fingers on my breasts?"

I tear my fingers away from my clit, unclasp my bra, tease it off my shoulders, then pinch my nipples between my thumb and forefingers. Getting lost in the moment is easy while I rub my palms over my peaked buds, pulling and tweaking until I've built myself up into an inferno. I sneak my fingers under the elastic of my panties again, searching out my clit.

Rough hands grab my panties, and in two seconds, they fall to the floor, ripped in half.

I suck in a breath, staring while he slowly backs up, dick still in his grip. "I said I want to see."

My heart beats like crazy. "You always get what you want?"

"Never," he breathes, running his fist from base to tip. He traces a finger over his slit, then slides it down his shaft, his chest hollowing out.

Since I'm completely naked—by force—and I have his full attention, I just do what feels good. I close my eyes, remembering the pleasure of the mystery tongue while it dove between my folds.

"Open your eyes."

They flutter open of their own accord, zeroing in on him again.

"Eyes on me, Eden. Got it?"

I nod, staring at him while touching myself. When his movements quicken, so do mine, matching him like we're touching each other. We feed off one another like lovers. I watch the tension in his jaw and the pout of his full lips to urge me forward. My harsh breaths fill the room while his strained movements become jerky, the muscles in his abs shifting and clenching.

He stands suddenly. "Where do you want it?"

For a brief moment, I think he means vag, mouth, or ass, but it's clear when he keeps stroking himself what he really means.

"Where do you want it, Eden? It's yours."

No one's ever come on me before. It seems so... dirty. Wrong.

My pussy begins to clench, and I pull my shoulders back, offering up my breasts. Leo doesn't hesitate. He strokes himself into a frenzy, slowing just as a line of cum shoots from the tip, hitting me in the chest. I blink, my own body taking over, sending me into an orgasm that hovers and intensifies while more ribbons of cum drip onto my sensitive nipples.

He inspects me, like an artist approving his work. "You should be wearing my cum all the time."

My fingers still work over my clit, eking out every last ounce of pleasure. "Like a mark?" I ask, breathless.

"Like I own you, Eden Astor."

The pulse at my neck thrums. Aftershocks spark inside me, and I let out a desperate cry.

He watches me before turning and walking away. The bathroom door closes, and I sit back on the mattress to catch my breath.

I'm not sure what the fuck just happened, but I liked it. Every interaction with Leo is like the sharp prick of a needle and the flood of relief as it pulls away. I want to get close enough to feel the sting, but not stay long enough to become permanently damaged.

I choose not to dwell on why I liked that so much as I grab my shirt, cleaning up after Leo just as the water turns on in the other room.

Discarding my shirt on the floor, I lie down to wait for him, but I pass out before he even finishes his shower.

24

Oliver

*L*eo keeps staring at Eden's tits, and I'm dying of jealousy. That's how this morning is going.

I didn't hear anything going on from his bedroom last night, but then again, I'm two floors up.

Of course something happened between them. Otherwise, he wouldn't be ogling her, and she wouldn't be actively trying to ignore him.

I've gotten myself into a real problem. It's obvious she's craving the bad guy—the type that will more than likely break her. I've whittled myself into a corner where I'm the guy she can cry to. Where I'm the one who makes everything better. I've basically placed myself in the friend zone and barricaded myself inside. Nothing I did the other day seemed to help my case. I probably just reinforced it for her; padlocked that shit closed forever.

"Two things are about to happen today," Alaric finally speaks up. He's the only one of us not acting out of the ordinary. "One, you're both going to get your reward for passing the Trial yesterday."

"Ooh, a reward," Eden says, rolling her eyes. Like the Knights would be able to give her anything she'd actually want.

"If your reward is cock, you're rejecting it," Leo bites out.

"Can I reject a reward?" she asks. "That doesn't seem like the Knights' style. Besides, I should be able to accept cock if I want it. Not as if I got any last night."

Instead of placating me, her words make me stiffen on the barstool in the kitchen. She definitely wanted some from him then. The jealousy cycle starts all over again.

"For vastly different reasons than Leo, I also think you should reject it if it's in the form of a guy. We can't trust anyone, remember?"

"No, *I* can't trust anyone," Eden says. "Including you two." I clear my throat, and Eden's face colors. "You were implied in the people I can trust. Besides," she says, peering back at the other two. "Do they really reward with sex? That sounds so—"

"All the time," Leo and Alaric answer.

I glare at her, knowing she knows the truth too. We've spoken to someone about this already—the cute college girl who was part of the entertainment for the party her sister died at. If they weren't there for sex, or at the very least, a sexy show, then I don't know why else they would've been invited. Outsiders are too much risk. Like a lawsuit waiting to happen. Their contracts must be airtight.

As if she's thinking the same, she turns to me, finally meeting my gaze for the first time this morning. My heart squeezes. I've got it bad. So fucking bad. I'm angry as hell, but it doesn't stop the bubbling emotions pouring through me when she looks my way.

I wanted to hold her last night. Wanted to make sure she was safe, being cared for. What happened in the river had to have fucked with her head, and I was the one who was supposed to make her feel better.

Not him.

"Do I have to sit around waiting for this reward?" Eden asks. "Will it just drop on my doorstep?"

"You'll be waiting forever if it's cock," Leo grunts again. I'm beginning to think he has more of a stake in this than I originally assumed. Could she be breaking the tough guy down? Is he also jealous as fuck?

"I get a reward too, don't I?" I ask, drilling Eden with an amused gaze. It wouldn't surprise me if the Knights rewarded the guys with sex and the girls with something else. Maybe a frilly apron? Maybe the opportunity to suck their cocks? That sounds more up their alley.

Eden blinks at me, tilting her head as if she's trying to figure me out.

I'm not an idiot. Having sex with someone else right now would ruin my chance with her—if I even have one. But the idea that I might be able to make her jealous is like a wrapped present in my lap.

Alaric and Leo peer at me quizzically, but I just shrug. "We'll see how this plays out."

Eden takes a deep breath. I wish I could see inside that brain of hers, understand why she didn't pick me yesterday after I had her creaming on my thigh under the stairwell.

Maybe I just don't understand Eden Astor as much as I thought I did.

I glance at Alaric. "Did you ever say the second thing that's about to happen today? Or did we all just get sidetracked?"

"We'll put our Anne-Marie plan into motion."

"That's a reward too," Eden grins.

"Yes, but it's not a Knight-sanctioned one. No one can know we've done it," he warns.

"I'm sure plenty of people want to put that princess in her place," she muses.

Anne-Marie's squeal of laughter at Eden's scream still hardens my bones. Bitch deserves whatever she gets. Why in the fuck would you celebrate someone else's sorrow? There's no reason for it. Especially since I know Eden's never done anything to that uptight cunt. How could she? She's been living across the country for two years. Plus, she doesn't have a mean bone in her body. She's run away from shit like that her whole life.

Alaric checks his watch. "Well, if we want to do that thing we discussed, we really need to get going."

"Aren't you guys breaking some Knights rules here?" I ask, contemplating the plan we came up with last night. Apparently, Alaric knows that Anne-Marie's father gets a happy ending from his secretary every day after lunch.

When I questioned why we were going after her father instead of her, the unanimous reply was that if you want to hurt her, you go straight to the top. Right now, Anne-Marie is sitting high and mighty in the eligible-wifey category. She'll be the next to get swooped up, driven in a Bentley to her new mansion where she'll more than likely decorate it with something akin to pink unicorns. In Anne-Marie's world, that's what she was bred to do.

"Plenty," Alaric stews. "That's why I said we have to be quiet about this."

Even if I don't trust Leo, Alaric is growing on me. The way he took care of Eden after yesterday's Trial made it clear he's on our side—at least for now.

I check on Eden again, gaze dropping to her feet. Mine are killing me this morning, but at least the worst of it is gone. "You sure about this?" I ask her.

She nods.

The thing about anyone with power and prestige, everyone likes to exploit it. No one ever wants to be outed, though. If we gather evidence of his affair and pass it around, her family will have to draw back for a little while, which means Anne-Marie gets dropped from the shining-diamond category and goes back into the hole where she belongs.

It's actually quite devious.

It's hitting Anne-Marie right where it would hurt most.

Eden and I leave to get dressed. We're posing as a power couple that has an important meeting with the head of the Kennedy family. When we drop by unannounced, it'll be the perfect opportunity to get our evidence. Alaric and Leo were out of the question. Alaric would get recognized if he walked into the building, and Leo would be turned away at the door. When you look like a ruffian, you get treated like one. Instead, those two will be working in the background, making sure nothing will be traced back to us.

After I dress, I knock on Eden's door. "Come in," she says, her voice barely above a whisper.

Entering, I drink up her form. She's swathed in a forest green, knee-length dress that wraps around her midsection and flares out. Flicking those beautiful blue eyes at me, she looks like she could cry at any minute.

Swallowing, she turns away. "It's Dee's."

"You look beautiful in it, and I'm sure she did too."

Her shoulders slump. "I went through the dresses we bought the other day, but nothing screamed *ruin someone's life for the time being,* so I went looking through her things and found this." She curtsies, and I spy her throat working in the reflection of the mirror.

"But," she says, slipping a piece of paper toward her that's lying on the dresser, "I also found this." She hands me a square card with writing on it.

THINKING ABOUT YOU. GETTING READY FOR YOUR big day. Trust me, I've memorized every part of your body, Delilah Astor. I'm ready.

. . .

"Keegan?" I ask, thinking it looks exactly like a note one would leave in a bouquet of flowers or something. Maybe he and Delilah had made up.

"I thought so at first, but 'your big day'? What does that mean?"

"Graduation to the Knights? Wedding...?"

She shrugs. "I don't know. I don't like the feeling I get when I read this, though. It sounds stalkerish. I don't see Keegan leaving her a note like this." She sighs, reading from the card. "'I've memorized every part of your body.' 'I'm ready.'" She shakes her head. "I don't think it's his style."

"I don't know," I tell her. "I wish I did."

"I'm wondering if it means something," she says, taking it back and hiding it in her dresser. "After finding this, I really have to go through her boxes. If there are more things like this in there, I'm just sitting on them."

"It could be a love note," I suggest. "Maybe she'd found someone else? Maybe that's why Keegan looks so fucked up." She shrugs lifelessly but I trudge on. "I say we ask him. What the hell? See if he knows anything about the note. It's the only way we'll know for sure."

"We'll have to do it without them," she says, switching her gaze to the door. "They can't know we're asking questions about Delilah. They're still Knights."

The part where she wants to bang them must be implied. Even the mention of them makes my skin crawl. When it's the two of us, I can almost forget they're even here.

Her suggestion works in my favor, though. "Absolutely. Just the two of us. We'll figure out a way."

She smiles at me. "Are you...mad about last night?"

"I'm not mad," I say hesitantly.

She raises her brows. "Is this the part where you say you're not mad, you're disappointed, so I feel like shit?"

God, this woman drives me nuts. I'm supposed to be mad, but how can I when she says things like this? Stepping forward, I slowly reach for her. She doesn't stop me, so I keep going until I curl my fingers around her ear, taking some of her blonde strands with me. "I made it clear how I felt the other day. Now, it's up to you."

"It was easier to choose him," she murmurs. "And probably not for the reasons you think."

My stomach tightens. Right now, what I think is that she wants to fuck him more than she wants to fuck me—if she even wants to fuck me at all.

She wrings her hand in front of her. "It's just that I don't know what this is yet, Ollie. If I chose you, it would be like telling you I was sure, and the last thing I want is to hurt you. So, it was easy with him. I know where I stand."

I bring my hand back, letting it drop to my side. In a convoluted way, her reasoning makes sense. "This was never going to be easy," I tell her honestly. "We've been one thing for a long time, and I'm asking you to see us differently. You weren't going to magically catch feelings for me. And I know you find his hardness attractive, but I can be a dick too."

She chuckles. "You think I'm..." She makes a disgusted look. "Ugh, well, I don't like that self-assessment. Can we change the subject?"

I hold my elbow out to her. "We have to get going, anyway. I'm sure Professor is down there checking his watch."

"And the other one's head will probably explode if we make him wait."

She loops her arm through mine, and we head for the door. Once we reach the landing, I lean over and whisper, "Are you up for this?"

Her face clouds over. "Bitch has no heart. It's not like we're fucking over innocent people. Her father's scum, and she's a caustic skank."

"Caustic skank, huh? I don't know why, but I kind of picture that as a good boat name. You know, instead of, like, Waverunner III."

"You want to captain Caustic Skank?"

I shrug. "I wouldn't say no to the idea."

"You're unbelievable."

As predicted, once we get to the bottom of the stairs, Alaric stands like he hasn't been watching the clock, and Leo marches out of his room. But the two things that I wasn't ready for are the matching looks they give my girl. Leo even pulls up short at the sight of her. I tug her closer, as if that would mean anything to these two.

Leo, I'm not surprised about. He considers every woman a conquest. But Alaric? I don't like the slight change in him. The way he worried over her feet; the way he stared at us on the bus. Now this? I take back what I said about trusting him more.

It's not shocking that people would fall for Eden Astor. I did so many years ago, and she's gotten nothing but brighter and more beautiful. But when they're ruining something I haven't even had the chance to have, that's when I'll fight.

I'll be whoever she wants me to be because nothing has felt as sacred as her standing next to me.

25

Eden

*O*llie holds my hand in the backseat of Alaric's more sensible SUV. Leo was outnumbered. Oliver said he could have a driver take us in one of his Minis, but really, the least amount of people who know about this, the better.

I'm not nervous as we make our way toward downtown where Anne-Marie's family's offices are located. I highly doubt her father will recognize me. People in my world dismiss children as soon as they're introduced.

If anyone should ask, Oliver and I will tell them we have a meeting with the CEO. We'll "accidentally" walk in on them, snap a few discrete pictures, and leave. No one will be the wiser. Especially since Alaric and Leo are going to make sure we're never caught on camera—which will probably be easy since, if Kennedy has half a brain cell, he won't have the cameras on in his office while he's sleeping with someone who's not his wife.

It was kind of scary listening to Alaric and Leo know so much about how to do this sort of thing. I had the brief thought that I was glad they were on my team, but on the other hand, they're not really on *my* team. They're on my make-believe team. The thing I'm doing right now to make sure I get to do what I came here for.

Alaric pulls into a space in an outdoor parking lot. He turns in his seat, gaze falling to my hand entwined with Oliver's before lifting again. Behind him, two men in suits and ties walk by on the sidewalk, and a woman passes them, walking her dog who practically struts, swishing its poofy tail around. "Leo and I will go in. Wait five minutes, then do your thing."

"I should be going in with her," Leo butts in, peering disdainfully at Oliver. He swipes his palms down his thighs and sighs. "Just make sure we get the picture we need. She's never done anything like this before."

"And you have?" I snap. I quickly back down. Obviously, he has. That's why he has the reputation he does. "Okay, okay," I give in. "Don't worry. I'll turn my phone to record, just like you said. I'll just pretend I have it in my hand like every other person my age if they see us. We can screenshot the incriminating pictures from there. I got this."

Leo's brows lower over his hauntingly dangerous eyes. The way he stares at me pricks at my skin. "Just get them in the frame."

"Yes, sir," I say, thinking about saluting him, but ultimately choose not to for my safety.

The words are meant as a fuck you, but Leo's answering smirk tells me he didn't quite get that memo. Instead he drags his gaze down my body, bringing along goosebumps with it. My nipples peak as if I still have his cum marking me. He said he owned me yesterday, and for some fucked-up reason I haven't been able to comprehend, it didn't make me want to run away.

Alaric throws his door open. "Let's do this."

Oliver and I heave a sigh after they leave. Watching them walk together toward the large building makes my stomach clench. They couldn't be more opposite in some ways. Leo with his tattoos and bad boy style. Alaric with his handsome façade. Only, he can't be as perfect as he looks. He's a Knight, and every Knight I'm aware of has a dark side. Leo just carries his where everyone can see.

Passers-by on the sidewalk give them a wide berth,

and I have a sudden thought that it's not just me. These two exude power and confidence. Living in this world, I should be used to that, but escaping to California and then returning has put a giant spotlight on some of the wilder aspects of this life.

When they disappear on the other side of the glass doors, I turn toward Oliver, doubt settling in. "I'm not backing out, but Anne-Marie better have done what we're accusing her of." Just thinking about that mannequin head gives me chills. It was a direct hit at me and whoever did it deserves to be punished. But...

"Are you kidding? It was Anne-Marie," Oliver fumes. "I saw the evil glint in her eye. She thought the whole thing was so damn hilarious." He shakes his head, turning ice blue eyes to me. "She wants to be the first full-fledged female Knight, so she's sabotaging you. Trying to, anyway." Ollie's protective side is shining through, and I love him for it.

"Do you think we're like them?" I ask, motioning toward the spot I last saw our teammates.

"Those two?" Oliver frowns, peering away. "I don't know, Edie. Yes and no. But you—" he says, turning back. "—are far and above better than all three of us." He squeezes my hand and lowers his voice. "Do you think they knew about the Dee head? They *are* Knights."

Shit. I hadn't thought of that. My gut tells me no,

though. They're the ones who brought up making Anne-Marie pay for the stunt. They seemed just as pissed as Oliver and me. "No," I tell him honestly. "I don't. I'm beginning to think they're as in the dark as we are when it comes to Trials stuff."

He checks his watch and sighs. "Let's go get the bitch, then."

Stepping out, I wait for Ollie near the front of the SUV where he loops my arm around his. To any outsider, it looks as if we also work downtown, maybe meeting up with our partner for lunch. Instead, we head into the brick building that has *Kennedy* emblazoned on the outside. Anne-Marie's family has been running businesses out of this one building for as long as I can remember.

Pulling out my phone, I find the text Alaric sent with the directions to Kennedy's office. It's pretty simple, actually. It's in the Penthouse, so we only need to find the elevator and take it all the way up.

"What if Anne-Marie is here?" Oliver asks.

"Please," I scoff. "I'm willing to bet she stays as far away from his office as possible."

I only go into my father's office if I have to. She probably does the same. It was Delilah who never minded shadowing our father, preparing herself for her eventual career.

The last job I want is to be stuck in an office building all day.

Being here, though, makes me think about my parents. I should call them. Answer that text from my mom that I'm currently avoiding. The truth is, I feel bad for them. They lost the one good person in this family who wanted to do all the things they wanted her to do. Sure, she wasn't going to do it in a conventional way. Not Dee. I smirk at that while we walk into the building. But she wanted the same things they did. Mom would've been happy if she became Keegan's wife and nothing more. Of course, there was more. With no son, her taking over Dad's businesses would've made all of his hard work worth it. She was going to do so many great things...

Not me. I'll never make them proud.

Unless I marry a prince. Mom would die happy, at least.

I peer at Oliver and chuckle. He presses the button on the elevator and glances over. "What?"

"Nothing," I tell him. "I was just thinking about my mom."

He grins. "Your mom loves me."

"I know. I should probably break the news that you're in town, but she'll come visit if I do."

"Your mom's not so bad," Ollie placates.

I peer away. The respect I had for my mother is

long gone. She struts around the house worrying about arbitrary shit when she has bigger problems than that. "Yeah, for a woman who loves burying her head in the sand…"

Oliver nods knowingly. He's listened to me bitch about my parents' circumstances more than a few times. My hands turn to fists, the guilt about what we're doing here fading. If one more asshole gets what's coming to him for cheating on his wife, good. Sometimes, I wish my father would get called out too. Unlike Anne-Marie, I couldn't care less about my standing in the marital pool full of arrogant assholes.

Weirdly, when the elevator doors open on the top floor, no one is in sight. The reception desk in full view of the elevators sits vacant. Oliver squeezes my hand as we take a left. There are no security personnel walking around, but I spot cameras in a few corners. Oliver and I walk with our heads down or turned away. I know we're getting close to Kennedy's office when a short cry sounds.

The quick breaths come next. My hair stands on end when I spot the door at the end of the hallway ajar. Not very smart, if you ask me. We might be able to get our pictures and go without even showing ourselves.

Oliver and I tiptoe the rest of the way. My pulse slams at my wrist, my heart beating like crazy now that we're so close. Not only is the door open a crack, letting the sound filter through, but the blinds hanging on the door for privacy have a gap in them just wide enough to take in the scene.

Oliver and I grin at each other. Quickly, I turn my phone on video and peer through the gap in the blinds. At first, all I see is a mess of black, curly hair. I hold my phone up, checking the screen as it records. Anne-Marie's father is laid out across his desk, the woman on top of him going to town on his dick.

He's wrinklier than I expected—

Another cry escapes the woman's throat, and I nearly drop my phone when I recognize who it is. It's not Kennedy's secretary at all, and it's not Kennedy getting fucked. It's Anne-Marie and... Holy shit. It's Franklin Jarvis. Fucking on her father's desk.

Oliver makes a small sound of surprise. He must be seeing what I'm seeing, but when I follow his gaze, he's not watching the action, he's peering toward a figure in the corner. I slap my hand over my mouth when the man moves.

My stomach clenches, nausea roiling inside.

It's Kennedy.

"Holy shit."

Oliver grabs my hand, knocking the phone out of it. He quickly scoops it up and drags me away. We nearly run down the hallway, and he taps the button for the elevator over and over until it dings, the doors finally opening for us after what seems like an eternity.

"Hello?" a voice calls out from down the hall. We scamper into the elevator, gasping for breath.

My heart soars into my throat, waiting for someone to appear in the gaping mouth of the elevator doors. The hold Oliver has on me tightens, the seconds ticking away painfully slowly.

The elevator dings, and with it, the doors finally close, hiding us away.

"What the fuck?" I yell. "What the fuck?"

"Shh, shh."

"Don't try to calm me down! Did you see that?"

Oliver grabs my cheeks, sending me a warning look as if to say *not here*. My stomach lurches again, and I grip the cold steel of the elevator behind me. He swallows, stops the recording on my phone, and tries to hand it back to me. I shake my head, refusing to take it, so he slips it into his own pocket before squeezing my hands. "Relax, okay?"

Tears gather in the corner of my eyes as my brain tries to make sense of what I just saw.

Anne-Marie was fucking Franklin Jarvis.

While her father watched.

What the fuck is going on here? These people are sick. This is way more than finding her father cheating. This is— Jesus. I don't even know.

Oliver pulls me close, holding my head to his chest. His heart beats rapidly, but the longer he holds me, the more it calms. I try to follow his rhythm, so that by the time we walk out of the elevator on the first floor, I'm able to gather myself enough so I don't scream to the world what I just saw.

Down here, everything is normal. Staff are going about their day. Jobs are being completed. Employees are returning from lunch, laughing, joking.

In there...what I saw...it was disgusting. On every level. Maybe it shouldn't, but my heart goes out to Anne-Marie. This sick, twisted world, it...corrupts.

It's not as if she was being raped, I have to remind myself. She was on top. She was the aggressor. There certainly was no doubt that she was enjoying it.

"Fuck, Oliver," I groan, not knowing what we're going to do with this information.

A man stops in front of us, blocking our path. "Hello."

My gaze darts up to the intruder but I dismiss him as an overeager greeter. "Hi," I say, attempting to pull Oliver around him so we can get back to the car and get the hell out of here. I need to bleach my eyes.

"Were you just up in Kennedy's offices?" the man asks, sidestepping right in front of us again.

I blink at him, mind racing. I certainly can't say that's where we were. What if—

"Leave them alone. They're with me."

To my surprise, it's Leo speaking up, Alaric at his side as they walk toward us. The man blocking our path turns his head and greets Leo with a condescending smirk.

"Well, this is interesting..." the man states. He looks between us four as if he's trying to make the connection of why we're all together.

"Don't fry the few brain cells you have left. I'm sure Grandfather's told you I'm back in the Knights. This is my Pledge group."

"Oh, right," he says. Turning toward me, the man gives me a wide grin. "Eden Astor, right?"

"Right," I say, ignoring his outstretched hand. I'm not sure I'm going to want anyone to touch me for a while after what I just witnessed.

Oliver takes his hand instead, introducing himself. Alaric is next. "Vincent," he greets. It clicks then. This is Vincent Jarvis, Leo's cousin. Judging by the way they're sneering at each other, I can tell there's no love lost between them.

"What brings you four here?" Leo's cousin asks.

Leo growls, "Pledge business."

Vincent doesn't balk at the simple answer, and I'm left wondering how in the hell that's an excuse he accepted.

"You know how it is," Alaric says conversationally. "Always something when you're in Trials."

"Well, good luck with that, you two," Vincent says, looking me up and down and ignoring Oliver altogether.

I can see some of the resemblance between him and Leo in the mouth and cheekbones, but I'm thankful now that I actually see no familiarity between Elder Jarvis and Leo.

My body convulses, and I hurry outside. Stumbling over my feet, I gulp in the fresh air, ignoring the images bombarding me. Did Dee know stuff like this went on? Has Dad watched her fuck someone in his office?

It's disgusting. Deplorable.

There's no way in fucking hell I'm fucking an Elder to get into the Knights. I draw the line there.

"Alright, what the fuck happened?" Leo spits. "You two look...fucked up."

Oliver wraps his hand around my waist, leading me to the car. He helps me in the backseat, but when he attempts to sit with me, Alaric tugs him out of the way and takes his spot.

All four doors slam, Oliver cursing under his breath as he sits up front with Leo. "Let's go," he directs. "We don't want to get caught having this conversation on any cameras."

"That bad, huh?" Leo asks. "Did you see his

wrinkly cock?" He peers into the rearview mirror at me. "Is that why Eden looks like she's going to puke?"

"Go somewhere private," I hiss. "Somewhere a Knight would never set foot."

"I've got just the place," Leo promises.

He holds his palm out, and Alaric drops the keys there, not taking his stormy green gaze off me once. When I finally shift to peer at him, he frowns, jaw pulling taut.

I move to reach out for him, but stop myself. He's a full Knight. If anyone knows these kinds of things go on, it's Alaric Barclay.

Maybe we shouldn't tell these guys what we saw...

Ollie turns around from the front seat, and I move my attention to him. In his eyes, I see all the same questions I'm asking myself.

What will the knowledge of what we just saw do to us?

26

Eden

*L*eo's idea of somewhere private *and* a place the Knights would never go is a go-kart track outside of town. It's pretty rundown with a shitty food court area that consists of a hot dog and hamburger place inside a jerry-rigged Airstream.

"You take your dates here?" Oliver scoffs, turning his nose up at everything he sees. He may be the royal disappointment, but he's still enjoyed a life of privilege. We all have.

Which is why this place is perfect.

The Knights wouldn't set foot in here. They probably don't even know it exists...because peering around, hardly anyone else does either.

"I don't date," Leo grunts. "And don't knock this place until you try it. The chicken fingers are delicious."

Correction. Only assholes like Leonardo Jarvis know a place like this exists.

Just thinking his last name makes me squirm as we stride collectively toward a bright yellow picnic table on the edge of a sea of picnic tables painted in all the colors of the rainbow. A few in the middle boast sun-faded umbrellas running through their center—a remnant of summer left behind. Or, who knows? To match the rest of the decor, they may leave them up all year round.

I study Leo. If he has any inclination as to what we saw in that office, he doesn't show it. I'd like to think that if he knew there would be more of a reaction other than complete calmness. It was just wrong in so many ways.

He walks casually across the rocky area and moves to the tin can of a fast-food place, knocking knuckles with the worker inside. Wow. That's the first time I've ever seen Leo be friendly with anybody.

Is that a smile?

I didn't know the big guy had it in him. He's a weird sort of contradiction right now. He's the poster boy for danger with his tatted-up body, t-shirt that hugs his muscles—even his dark hair helps maintain his shadowy personality. But with him smiling like this, all of that lifts, and he looks like a normal dude out with some friends.

"You guys okay?" Alaric asks. "You're acting funny."

I tear my inspecting gaze away from Leo and instead, lock eyes with Oliver, wishing there was a way we could pause time to talk privately and figure out how we want to play this. Make something up? Tell them the truth?

If only we knew we could trust them...

The possible, awful outcome of telling them the truth is two-fold. One, if they're not shocked by this, I'm not sure how I could go on fantasizing about either of them in the bedroom. Two, if they're in on it, and we saw something we definitely should not see, we could be fucked.

Maybe Delilah witnessed something she shouldn't have? The Knights get rid of problems like that. To my knowledge, they never murder anyone, but that could be my complete naivete talking. Maybe they do shit like this all the time.

"I take it you saw something more than just Kennedy screwing his secretary?"

Alaric waits for an answer, but I'm still at a loss for

words. Trusting people when your sister's murder was ruled an accident is difficult, especially when the people asking questions are a part of the organization that is your biggest suspect.

After a few minutes, Leo returns to the table with several baskets of chicken fingers and an array of sauces. Oliver sneers at them, but Leo only shrugs. "More for me."

I pull one of the baskets toward me with a gold sauce that looks like honey mustard. I tear the chicken finger apart and taste test the first bite. When I gaze up, the guys are all staring at me, and I'm pretty sure it's not because they're waiting to hear the verdict on how good these damn chicken strips are. Sidenote: They're amazing. But what they really want from me is to start explaining to them why I freaked out at Kennedy's office building.

Taking my time chewing, I lick the tips of my fingers then give my audience a thumbs up. "Leo's right."

"Hell yeah, I am," he says, digging into his own basket. So maybe *he* was the only one waiting to see what I thought about the chicken. This guy is a puzzle.

"You can tell us," Alaric prompts, as if he's putting out feelers for what we're going to say.

"You guys didn't see anything from the cameras?" I hedge.

"The whole Kennedy system was completely turned off." Leo wipes his hands on a napkin he picks up from the pile he dropped onto the center of the table. "All the way from the front of the building, the elevator, and the entire penthouse floor. We didn't mess with it since that's what we wanted anyway. So," he says, chewing the last bit of his chicken, "what did you guys see?"

I try to rationalize myself out of this. Maybe it wasn't a big deal. Dads watching their daughters fuck old dudes like their life depends on it is normal, right? This wasn't some sick...thing.

Despite my attempts, this travesty has the Knights written all over it, and despite not caring for Anne-Marie one iota, I'm chilled to the bone seeing her do that. I can't help but think something truly sinister was going on at that very moment.

"They're scared," Alaric points out, switching his attention to Leo.

"No, we don't trust you," Oliver explains, laying it out for them. I kick him in the shin, and he glares at me.

Alaric presses his lips together, nodding slightly. Leo, however, isn't so quiet. "Well, that's bullshit. We all went there together, and you trusted us then."

He's got a point. We trusted him to shut the cameras off. They could've recorded us spying on

Kennedy and turned us both in. Hell, maybe they actually will do that. We have no idea.

"We can't help you unless you tell us," Alaric reasons. "I meant what I said. We're in this together. As soon as they grouped us up, it became my mission to make you a Fledgling. If we need to worry about something you saw, you have to tell us."

Leo rolls his eyes. "Jesus. When did you turn into such a pansy?"

Alaric glares at him. "Wow. I can't believe they don't trust us. I'm in utter astonishment."

Leo grins in response, then addresses me. "Tell us or I show the video I took of you to everyone I know."

I suck in a breath, and Oliver straightens. "Video? What video?"

"You won't," I bluff, fury icing my veins. "How will you be able to jerk off in the future?"

"Oh, you misunderstand," he says, danger dancing in the haze of his blue eyes. "I'm not going to delete the video afterward. It will be added to my personal spank bank, and so many others'. So. Many."

"Fine. Do it," I challenge, daring him with my eyes. I may be playing terrible odds here since this seems like something he does for shits and giggles on a Tuesday morning, but I really don't think he will. Why? I have no fucking clue.

Leo pulls his phone out of his pocket, and Alaric

places his hand over it. "You're going to delete that video as a sign of trust. And I'm going to deal with this like a Knight. If we want a secret, we divulge a secret."

Oliver and I peer at each other. It *could* work. That's how these games are played, right? Everyone has something on someone else, and that means everyone keeps quiet. Which is probably how Alaric knew Kennedy was screwing his secretary. What does someone have on him to keep him quiet, though?

I expect Leo to laugh at Alaric's idea. He doesn't. His throat works, staring at Alaric as if he's wondering if his secret will be worth deleting the video along with hearing the information we have. In the end, surprisingly, Alaric's secret wins. Leo taps his screen a few times, then turns the phone toward us while he deletes the file.

"From the cloud too," I add.

"Done," he states, shrugging.

Oliver touches my leg from under the table to gain my attention. When I peer toward him, he lifts his brows in a silent question. I give him a slight nod.

"Fine," Alaric continues. He rubs his temples, then slides his fingers through his beautiful hair. "I've got something that could get me kicked out of Carnegie. Record this next part," he instructs, dropping his voice low.

Oliver takes out his phone, but Alaric keeps his

stunning gaze on me, his green irises burning me up, sending my heart fluttering all over the place. "I went down on a student," he reveals. "And every time she's in my class, I want to rip her clothes off and devour her with my tongue."

I'm breathless. He's talking about me, which means it was Alaric's face in my pussy before that river Trial. My body heats at the admission, but Oliver growls. "Not good enough."

"I agree with the royal pain in the ass," Leo seethes. "The Knights would cover that up in a heartbeat."

"Fine," Alaric relents. He faces Oliver's phone camera. "The Knights think I'm back at Carnegie to teach. They're wrong. I came back for a very specific reason, and it has nothing to do with teaching." Glancing above the phone at Oliver, he says, "That should be sufficient. You lie to a Knight, they make you pay. You don't need to know the reason yet."

"Yet?" I ask. Yet implies he might actually tell us one day.

Leo catches my gaze. He nods, telling me that's a pretty good secret to divulge. For myself, I liked the other one better—the one where he wants to devour me.

Yes, please.

"Now, your turn," Leo states.

Ollie and I peer at each other before focusing back

on them. "How much do you know about your grandfather, Leo?"

Leo snorts. "I know he's a devious old fuck, and that's not a secret. I'd say that to his face." His shoulders straighten, and he fixes a pair of wild eyes on me. "Tell me you did not see something concerning him up in that room. Was he in that room?"

I nod slowly.

"Fuck," he bites out. He peers at Alaric, who looks as pissed as Leo.

My heart drops to my stomach. "What?"

"Vincent was there, and he saw us. *All* of us," Leo grinds out. "Vincent's my grandfather's next in line. He's like his little lapdog, so if you saw something you shouldn't, this could be fucked."

"Wait, you're not his next in line. I thought your fa—"

"No," Leo growls, putting an end to that conversation quickly.

Oliver sighs. "It was Anne-Marie we saw up there. Your grandfather was laid out across her father's desk, and she was—." He widens his eyes. "—enjoying him."

There's a beat of absolute silence, then Leo laughs like I've never heard him before. He does it with his whole body, as if the laughter itself is its own entity that he never lets out to play. Pure amusement threads through his entire being. "That's all? My grandfather just got head from a girl right after me the other day to teach me a lesson. He doesn't have game. It's called being rich. Money talks."

"Her father was watching," I add. "The whole thing. In the room with them."

"I mean, completely naked. Tits bouncing," Oliver explains, jumping in his seat as if he's going to do a replay for them. "Her father was just standing there, arms crossed, fucking watching."

"It was disgusting." I swallow the bile rising from my stomach.

"Well, that's interesting," Alaric agrees, peering over at Leo. "If Kennedy was watching..."

"An alliance of some sort," Leo agrees.

"Her reward?" Leo offers.

"Old cock?" I gag. "Oh fuck. He's not going to—" I space out, imagining having to fuck that old guy, and I nearly lose it.

When I come to, Leo's hand is under my chin, and he's staring me dead in the eyes, his face as serious as I've ever seen it. "That'll never happen. Understand?"

The certainty of his voice hardens my skin, setting me at ease. I believe him. Inexplicably. He keeps his hand on me as I regain my surroundings again. I peer around the table wondering if this is more than just the group that was thrown together by the Knights. I wouldn't stake my fortune on it, but it's starting to feel less like the partners you don't want in Science class, and more like the people you want to chill with because they mean something to you.

Leo, for all his tough exterior, has been put through the wringer by this world. I can see why he would hate his grandfather and everyone else but be stuck here at the same time.

Alaric... I don't completely understand yet. His secret does say a lot. Sure, we don't know why he really came back, but if he lied to the Knights, it's either something he doesn't want them to know or it's something that could hurt him.

Oliver is always on my side. Currently, he's glaring at Leo like he could rip his arm off, but then he turns to me. "Never going to happen," he mouths.

Alaric sighs. "What are we going to do about Vincent?"

Leo finally releases his grip on my chin. "I'll have a talk with him. He may be Grandfather's favorite, but he's also a moron. I'll figure out whether we have a problem or not."

"Leo, this is—"

"I'll be able to tell," he growls. "I've been outsmarting that fucker since we were kids. If he thinks Eden and Oliver saw anything, he won't be able to shut up."

"You think Vincent knows what was happening up

there?" I ask, still not able to rid myself of the cold chills every time I think about it.

Leo swallows. "I don't just think he knew, I think it was for him."

"What?" Oliver and I gasp out at the same time.

"My grandfather fucks all the women who marry into my family. It's to prove that he's still head of the family, no matter what."

"But she—"

"She would want to do a good job," Leo says, cutting me off. "If she's a lousy fuck, she may not make the cut."

My face must say what I'm thinking because Leo turns away.

That's fucking sick.

"And Kennedy?" I question.

"A witness," he whispers. "I wish I could say it was because Kennedy wanted to make sure his daughter was treated well, but it was probably more about the transaction." He peers back at me with his thunderous blue eyes. "To make sure it was done—and done to satisfaction."

27

Eden

*A*rriving back at Jarvis Hall, I begin to limp. The pain reliever I took this morning and the fresh bandages wrapped around my feet are not cutting it after all these hours on my feet. Overall, the worst injuries from the night before are the mental ones. Thankfully, I've been able to distract myself from those well enough.

Leo leads the way to the building. He frowns when he opens the door and the alarm doesn't go off. I try to peek around him, but he steps in front of me. "What the hell are you doing in here?"

"I've been trying to get a hold of your group all day. I should be asking where *you've* been."

That's the last thing we want anyone to ask, I don't care that I can't see who it is.

Alaric pushes past Oliver and me, walking in casually. "Team-building exercises," he says.

I peer around Leo's huge shoulders to find Alaric pleading me with his eyes to move into the room. I do as he asks, and Leo shuts the huge door behind us, crossing his arms over his chest. "Oh, don't look so pissed, Jarvis. You're just like your grandfather."

Leo's jaw tightens, and his whole body seems to thrum with anger. No doubt he wants to tell this Knight that he's nothing like his grandfather, and honestly, I believe him. It's almost as if the elder Jarvis tried to grow Leo in his image, but he rebelled. Hardcore.

"Miss Astor, Prince Oliver," the voice greets as we walk in.

Jack Greene stands from the recliner in the small living room, leaving the business section of today's paper folded on the arm of the chair.

Unsure how to greet him, I just nod back. His son is a Fledgling teamed up with another girl. He's a regular at my father's parties, and we've been going to his fancy garden soirees since Dee and I were little. But we're in Knight territory now, everything is different.

"I'm here to tell you your current rankings among the Pledges."

My stomach bottoms out, my mind at odds with itself. Part of me is screaming it's wrong to want to have done well, but the other part is telling that voice to shut up because it's the only thing that will get me closer to answers.

"You've done pretty well for yourselves so far. You're running fourth from the top, respectively. Two teams were eliminated as of the last Trial. Everything will be more challenging moving forward. I've left a burn ointment on the kitchen counter for you two."

My gaze flicks to the kitchenette, and I wonder what the hell else he got into while he was here. Hopefully not Delilah's boxes. We started using the security system so shit like this wouldn't happen.

"We'll work as hard as we can," Alaric assures him. He's standing with his arms behind his body, addressing this Knight like he's someone to respect. I don't know much about Jack Greene, but what I do know is no one has gotten through the Knights unscathed. They change you in some way.

"Excellent. We love to hear that. Now: your rewards. For this Trial, we thought it fitting that you receive your greatest sexual fantasy."

I almost groan. Leo and Alaric were right.

"If you are unaware, sex is the greatest stress

reliever. And when you have jobs and relationships as complicated as Knights, there's nothing that beats a carefree romp." His words sound like he's reading from a textbook. "It's also a big responsibility," he adds. "Sex is power. Sex is a tool. I suggest you use it wisely." He peers at Alaric and Leo. "You'll notify us when they receive their rewards and if there're any strings we need to pull to make it happen."

My babysitters both nod while Greene steps around us and reaches for the doorknob. "Keep up the good work and enjoy."

After he shuts the door behind himself and he's out of earshot, we all talk at once.

Leo bitches about the fact that he somehow got around the security system, and he's berating Alaric, who was supposed to set the alarm when we left.

I'm still moaning about the sex thing, and Oliver is asking what world he's living in.

"Just lock the door," Alaric finally grinds out after promising Leo that he, in fact, did set the alarm before we left earlier. "We'll work on the security system later."

"You didn't set it," Leo gripes. "That's how he got in."

"I set the fucking alarm," Alaric bites out. "Jesus. Do you ever shut the fuck up?"

"Anyway," I almost explode. I'm harboring enough

secret sexual fantasies that I don't want to share. Couldn't we have gotten something else for doing a good job? "Anyone heard of..." Time and time again, I bring up an idea of other rewards, but I shoot it down before even voicing it. The truth is, we all have money. We have vacations whenever we want them; we have the means to make almost anything happen.

Which is why he said sex is a tool—a weapon, some might say. Old Wrinkly Cock Jarvis uses it against his entire family. It's the one thing we can't control. And when we can, it's not all that fun. *It's easy to jump in the sack with someone who wants to fuck you for your money*, I think, peering at Leo. It's most likely why his appetite skews in a different direction. Which explains why he hangs out at rundown go-kart tracks instead of places where people would recognize his face and name.

"Fine," I say, admitting to myself that I won't be able to avoid this.

Leo can't let my outburst go, though. "What? You got something against sex? You seemed interested last night..."

"No," I say with a little too much barb. "It's just, sex shouldn't be a tool or whatever Greene said. It makes me second-guess everyone's intentions."

"Well, we all know what Oliver's intentions are,"

Alaric rasps. "Greatest fantasy? Must have something to do with Eden."

I gulp. I hadn't thought past my own reward, and I'd forgotten about Oliver altogether. Peering up at him, I wait until he slides his gaze to mine. "It does."

There's something different in his blue hue. It's not the normal, shining eyes of my best friend wondering what kind of trouble we're going to get into next. This is excitement in its purest form.

"Eden Astor," he orders, his breathy voice cloaked in a physical manifestation of sex. "Wait for me in my room."

I blink at him, a small smile forming on my lips. He must be joking. "Oliver..."

Moving forward, he bends to get in my face. "In my room. Now. Or I'll throw you over my shoulder and take you there."

The distinct features on his face tighten, his commanding stare searing through me until my legs feel like jelly.

I don't know whether to call his bluff, possibly humiliating myself in the process, or to go upstairs like he says—which is also humiliating. Either way, I'm in for a bout of shame, so I do as he says, glaring at him as I walk by. Once we get up there, he'll drop this charade. We'll just sit and talk, make it seem like we did something because there's no way Oliver would make me have sex with him. It's just not in his nature.

My feet sting a little as I walk up the stairs. When I get to the landing, I slip my shoes off and place them next to my door. Despite us being here for a few days, I haven't even been up to Oliver's room yet. I've seen his place in plenty of other houses, though. His style is always distinctly masculine with a mix of old and new.

My heart beats as I hear their voices drifting up the stairs. I'm too far away to hear what's being said, though, so I keep moving to the top floor where Ollie's is the only door. I push it open, and his scent bombards me, skating over my skin.

When I lost my virginity to Oliver, it was...fun. Amazing, actually. Since I was inexperienced, I'd wrongfully believed all of my sexual encounters would be equal or better, but after a few less-than-stellar experiences, I realized sex with Oliver was actually stellar. Which is why we started experimenting with each other when we got older and more curious.

Much like Greene said, life can be stressful, and people need an outlet for energy that there's no other healthy way to expend. Turning to Oliver was easy. No strings attached. Only pleasure. And he's *good* at it. Finding someone to fool around with and hope for the best is exhausting. He was a sure thing.

It wasn't until recently that I suspected he may

have felt like what we were doing was more. And then very recently—as in the other day—that he confirmed it for me.

I haven't had time to do a deep dive into my feelings for him. I haven't—

The stairs creak. I turn, my back to the bed now, and shuffle backward. I see his head first, then he zeroes in on me like he has me in his sights. My chest flutters. The way he's staring at me doesn't say he's about to drop this.

"Oliver," I hedge, taking a step backward.

He slowly shakes his head. "It's my time, Edie."

"You can't think—"

He moves forward, blue eyes taking me in greedily. He starts working the buttons on his shirt, the top of his chest peeking through. We'd only ever gotten naked-naked that first time. The subsequent times were about just getting the act done, only taking off what we needed to climax. It wasn't about exploring each other or passion. It was all about the high.

That doesn't look like what Oliver has on his mind now.

He works his arms out of his shirt and lays it over his ornate dresser. It's a big monstrosity of a piece that is out of place in this room, yet somehow fits Oliver perfectly.

"Here's what's going to happen," he informs me.

"I'm going to take you like I've been wanting to take you. I'm going to kiss every inch of your skin, pushing you higher than you've ever gone before. I'm going to make you scream my name, Eden Astor."

My insides twist. His words heat my core, but my mind doesn't want to admit that he's having an effect on my body. "We can't. We're friends," I argue.

"Not when we're talking about my reward. We're not friends. We're lovers. And you're going to want it so badly. You'll scream for me so loudly, that it'll be evidence enough for those guys downstairs to back the fuck off. Because I had you first, Eden. First...and always. Now, take your dress off so I can see those beautiful breasts."

I swallow hard, my mouth dry and scratchy. Images of Oliver and I over the years flip through my head. He was the cute, awkward kid with the accent and the penchant for telling adults what to do. I was taller than him for a few years until he hit his growth spurt. Our relationship grew and grew. First, pen pals and telephone dates. Then email, instant messaging, and Snap Chat. Every opportunity we could take to see each other, we would do it. Summers in England and Winters at my house. We're inseparable.

"It'll change everything," I warn.

He swallows, meeting my gaze again. "That's the plan."

"But maybe not for the better," I retort, doing as he asks. I slip the side zipper of my dress down and peel the fabric over my head. I leave the green dress to fall to the ground while my best friend stares at my cleavage, licking the inseam of his mouth.

He pulls me to him with a firm grip on my hips. I crash into his chest, and he immediately fuses his lips to mine. Kissing is something we never did. Never. I stand there, refusing to kiss him back. He growls into my mouth, working his lips over mine earnestly, but I don't back down.

He can't see that I'm trying to save us, but I am. Him and Delilah have been the two constants my entire life, and now I only have him. The backside of my eyes heat. Inside, I'm breaking down.

Fear. I feel it, palpitating through me.

Wasn't it just the other day that I said I wasn't afraid of anything anymore because the worst thing that could possibly happen had already happened? I was wrong.

"Kiss me," he grinds out, and he doesn't sound like my best friend anymore. He sounds like a man starved.

When I still won't open for him, he breaks away, fingers still digging into my hips. He pushes me, my back hitting the mattress.

He works on his own pants as he stands above me. "Let yourself see me. Feel me."

What I see is our friendship deteriorating, and it pains me.

His jeans hit the floor, and his erection bulges from his flimsy boxers. He climbs over me, trailing his hand up my side to cup my breast. Flicking his thumb over my nipple, my body immediately responds, and I arch into him. He knows how to get me hot. He's had a front-row seat with me for years.

Peeling back the cup of my bra, he rubs his fingertip over my nipple until it pebbles under his attention. "Look at me," he pleads.

I peer down, trying to keep myself from falling under a spell. While I watch, he takes my breast into his mouth, eyes closed as if he's indulging in a delicacy. He flicks his tongue repeatedly before drawing me out again, gently scraping his teeth along my nipple.

I squirm at the sensations building, the area between my thighs heating, needing touch. The worst part is I know Oliver will make me feel good. I just don't think I can give him the other thing he wants.

"It's been too long since I was inside you," he moans as he drags his cock between my legs. "You were so perfect."

Reaching around my back, he unclasps my bra and slowly reveals my breasts, dropping the lacy fabric off the side of the bed.

"You've grown, though," he murmurs, drawing

back to look at me. "You've matured into someone so beautiful, Edie."

As promised, he lowers himself and turns my whole body into a canvas for his lips. Sometimes they're slow, caressing, and sometimes hard and rough. Not knowing which one I'm going to get makes me wet. My fists clench as he flicks over my belly button on his way down. Flirting with the line of my panties, he drags his tongue across my entire waist, moving lower until he nibbles at my clit over the fabric of my underwear.

I let out a cry. A rushed sort of excitement builds out of nowhere. Little by little, he lowers my panties, flicking his tongue, dragging his teeth, kissing my skin as he goes. I'm shaking when he pulls them past my ass and down, discarding them afterward.

Oliver hikes one of my legs up, keeping the other dangling off the bed. He opens me wide, bare for him as he stares down. "You're glistening for me." He sucks my clit into his mouth until my hips come off the bed, chasing after him.

"Oliver..." His name comes out half in a pant, and half in a warning to not take this too far.

"Not enough," he exhales. "You know I can make you feel good. I'll turn you inside out. You won't know what to think anymore."

Leaning up, he rids himself of his boxers. I've seen

him recently, obviously—even had my hand wrapped around him—but there's something intimidating about his cock right now. He starts to run his hand down his shaft, and I watch intently. This is the part of Oliver I don't see. I've sucked his cock before. I've worked it like a job until he was ready to spew, and I'd remove my mouth to let him come on the sheets.

Now, though, I spot the bead of precum on his dick that's strictly because of me.

"There are so many things I want to do with you," he murmurs, stare trailing across my body. My skin buzzes from his attention, but the worry remains.

He holds out his hand, and I take it, wondering if he's about to end this. Instead, he pulls me to a seated position. He stands in front of me, and I'm eye to eye with his cock. "Suck it."

I look up defiantly. He's never asked me to do it like that. In fact, he rarely ever makes me reciprocate.

Oh, shit. My heart races irregularly. I hadn't noticed—maybe because I didn't care—but he hardly ever asks me to pleasure him. It's only ever for me.

He takes my chin in his hand. "Open up, beautiful. Take me inside that mouth of yours."

I purse my lips, then open them slowly. When there's just the barest of space, he pushes forward, the head of his cock hitting the back of my throat. Tears spring to my eyes at the intrusion, but he keeps thrusting, his hand slipping to the nape of my neck to hold me in place.

"Fuck, Edie. Suck me hard. Just like that. Suck me like you can't wait to see where I'll take this next."

Holy shit. My body flames, burning in the embers of Ollie's words. He told me he could be a bad boy, too, and he wasn't wrong.

I brace my hands on his hips, and he pushes forward. I gag, my nipples peaking, my pussy spasming with pleasure.

"Take all of me. That's it," he praises.

I groan onto his cock, unable to hold it in anymore. His eyes widen. Staring down, his blue eyes light with excitement, thrusting into my mouth.

"You're so fucking good at this. It's hard for me to stop," he admits before pushing me off him, his cock bobbing free in front of me.

I'm drunk on his taste. I lick my lips, looking at him, waiting for him to tell me what to do next.

"How wet are you?" he asks, standing with his hands on his hips. "Check."

I swallow, moving my fingers around to my front. After forcing my knees wide, I dip them between my folds and moan. "Wet," I confess, unable to stop my exploration.

"Dripping?"

I nod in agreement, and he tears my hands away.

"Don't get too greedy. This is my show."

His brown hair falls in front of his face. Keeping my gaze, he crawls over me, shifting my legs further apart with his knees. His cock finds my entrance but shifts over it as I gasp. I move my hips up, searching out the friction, and he gives it to me, slicing his thick cock over my clit.

He kisses my collarbone then works his way up my neck. After placing chaste kisses along my jaw, he tugs at my lips, teasing them with his teeth. "If you want my cock inside you, you're going to kiss me. You're going to let everything you thought you knew about this relationship go. You're going to treat me like some guy you want to make you come. Understand?"

He doesn't give me a chance to respond. He attacks my mouth again, catching me off guard. Sliding his tongue over my own, he massages it with a deep kiss that takes my breath away.

Blitzed out of my mind, I kiss him back. I let him plunder my mouth, opening up wide for him as he builds me into a frenzy. He pinches my nipple, and I yelp before the spike of pleasure sets in, allowing me to moan into his mouth.

Grabbing his ass, I knead my palms into him, digging my nails into his skin and lifting my hips at the same time. I want nothing but to feel him inside me, teasing me, filling me.

"Let me hear you say it."

"What?" I ask, searching out his mouth again, tangling my tongue with his. I grab hold of his ass and push up again, rubbing my clit over his cock.

He pulls away. "Say you want me to fuck you."

"Oliver..."

"Say it," he demands.

I growl, caught between the defiance and pleasure of his commands. "Fuck me," I grind out. "Fuck me hard."

He sucks in a breath, staring down at me in surprise. In the next moment, determination clouds his features. He lifts his hips back, pins my own to the bed, and then slides inside, filling me in one swift motion. I can't help the cry that escapes the back of my throat like it rose from the depths of my fantasies.

He mutters something to himself that sounds suspiciously like he hopes he lasts, but then he's back in sex-god mode again.

He grips my ass while he sits on his haunches, bringing me with him until we're face to face and I'm riding his cock. But he's not just taking it, he's giving it right back. We're slamming into each other, hammering away at the pent-up passion between us.

"Ride my dick. Fuck. Yes." He slams me down over him hard, and I cry out again. My pussy spasms, clenching onto him like she never wants him to leave.

"Oliver!"

"Yeah?" he teases. "Like this?" He does it again and again until I come apart on his cock, screaming. I cling to him for dear life, but he barely lets me have a moment to comprehend what just happened before he flips me around. "Hands and knees," he instructs.

I do as he tells me, my pussy still spasming. He fills me from behind, his fierce grip on my hips biting into my skin. I'm angled toward the door, and I only now realize it's wide open.

He grabs a handful of my tit, squeezing. "This is the part where you let them know, Edie. Tell them I've owned you forever." He thrusts inside and pinches my nipple at the same time.

"Oh, God." My body is still at inferno levels. I never came back down from the climax. He uses his rough grip on my breast as leverage to fuck me from behind, squeezing and releasing with the thrust of his hips. "Oliver," I call out.

He gives a low, hard groan. "Yes, baby?"

"Fuuuuuck."

"Are you enjoying yourself, my little Edie? Do you like being filled with my cock?"

"More," I gasp. "Don't stop."

"Wouldn't dream of it."

My rough pants fill the room, interspersed with

cries I can't contain. If Leo or Alaric are still down-stairs, they're hearing all of this.

For some reason, that only makes it hotter.

Oliver gives up one of my breasts to settle his hand between my legs, working my clit in circles.

"Oh, shit," I breathe out, gasping at the friction. He really does know me inside and out.

"Come on my cock again. Let it out."

I close my eyes, just feeling him. Letting the push and pull, the slide of him take me over the edge once more. I grip the sheets in my hands, throwing my head back when my climax hits. He rides it out, slowing his movements, which makes it that much more profound.

"Oliver, I'm—"

He pulls out, and I almost sag to the bed, but he's not done with me. He's had this pent up for ages, who knows how long we'll be at this. I'm his reward. His fantasy.

He hovers over me, watching me with a different sort of look. It's not lust anymore. It's...love. "Open up for me, Edie."

I do as he says, dropping my knees to the bed. He slides inside, pushing up on his elbows to hover over me as he takes me nice and slow. Gentle.

Tracing his fingers over my cheekbones, he stares, gaze hitting every corner of my face—every hidden shadow, everything I try to hide. He moves my hair out of the way, curling it around my ear as he continues his slow rhythm.

I start moving against him, joining him in the middle, and his jaw tightens. "Edie, love, do you feel that?"

I swallow, beads of sweat cooling my heated skin. He's glistening with it as I reach my arms around him, letting my fingertips explore the muscles of his back.

"It's my love for you." He pushes forward again, eyelids fluttering closed as he groans. "It'll be here for you no matter what."

"Oliver," I sigh, letting his name hang in the air between us.

He makes love to me, taking his time, reading my body. We've not come together like this in so long. It's better than I remembered. It's startling how real this feels. How profound. Life-altering, even.

"I love you," he says, blue eyes blazing. "A part of me always has. I want to take care of you. I want to hold you when you're sad and fuck you when you're horny. I want to be your biggest cheerleader and your strongest defender."

A bead of sweat drips from his pecs and slides down the middle of my breasts. He lowers to lick it off me, leaving his lips there and pressing a kiss against my sensitive skin.

He continues silently as he fills me time and time

again. His jaw twitches when he gets close, grinding his teeth, like he's trying to make it last. His movements become jerkier.

But this is the part that undoes him. The slow, the caring.

I lift my hips, urging him forward to meet me. I slide my fingers up and lace them behind his neck, bringing him down until we're nose to nose.

"Oliver?"

"Hmm?"

"Fill me with your cum."

Almost instantaneously, he jerks; his cock hitting that perfect place inside me. He holds there while he spasms. His climax lasts forever, the pinch between his eyebrows deepening. He lets out the last of it with an exhalation that's half grunt, half relief.

His body collapses over mine until we're just two hearts beating against one another's.

That was unequivocally the best sex of my life. The heat, the passion...the *feelings*. I felt it all.

And I want more.

"I'm staying here and never leaving." He takes in a deep breath, letting it out slowly. "I'm afraid that when I pull out, I'll never get this again."

I close my eyes, tears gathering in the corners. I can feel his desperation, and I hate it. "Oliver look at me."

He hesitates before retreating just far enough away

to look me in the eye. When he does, I don't think, I react. I lift up, sealing my lips to his in a searching kiss. Exploring. Waiting.

Butterflies erupt in my stomach, fluttering, making me thread my fingers through Oliver's hair.

It's fucking scary, and I know I should stop.

Nothing good ever comes from relationships like this. Why couldn't we have just kept the status quo?

It was so much easier than the fear currently clawing at my skin.

28

Leo

$\mathcal{M}$y Hall has been quiet. It's been a week or longer—honestly who knows what time is anymore—since Oliver brought the house down, proving to Eden that she wanted to fuck him as much as he wanted to fuck her. Honestly, I didn't think the little fuck had it in him.

He's a quick learner, though. He realized Eden didn't want the princess-on-a-pedestal relationship, so he took control and now look what's happened. The entire house is in disarray.

I never thought I'd be intimidated by a guy who sounds like he belongs in an aristocracy. Eden's avoiding all of us. The Knights haven't come calling again, and Barclay has been keeping to himself, pensive as fuck.

I'm bored as hell, but I've been sticking around, only answering my grandfather with texts.

Fucking Anne-Marie. I have to give her credit, though. She knew exactly what she was doing to score a Jarvis. It's why women like Eden and her sister won't go anywhere in this world. They're more apt to marry for love and then have their families siphon money to them. The entire society will talk about them behind their back when they show up at their parents' parties with a pity invite.

I should know. My father was that guy. Disgraced in front of everyone but walking around, trying to keep his head high.

Upstairs, I hear movement while I sit at the kitchen island. The attraction I felt toward Eden hasn't wavered since that first day. Every time Grandfather texts, I respond with the bare minimum, doing everything I can to keep him off her trail. I'm rooting for Eden, and as far as I'm concerned, the Knights can all go suck a huge bag of dicks. Their elitist bullshit has never done anything for me other than make me feel shit and take my father's life.

But Eden? Damn. The girl is strong. The more I learn, the more I respect her for things other than her banging legs and tight ass. She's living in her dead sister's room, pledging her society, practically walking in the ghost of her footsteps. Not once has she mentioned uprooting her whole life, but that has to be the case. Doing it for her parents since Delilah was the good girl. The one who—even if unconventionally by our society standards—was going to do something with her life. Eden was always the sister they brushed under the rug. Out of sight, out of mind. People telling jokes about how she was probably pregnant on the West Coast because she never showed up to shit.

Instead, she was living her life. Like me. Until I got dragged back, and she did too. We're more alike than she thinks and I care to admit.

Barclay walks into the room. He's dressed in his normal class attire—button-up shirt, suit jacket hanging open. I'm still trying to figure this motherfucker out. He's not here to teach Economics, and the reveal of his secret clearly says he's not here for the Knights either.

So, why the fuck is he here?

I can't just ask him because he'd laugh in my face. I haven't told Grandfather about his secret, and I don't plan on it either. Barclay isn't my concern, but the more he's around, the more I understand him too. He was always such a gigantic asshole, walking around like he was God's gift. Still does, actually, but in Jarvis Hall, it's mellowed.

He doesn't greet me with a smile, but he does peer up the steps, searching for the girl we've all been orbiting around. "The Knights won't stay quiet for long."

"Maybe they're waiting for their feet to heal?"

He chuckles. "Like they give a fuck. I think it just means their next test will be hard. The anticipation is killing me."

I grunt in response. It's hard to compare these Trials to my own. Everything was a blur back then. I didn't take shit seriously. I was in my burn-the-world-down phase, acting out because Grandfather was trying to take pity on me, and I really didn't want anything from him except an explanation as to why my father was no longer around.

I never got one.

It wasn't until I got kicked out of the Knights while a Fledgling that I understood he'd been trying to help me in his own way. But even then, I saw it as him trying to make me in his own image. He wanted me to be the rule follower, to toe the line, to be the perfect Jarvis.

That's when I lost my shit and left, rid myself of this fucking world. I had no parents to track me down. No one to look after me. A year later, I came crawling back like a little bitch. I should've stayed gone. Now, here I am, getting a second chance, and I'm back in the same boat. I should be taking everything I know about Eden right to him. Instead, I'm keeping it close to the vest. A crisis of fucking conscience is the only thing I can chalk it up to. Every day, I tell myself I'm going to go to him with every scrap of information I know, only I don't. She'll come downstairs looking sad or like she has a fire inside her, and I can't extinguish that. No matter how hard I try to talk myself into doing what Grandfather's asked of me, I can't.

He'll get suspicious soon, though. He's an untrusting old fuck, but I don't suppose you get to where he has by trusting anybody.

I hate him. I've dreamed about putting a bullet in his head and carving my name into his body so he knows it was me...along with the message *For Dad*.

"You seem grumpy," Barclay notes.

"Aren't I always?"

"Yeah, it's just worse today. You have this whole *don't fucking talk to me* look on your face."

"Yet, you're still fucking talking..."

He grins. "I'm not pandering to your tantrums, Jarvis. We're here for Eden, and that's it."

"Are we, though?" I ask, anger building inside me. I guess I am in a damn mood. "Because it sounded like you were here for a different reason. I mean, other than the revelation that you want to fuck our little charge up there."

Barclay's face hardens. "Get over yourself for one fucking day. Go get fucking laid."

"That's another thing," I growl out. "How long are we going to wait to give Eden her reward? We all know what it is."

Barclay shakes his head. "You're a caveman."

"No, I'm a realist. They obviously had a good time, but he alone won't satisfy her. You saw how she—"

"I felt it," he grinds out, hands turning to fists. "I tasted every last drop, so I know."

Standing, I go toe-to-toe with him. "It should've been me."

"Except you backed away like a coward, so a man had to do the job."

I swing. It's reckless and uncontrolled, and Barclay easily shifts out of the way as if he was avoiding a darting mosquito. I roar, angrier that I missed than at what he said. "Don't push my fucking buttons."

His jaw hardens. "Think from her point of view, Leo. Her best friend revealed his feelings and fucked her. Whether she liked it or not, she doesn't need to worry about two other cocks right now."

"Even the prince said her fantasy was all of us. It was his idea." I don't know why I'm so irate about this. Maybe because I think if I fuck her, I'll be able to get it out of my system and *then* go to Grandfather. That would be ideal. My body just wants to sink inside her so bad.

Enough teasing.

Enough waiting.

I haven't hung around a girl this long to get laid. I would've had her that first night if Oliver hadn't shown up. Now, here we are, weeks later. "Besides, since when do you fucking care? Your reputation is about as bad as mine."

"I don't know. Maybe since I have a heart."

I scoff. "Not one Knight has a heart, and you know it."

Barclay's jaw snaps closed, and oddly, it's as if I've gotten to him. Those words shut him up.

Tiny footsteps interrupt our stare down, and I turn to find Eden at the bottom of the steps, hands on her hips. "I love how you're talking about my sexual fantasy, and I haven't even brushed my teeth this morning."

Her hair is up in a messy bun. Little by little, over the course of the days since she slept with Oliver, she's started to look more like the girl she was when she got here. Sure, she wears the clothes that are expected of her, but they're a costume now, where before she was more than just going through the motions. She's not as polished or put together; her makeup is lighter, making her look more natural. She's beautiful both ways, but like this, her raw beauty shines. She's absolutely stunning. Together, she and her sister must have been a sight to see.

"We can tell. You going to class like that?"

"No, I'm just fucking hungry. Then I come downstairs to you two fighting like little bitches."

"To be fair, he was the only bitch fighting," Barclay mutters.

She moves into the kitchen, and I get a perfect view of her ass as she bends to retrieve the milk from the fridge. When she turns, I try to look anywhere but at her while she gets out cereal and makes her bowl. It's obvious something is different with her. She's retreated more inside herself. Scared, even. It won't bode well for whatever the Knights have cooked up next.

I say as much, possibly even more unflatteringly than I said it in my head, and she glares at me. "Can't a girl eat her breakfast in peace? Shouldn't you be off burying yourself between two legs about now?"

I snicker. "You don't want me to do that. You'll get all jealous, just like before."

"I wasn't jealous," she protests, but it's a feeble attempt that fools no one.

"Listen, if you want us, you're just going to have to tell him," I offer as the perfect plan.

She peers up the stairs, a worried expression on her face. Something shifted between them, but I don't think she even knows if it was enough to change them completely. When she turns back to me, though, her face is pinched in anger. "That would work if I actually wanted you."

"Do you hear that, Barclay? She's lying to herself."

"I hear her," he says, voice low and dangerous.

I grab the cereal bowl from her hands and set it on the counter. Barclay and I sandwich her, moving in. "Do you think she knows she's lying to herself?"

"I do."

I angle my hips into her ass. In response, she reaches up and grabs Barclay's lapels as if to hold on to something.

I spread her ass cheeks, giving myself a tight little pocket to rub my dick between. I'm such a horny fuck, but I can't help it. I expect her to pull away, but instead, Barclay steps closer and she ends up sticking her ass right back into me.

"Fuck me."

My words must pull her out of her sexed-up stupor. "Okay, that's enough."

"Yeah," Barclay agrees, throat thick. "Oliver should be down soon."

She wiggles out of our grasps. "Actually, Oliver left last night. He needed space."

"Wait, what?"

"Yeah, he left," she whispers.

Barclay reaches for her, but she steps out of the way. "And guess why," she snarks, shaking her head. "Because...fuck," she growls before turning and running up the steps.

When she's out of sight, a cruel smile carves my face.

"What are you grinning at?"

"He wussed out. It's our turn now."

He doesn't answer as he retreats to his room, shaking his head.

I'm not going to let this opportunity pass me by. I take the steps two at a time, opening the door to her room. Her back is to me, her head tucked into her shoulder. Her voice rings out. "Yeah, Oliver, it's me. Just making sure you're okay. Call me."

Suddenly, I'm not in the mood to get my dick sucked anymore.

The doorknob creaks under my grip. She turns, glaring at me. "What do you want?"

"Just wondering when you were going to get your ass ready since apparently I have to walk you to class this morning."

"Alaric can do it."

"Fine," I grumble, stepping back to leave, but something makes me pause. "Are you mad because you want to fuck me? Is that it?"

She presses her lips together. It doesn't take her

long to think about what I've asked, though. "Yeah, actually, I am. And I'm hurting my best friend in the process, so save your whole fantasy sex talk for another time."

I heave a sigh. "Listen, Little Astor, there's no way he won't come back, so calm your tits. Just figure out what you want."

"Easy for you to say," she mumbles, then moves forward to slam the door in my face.

29

Alaric

I start across campus, but a student calling out, "Professor Barclay" halts my steps. Turning, I find Eden power walking toward me. I stop to wait and she hikes her bag up over her shoulder. "Didn't Leo tell you I was walking with you?"

I peer at her as if to say *Really?*, and a smile teases her lips.

"Of course not. He's kind of a dick."

Those are tame words for Leo Jarvis, but... "He's had a shit life."

"Apparently," she says, but there's no malice behind it. A cute little wrinkle forms between her eyes that I try not to stare at as we make our way across campus.

I wasn't expecting to be so curious about this girl when I decided to come to Carnegie. It's so fucking cliché, but there's something about her. Her refusal to give up; the way she pulls her shoulders back and trudges straight ahead no matter what she's gotten herself into.

Men like me aren't taught to respect women, and I'll be the first to admit that I've been an ass in the past. Many, many times.

I drop my gaze to her gait. "How are your feet feeling?"

Despite what she came down wearing first thing this morning, she's dressed completely different now in Knight-appropriate attire, complete with little black flats, one rhinestone twinkling in the middle of the bow. "Fine," she says. "My feet are the least of my worries."

"You like Oliver, then?" I ask. It was apparent the other night, but if Oliver's gone, maybe she had second thoughts.

She narrows her gaze. "Are we really going to talk about this?"

I shrug. "Not if you don't want to." Maybe I'm taking my professor role a little too literal. It's actually not a terrible gig. The part I like best is

325

living at Jarvis with Eden, helping her through Trials.

Leo grates on my nerves, but for as much as he likes to play, he's in this like the rest of us. I've seen the way he looks at her. He may be too stubborn to realize it, but he's worried for her as well. It's not all about jumping into bed with her like he tries to make it out to be.

It's not easy for guys like us to care about someone. When it happens, usually someone tries to take it away. Or test it. Or just ruin it completely.

That's why most of us have surface-level lives and something else altogether in secret. Something no one else can touch.

If Eden was smart, she'd stick with Oliver and get the hell away from us.

"Why are you here?" I ask. "Really?" When she looks up at me again, I continue. "I can't imagine your parents are happy with you being at Carnegie after...everything."

Eloquently put, asshat.

"They're not." She peers away, sending the sidewalk in front of us a withering glare. "But someone has to do it, right? Dad didn't get a son like the other elite families. All he had was Delilah, and now she's gone."

"I'm sure he wouldn't—"

"You don't know anything."

My jaw tenses. I know more than she thinks I do. Males in this fucking society dominate. I get it.

She sighs, and it's that bit of childish behavior that sets me off. I stop, pulling back on her hand and making her whirl toward me. "You're not the only one who's gone through shit."

She blinks at me, then glances at my grip on her arm. People walk around us, and I immediately let her go so we don't make a scene.

We fall back into walking together toward class when a feminine voice calls out, "Alaric!"

I already know its owner, and I groan. "You know it's Professor Barclay," I grunt.

The girl that walks up to us may look like Eden on the outside—polished, put together, the whole package —but she's nothing like her. She's like a cardboard cutout, whereas Eden doesn't know how to be anything other than 3D.

"You look handsome today," she says, ignoring my comment.

"Inappropriate," I tell her as I sidestep around her, forcing Eden to move out of my way and follow me.

The girl quickly catches up once we're inside the building. She's always the first to class, and I hate it. I turn to ask Eden not to leave me alone with her, but she's already gone. Left me here with this fake.

"I'm looking forward to you teaching me something today."

The innuendo is all over the place in that sentence. An earlier version of me would've acted by now. Maybe the guy who showed up here on the first day of this term would have, also, but not now. "I teach stuff every day," I tell her, stopping at the entrance to my classroom to search for a blonde head of hair amongst the students walking to their respective classes.

"Yeah, but nothing I want to know," she says, trying to act coy but only coming off as desperate. I'd have to check her last name again, but I'm pretty sure she's one of the lower-rung families. Got here on good grades instead of her last name. Those types are always attempting to move up the ranks. I may not be a Jarvis or an Astor, but Barclay isn't some schmuck name either.

Before, it'd be so easy to use girls who were just worried about status, then pull some lame excuse like they didn't do it for me. But it's getting more difficult the older I get. I'll be expected to pair off soon. Start churning out male heirs so the rest of my family can calm the fuck down.

I push past her and head to my desk. Thankfully, more students begin to file in, so I don't have to pretend to have a one-sided conversation with this girl.

I pull my chair out, set my briefcase on the desk,

and sit, attempting to assimilate into professor mode instead of wondering what Eden's up to and whether I should text Leo to follow her since she bailed on me. My stomach clenches. We're supposed to watch her at all times. I'm wracking my brain, trying to remember where her class is. Student schedules are in the faculty portal, so I pull out my laptop. I'll send her schedule to Leo so he can find her. We don't need another instance of the Knights getting the drop on us.

Fucking Oliver. At least he was always around to make sure no one could get to her. Now we don't even have—

I'm yanked forward, my chest almost slamming into the desk. A hand cups my cock and I jump. Sliding back, I find a heavy-lidded Eden seated under my desk.

She gives me a mischievous grin, before reaching for me again. She grabs the end of my pant leg and pulls me forward, fingertips sliding over the sudden bulge in my pants.

My hands turn to fists, and I snap my gaze up to see if anyone is paying attention.

"You alright, Professor Barclay?" a student asks.

I nod, throat working. "Rammed my knee into the desk. All good," I say as Eden strokes me through the fabric of my clothes. It isn't just my cock she's paying attention to, but massaging up my thigh, fingertips grazing my now massive erection.

I don't know what's come over her, but fuck. This is both highly inappropriate and something I've been fantasizing about when it comes to her.

More students saunter in. The veins on my arms pop as I try not to let my face hint to what's happening below. Thank fuck for these intimidating, ostentatious desks Carnegie has in every room.

Pushing on the inside of my knees, she forces my legs wide. I shift in my seat, allowing her space. Her fingers move upward and grasp onto the top of my pants.

I should tell her to stop.

I should definitely tell her to stop.

But I'm sure as hell not going to.

Her hot breath filters over my crotch. I jut my hips forward, and in the next instant, she scrapes her teeth down my pants, just over my cock. I grab the edge of the desk in front of me as pleasure spills through my veins.

"You look a little flushed," the same annoying student observes.

"I'm fine," I bark, and nearly the whole class turns toward me. I chuckle and peek at the clock on my laptop. Class starts in two minutes. I'll be mid-lecture before I'll be ready to empty my cum down her throat.

I peer out at the class. There's just one more student left to arrive—

That thought quickly obliterates as Eden unbuttons my pants. The zipper comes down next, thankfully drowned out by another student regaling half the class with a story of what he did last night.

She moves my tucked-in shirt up, cupping my cock through my boxers again, her breath hot above my eager dick.

I'm so getting fired, but I couldn't care less at the moment. She starts to stroke, and my toes curl in my shoes. What I wouldn't give to see her face right now. Her pretty pursed lips, her stare of concentration. How far does she want this to go? Does she want me to tell the class to leave? Or do I let this play out?

I really didn't peg her as an exhibitionist, so maybe she's just trying to tease—see when I'll put a stop to this. Or maybe the flirty student pushed her over the edge. That bitch is definitely getting an A now.

Actually, I don't need to know why Eden ended up under my desk, only that she did.

Precisely on time, the last student enters, and I think quickly. Eden's fingers brush the tip of my cock, and I have to wrangle my control.

"Pop quiz," I say in greeting. The whole class groans, and I give myself a moment to indulge in one too as Eden fists my dick, pulling it free from my briefs. "Who read last night's chapter?"

A non-committal sound comes from most of the class. I choose the smartest student so I don't have to pay attention to what I have planned. "Gary, you're up first. Pick a lesson from last night's chapter and teach it to the class. When you're finished, pick the next person, and so on. You'll *all* be evaluated," I relay, nudging Eden with my foot.

A chuckle comes from underneath the desk, but it was drowned out by more disgruntled sighs. I smirk, hoping she got the message that I'll be assessing her too. From the fact that she didn't just shove it into her mouth and start sucking means she's off to a good start.

"Can we use our textbook?" Gary asks.

"Yes, whatever you need. Begin."

Gary stands at the front of the class, and he's the exact distraction I needed as Eden strokes me. The anticipation of feeling her tongue slide along my cock is exhilarating, heightening my own responses.

Gary begins to lecture, but my mind is on Eden, conjuring up images of her face, of her playing with herself at the same time she touches me. She drags her palms up under my shirt, spreading her fingertips wide over my abs, then back down again, enclosing her fist around the base of my cock.

She licks the tip first, and I inhale a breath. I have a

tremendous amount of willpower under normal circumstances, but this is anything but normal. I place my elbow on the desk, holding my head up with my palm and attempting to keep my face neutral while I sneak my other hand down. She reaches her free hand to connect with mine, tracing her fingertips over my palm and up my forearm at the same time she closes her lips around my cock, stroking and swallowing me.

She moans, and a few people in the front row peer around, but go right back to listening to Gary. I pitch my hips forward, using my hand to filter through her hair and cradling her head as she takes me deeper and deeper into her mouth. The chair rocks, and I have to spread my knees wider, using the side of the desk to keep from moving.

She takes me all the way in, my tip hitting the back of her throat where it sends a jolt through me. Her hand around me tightens as she increases her rhythm. Another moan escapes her, and I pull on her hair in warning. She opens her mouth wide, licking the underside of my cock as if to snark back at me, but then she's sucking me down again, fisting me into her mouth with the perfect amount of pressure.

Her free hand curves up my hips, biting into me almost for leverage as she increases the pace. It's becoming impossible not to react. I'm going to burst holding back.

She stays at the tip, sucking and sucking with little motion until my fingers curl into her hair and I force her all the way down. "Oh, fuck," I growl when she gets to the base.

Gary turns to look at me, as does the rest of the class. I have to think fast. "This is pathetic," I grumble. "The worst—" She scrapes her teeth down my cock, and I nearly come out of my seat. "I'm going to give you guys one more chance, but not today. Today, I want you all out of my class. Now. Go back, study the damn chapter, and be ready." The students look around stunned, mostly Gary. I honestly haven't been paying attention to a damn word he's said. He could be teaching the material better than me, but I'll never know. "Now," I growl out.

The students pack their stuff with wide eyes and low whispers. Gary sticks by the desk, but when I don't even look up at him, he stalks toward his seat to grab his things. It's the flirter that comes up to my desk next as the other students file out. "Can you tell me more of what you'd like to see from us, Alaric?"

"I'd like to see you get out of my classroom," I bite out. "Shut the door behind you."

She presses her lips together, but my harsh words do the trick. When the last student leaves, shutting the door behind them, I push away from the desk, and my dick pops free from Eden's mouth. She smirks, her fingers shoved down her panties and rubbing. "Do I get a bad grade?" she pouts playfully. "Pathetic, you called it?"

I groan, the sound almost foreign to my ears. I crook my finger at her. "Come here, Eden Astor. I need to watch you suck my cock."

She crawls out, gaze flicking to the door. "Should we lock it?"

"Says the girl who just went down on me in front of my entire class."

She eyes my cock, pure sexual haze dripping from her beautiful blue eyes. "You'll get in trouble."

"Not as much trouble as you'll get in if you don't get over here and wrap those perfect lips around me again." I shrug my suit coat off, fold it, and lay it next to my feet so she can save her knees. She places where I ask, running her hands up my thighs as she takes me in her mouth again. As exciting as the other was, the picture of my dick disappearing into her mouth is what does it for me.

"God, where did you come from, Eden Astor?"

She peers up at me, and the innocent look in her eyes as she takes my cock into her mouth makes my balls tighten.

I hiss in a breath, relaxing back into the chair as she takes care of me. "When you're done, I'm going to spread you out on my desk and eat you for breakfast."

This must thrill her; her movements accelerate with renewed purpose. I let her do her thing, watching as she brings me to the point of climax. I hold it back, living in the moment, wishing it would last longer. I lift my hips to meet her mouth, and the little cry she gives undoes me.

"Fuck. I'm going to—" I try to get my words out fast enough, but it doesn't happen. My cock fills her mouth before I can ask her where she wants it. She doesn't balk, though. She closes her eyes and drinks me down as if she's tasting the sweetest nectar, moaning in contentment. "That's right. Drink me up."

She opens her eyes wide as she takes my last drop, then pulls away, her lids fluttering as I leave her mouth.

Jesus Christ.

I don't waste time. Cock still out, I help her to her feet, then pick her up and set her on the desk, moving her into the perfect position. I roll the chair back to me again before sitting, reveling at the way she looks, laid out on my desk, my laptop tucked away in the corner. Pulling her pants and panties off, I spread her wide and lift her feet to rest on the arms of the chair.

I nuzzle her pussy. I've tasted its sweetness before, and I know once I start, I won't be able to relish in it. I'll want to keep tasting until she's coming apart on my tongue.

A kiss to the inside of her thigh makes her sigh. I

mirror the movement on the opposite thigh and juices trickle from her. I lap them up, unable to help myself.

She lets out a short cry, and I peek at the door to make sure we're still alone. This probably isn't my smartest move, but I don't care. I just want her. Pausing to lock the door would be a waste of my time with her. "In class today," I start, trailing my nose up her thigh, "we're going to discuss the power of women."

"Mmm," she moans. "My kind of class."

I lick up her length, stopping at her clit where I flick over her tight bud. She reacts much the way she did when we were on the bus, bucking into me, craving more.

"How you hypnotize us. Make us crazy with want until we're addicted."

"Are you addicted to me, Professor Barclay?" she asks.

Oh, fuck. This roleplay has me beyond excited. "You know I am," I tell her. "Now, let's see how good of a student you are." I drag my lips up her seam in a featherlight touch that has her searching for me with her hips.

"What do you want me to do?" she purrs.

"Just enjoy yourself."

She releases her hold on the desk and immediately reaches under her shirt. I watch as she grasps her breasts, moaning. "I can definitely do that. Should we lock the door now?"

"Too busy," I growl as I lick her, flattening my tongue against her bud. Her bra shifts with her movements. I reach up her sides and around her ribcage and down.

I won't be locking the door, but I probably should hurry in case someone decides to come back to class. Lowering my hand, I trace my thumb over her clit. She lets out a loud moan, and I keep it there, rubbing her, tasting every drop of her pussy. My attack is direct, going for speed rather than style.

"Tell Professor Barclay when it feels good."

She bucks into my mouth when I increase the pressure and tighten my movements. She forgets her breasts altogether and grabs the edge of the desk again. "Oh, hell. It's amazing," she says, breathless. Her knuckles turn white, and she begins to shake at my relentless pace. "Fuck. Please," she rattles.

I move my tongue to her clit again, flicking until her entire body locks up. Short cries pour from her mouth. She peers down at me with the most impassioned gaze when she comes, her hips rocking into me. I'm not going to lie, it makes me feel like a goddamn rock star.

She takes deep breaths in the aftermath, her chest rising and falling, her rumpled top saying everything about the encounter. "That might be a record," she sighs. "Wow."

"You're going to give me an ego."

A lazy smile crosses her face as I stand. I tuck my semi-hard cock into my pants, zipping and buttoning him away to safeguard me from wanting to use him. My buttoned shirt is still loose, and my suit coat is still on the ground, but I help Eden to a seated position first. She runs her hands through her hair, trying to get the blonde strands under control before nibbling her lower lip. "That might have been the best blow job decision I've ever made."

I narrow my gaze at her. Damn Leo pops into my head. He would never let her get away with saying that, and neither will I. I reach around, taking a handful of her hair until she's staring at me. "Eden Astor, don't ever talk about another guy after I've just had you screaming on my tongue."

She bites her lip harder, as if she's going to tease me more. Wisely, she thinks better of it.

Reaching down, I grab her discarded clothes. I start the panties over her feet, and she pulls them up after arranging her shirt and bra. I help with her pants, too, tugging them until all she has to do is slide down from the desk, zippering them into place.

She bends to grab for her bag, but I stop her. "What spurred this on?"

Shrugging, she says, "That needy bitch was annoying me. Then I remembered when you said you thought about me in your classroom, and I couldn't resist."

And I'm glad she didn't. I move past her to reach for her bag. "It's supposed to be *your* sexual fantasy we're making come true," I point out.

"We still have time."

My reminder puts a damper on the situation. She takes her bag from me and moves toward the door. Before she gets there, it careens open, and a very pissed Leo stands in the doorway.

30

Alaric

*L*eo's rough breaths halt as he makes eye contact with Eden. "You're not in your fucking class," he growls. His gaze shifts to me. "And shouldn't you be teaching a class?"

Eden presses her lips together, her entire body shifts into a closed off position. When she doesn't answer, I sigh. "I canceled class," I tell him, lifting my chin in the air. He's such a bastard, and he really can't help it.

He lunges forward, but not at me. At Eden. "So, the only guy you don't want to fuck at Jarvis Hall is me?"

She glares at him. "Get a hold of yourself, frat boy. I fuck when I want and who I want. Just because I'm attracted to your controlling ass doesn't mean you get to talk to me that way." She crosses her arms over her chest. "You're playing a different game than we're all playing. You think this is some sex ed course and the fact that your last name is Jarvis means you own my ass. It's so much bigger than that."

He grinds his teeth together in her face, and then storms from the room just as quickly as he'd come into it. She sighs. "Jeez, I'm just making everyone happy, aren't I?"

"Leo's being a dick. You decide what you want."

"Oh, I know," she says, peering over at me. "What we just did was probably a bad idea, huh?"

I swallow. I don't know how to answer that. Detangling all these conflicting feelings inside is going to be torture. "It depends on why you're saying that. Because of everyone else?"

She straightens her shoulders. "You're right. I'm sick of doing what everyone expects me to." A moment later, though, she drops her head. "Except, that's my MO, isn't it? I'm so fucking selfish. Always have been. Dee was the one who always did everything she was supposed to. She didn't even need a rule book. Or help. It's like she instinctively knew."

That sounds...a hell of a lot like me. I always

played by their rules before, so I don't know what my problem is now. Well, actually, I know what the problem is, I just don't know why this—of all things—has actually gotten to me.

"I don't even think it bothered her," Eden says, her voice gripping onto wonder.

"Some people are like that," I tell her softly. "Speaking from experience."

She rubs two hands down her face, searching for me over the tips of her fingers. "Would you always do everything the Knights told you?" She sucks her bottom lip into her mouth when her hands drop. "I just keep thinking about Delilah during her Trials. Some of this stuff doesn't seem like things she'd do. Rewarded with sex?"

"What? You think she was a nun?"

"I think my sister was holding out for one guy, and that guy..." Her jaw hardens. "I don't even know what to think about him."

"It's possible there was nothing like this last year," I tell her. I honestly don't know. Once you go through Trials, you're usually not privy to what goes on until you become an Elder. "And it's not as if someone sits there and watches while you get your reward." I hesitate to ask my next question because I think it'll say a lot about what she thinks of me. "Would you think less of her if she did take sex as a reward?"

She cocks her head, brows pulling together. "No, but I'd probably think she wanted this a lot more than I knew. It's not fair what happened to her."

"It's not," I say firmly. I'm always skirting the line between truth and lies when I talk to Eden, but this is one thing that I truly believe in. Delilah didn't deserve to die, whether it was Knights orchestrated or not. I keep trying to feel Eden out, wondering what she thinks about her sister's death. There are so many times I can read her like a book, but when it comes to Delilah, she keeps things close.

One day soon, we're going to have to lay all the cards out on the table and see what they show. Right now, I don't know where any of our quad stands. Is Leo really only here because his grandfather is trying to get him back into the Knights? Or is there another reason why he's been grouped with Eden?

I don't trust him. And maybe that's Eden's problem too. He's rough around the edges, like he wears barb-wire for show, but I've seen a different side of him recently. There's no way in hell I'm trusting him first, though. Despite the fact that he may have more reason to hate the Knights than I do. As much as Eden does.

And Oliver? He's obviously just here for Eden. Plain and simple.

I'm walking a tightrope of everyone else's lies. I let a partial truth slip the other day—and I'll gladly do it again as long as I know it's not going to come back and bite me in the ass.

You never know what will happen where the Knights are concerned, though. We're all in their game. They make the rules. They make the odds.

We're just their pawns.

31

Eden

J pull up to the address Oliver texted me. No context, just a number and street. I really didn't want to attend classes today, anyway. Not after Leo's outburst.

Leaning forward, I catch a glimpse of the large, stately house with manicured bushes surrounding its perimeter. In the front lawn stands a huge maple that's shed its beautifully colored leaves, only a few still hanging on, dancing in the wind.

The house itself is only a mile away from campus, but I don't know why I'm here. I trust Oliver with everything, though, so I park in front of the half-moon shaped steps and make my way toward the black door with a brass lion's head knocker.

I hit it once, and nearly jump back when a man in a bowtie opens the door for me. "Miss Astor, you'll find Prince Oliver in the drawing room."

It's one of the servants Ollie brought with him that first night. I'd never thought about where they were while he was staying in Jarvis Hall. I assumed they'd made their way back to Britain, but I guess not. "Thank you," I tell him, and when I walk in, he graciously shows me the way.

The large swinging doors that must lead into the drawing room are wide open, and I spot Oliver's halo of brown hair. He's sitting on a settee, one ankle crossed over his knee as he reads a book.

I sigh when I see him. I only knew he'd left when I found a note on my dresser this morning. Things had been weird between us since the epic sex we shared, but I never expected him to leave.

Anger tumbles through me. I charge into the room. "Just because you're a prince doesn't mean—"

Muffled cries come from the corner of the room, and I swing my gaze to find Keegan blindfolded, gagged, and tied up in a chair in front of a huge fireplace. He's sweating profusely, pit stains growing down his silver button-up shirt.

"Well, hello to you too," Oliver says in greeting.

I peer back at him. "What the fuck is this?"

He closes the book. "You want answers. I'm giving you answers."

"Did you...kidnap him?" I screech.

He beams. "I did. All by myself. The staff thinks I've gone mad." Just as he says it, a servant walks past the room, brows raised into her hair. Oliver glares at her, and she scurries away like she's stepped in a pile of red ants.

"This is what you left for? To get Keegan?"

Keegan's muffled sounds pitch higher, but we both ignore him. Oliver sets the book on a coffee table and stands, a sad smile pulling at his lips. "I want you to know I believe in you, Eden. I've been quiet and moping, but it isn't your fault. You have so much going on right now, and I'm only adding to it. So, this—"

"Is a present?" I ask, trying to guess.

He tilts his head. "I guess it is."

As presents go, it might be the most heartfelt one I've ever received. What the fuck does that say about me? I peer over at Keegan, who's in obvious distress. "So, what are we going to do?"

"We're going to interrogate him."

"Do we know how to do that?"

"If you've ever sat at a table with my grandmother, trust me, you're well aware of the gist."

I roll my eyes. "Ollie..."

348

"Ollie good or Ollie bad?"

"I don't know yet," I admit. I guess this is better than trying to track him down on campus and getting him to talk. "Let's do it."

Oliver's gaze sparkles and surprise ricochets through me. I didn't know kidnapping and interrogating was on a to-do list for him. Honestly, it sounds more like Leo's line of work, but...hey, whatever works.

Oliver moves forward and unties the blindfold first. When Keegan sees me, his eyes widen, and he starts talking faster. We still can't understand a word he's saying, so Oliver quickly unties the gag, letting it slip to the floor. I have to roll my eyes when I notice it's a fancy dinner napkin. He obviously hadn't thought this through, and I can only imagine the servant's reaction when he asked them to grab the fancy napkins when he dragged Keegan's ass in here.

The first thing Keegan says is, "You're a fucking psycho," while staring right at Oliver.

Oliver looks pleased with himself, standing back and folding his arms over his chest.

"Get me out of here, Eden," Keegan demands.

"Not so fast," I tell him.

"You're in on this?"

"Well, not until recently, but since you being here is kind of a gift to me, I have some things to ask you."

Keegan struggles against the duct tape holding him

to the chair. Oliver leans down. "Don't worry. He won't be getting out of those."

"What do you want?" Keegan growls.

Oliver slips the note we found in Dee's box out of his pocket and holds it in front of Keegan so he can see it. "Do you know anything about this?"

Keegan's face falls. "Whatever you guys are doing, don't."

"So, that's a yes," I growl. "What is this, Keegan? I deserve to know."

He grinds his teeth together, looking away. "You should go back to the West Coast. You should stay as far away from here as possible."

I almost laugh. "I don't trust you. You barely liked Dee, so forgive me if I don't heed your advice."

"Didn't like Dee?" he roars. "*I loved her.*"

The laugh that catches in my throat sounds like a drowning cat. "Please," I scoff. "I saw you with her during break. Remember?"

"A lot changed after that. A lot," he says, tears forming in the corners of his eyes. "I loved Dee, which is why I'm telling you to leave."

Not likely, though he's doing a good job of trying to sell it to me. "Tell me what I need to know, and I'll think about it."

"Ask your dad," he grouses. "He knows what it is."

His words are like a slap in the face. I take a step

back to steady myself, then read the note on the card again, my stomach clenching. *Trust me, I've memorized every part of your body, Delilah Astor. I'm ready.*

"Did you write this?" I ask, hand shaking.

"Me? No," he spits. He closes his eyes and shakes his head like the last thing he wants to do is tell me what this is. But when he opens his eyes, he looks resigned. "Listen, your sister got this fucked up bouquet delivered to her. Flowers were wrapped in one of those stupid gossip magazines, and it was a picture of your sister on your father's yacht...in her bikini."

Memorized every part of your body...

Well, that's disgusting.

"That note was in the bouquet along with a used condom," he relates darkly. "Your sister called me first. She trusted me, and so should you—"

"Who sent it?" I snarl.

Keegan sighs. "We never found out. We called your father to look into it, but there wasn't anything to go on. The DNA in the condom didn't match anyone in the system. We figured she had some psycho stalker."

"A stalker? Did anyone mention this to the police?"

"I don't know," he grunts.

Unbelievable. "Someone may have been stalking her, and no one said anything?"

"It wasn't my place to tell you or your mother. That was Dee's or your father's."

He's got a point, and I will be saying something to daddy dearest, that's for sure. My fingers trace over the note. "What's the big day allude to?"

"The wedding, I thought," he says. "On the backside of the picture was a section talking about celebrity couples."

Celebrity couples? I'm not going to unpack how much ego has to go into thinking he's that important. "But that doesn't make any sense."

"Listen, she didn't know, and neither did I. I thought it was that barista from the café at first. He had such a hard-on for her since she spoke to him one fucking time. It was ridiculous."

Oliver and I share a surprised glance. That has to be the same barista who'd tried to talk to me. He definitely looked at me like I was Dee, then Leo almost pissed on him.

Jesus.

If he sent this to her, he deserves that and so much more. She must have been so scared.

Oliver glares at Keegan. "Do you think her death and this stalker shit are related?"

More sweat drips down his face. He's turning ashen under the heat of the flames licking behind him. "I don't know," he states, but his voice sounds more broken than before. "I don't. I wish I fucking knew. I really do." His voice cracks. "If I could take back all the shitty things I did to her—said to her—I would. I loved her, Eden. I swear to you. I'd finally gotten my head out of my ass, and I only had one good week with her. One."

Emotion pours through me, unchecked tears filling my eyes. "You didn't deserve her."

"I know," he murmurs, and his voice is so lost. It's scary how fast men like Keegan can fall.

"What happened to Delilah?" Oliver asks. He's the only one of us who isn't crying.

"She drowned."

"How?" he seethes.

Keegan peers up at me. "Please, leave. Just go. I'll give you money. I'll help. This is the last place you should be."

"Why, Keegan?" I ask, chest fluttering. This is as close to the truth as I've been yet.

"Please..." he begs, before his head lolls forward and his eyes roll into the back of his head.

Horror grips me. "What the hell?"

Oliver strides up to him, leaning over. "I think he's just passed out. Maybe the fireplace was overkill."

I run my hands through my hair. "What are we going to do with a passed-out Keegan, Ollie? Shit."

"Calm down," he says in the only way a prince

that's fifth from ruling an entire country could say. "This is no big deal." He walks to the entryway into the drawing room and presses a button on the wall. "Please come remove my guest and return him to his residence hall."

"You're going to have your servants take him back?"

"Do you have a better idea?" Ollie asks. He flicks his gaze to Keegan's limp body. "He's not going to tell you what's going on, and we certainly can't have anyone know he was here, right? Leo and Alaric will ask questions if we come waltzing onto campus with a limp Keegan in tow."

"Fine... Fine," I exclaim. "Just—"

The servant who let me in the door walks in and unties the knots on Keegan's wrists and ankles. When another servant joins him, they both hoist Keegan into the air and start walking toward the foyer as if they do this all the time. "I'll text you the address, James," Oliver calls out as they leave.

"Sir," he says in response.

While he does that, I wear a hole into what is probably a ridiculously expensive carpet. When he puts his phone away, I ask, "What is this place, anyway?"

He peers around as if evaluating it. "I rented it for us. I figured you'd get sick of living in the residence hall and would want something else. Then, Leo and Alaric got thrown into the mix."

"But on the upside, it's a great place to bring kidnap victims," I chime.

"I suppose this room should have a little less light," he answers, gazing around. "Way too cheery for this kind of work."

I shake my head at him. "You're unbelievable, you know that?"

"I've known that forever. I've just been waiting for you to see it."

I press my lips together. "I didn't say it like it's a good thing."

"Really? Because that's the tone I got."

"You need to check your hearing. You've probably only heard muted mumbling for...how many hours?"

"A few," he says, smiling. "I wanted him to be good and worried by the time you got here."

I sigh, then drop back onto the settee where Oliver joins me. "So, she had a stalker?"

"Something like that," he confirms. "The barista?"

"Or a Knight. We've seen how they treat women." Instead of Anne-Marie's face, I place Dee's in the scene with Jarvis again, and the contents of my stomach threaten to expel. How far was she in this? "There's no telling what she got herself mixed up in while doing this."

"Maybe you should listen to Keegan," Oliver offers. He holds his hand up when I move to glare at him. "I know that's the last thing you want, but it would be safer. Now there are two things to be worried about. First, we were sure it was the Knights, now she may have had a stalker. What if the stalker—"

I gasp. "Remember the girl from the store said Dee argued with someone on the dock that night. Maybe that was him? The stalker?"

"So, basically what we did was make more questions for ourselves," Oliver deadpans. He peers down at his lap, frowning as if he's saddened by the fact that his first kidnapping and interrogation didn't yield better results.

"It doesn't matter as long as we find out what happened."

A minute goes by, and Oliver turns toward me. "We need to be wary of Leo and Alaric. What if one of them is a plant, paired with you because *he's* her stalker? I mean, hell, Alaric's already announced that he wants to fuck you in the middle of his classroom. That's kind of bold."

My face turns pale as the realization of what Oliver says strikes me. He thinks Alaric may be Dee's stalker. A man I just blew in front of his whole class.

Or Leo. I can't even count the encounters I've had with him.

"You two do look alike..." When I don't say anything, he nudges me. "You agree?"

I gulp, the acid in my stomach threatening to come out. "Things sort of escalated between me and Alaric this morning."

Oliver turns away, jaw tightening.

"I didn't do it to hurt you," I say immediately. "That's the last thing I want."

"I know you're attracted to them too. Just..." he hesitates. "Forget about all that right now. I'm thinking about your safety here."

"I don't know," I gush out. "I kind of trust him. He told us that secret."

"A half secret, which is really nothing at all."

"Don't you think your decision-making abilities might be skewed when it comes to them?"

"Don't you think yours are?" he counters.

Shit. I don't ever want to be one of those girls thinking with her pussy. But he may be right. "Fine," I relent. "We don't trust them until they deserve it."

"Or never. Whichever works."

"Or never," I agree. I bite my lip as I think back on my encounter with Alaric, second-guessing it all. He definitely didn't make me get under that desk. That was all me. But he refused to lock the door. He laid me out over his desk in view of everyone or anything.

What if he did it on purpose?

32

Leo

I pretend I'm not looking out for them as Barclay and I wait for the two Pledges on the front stoop of Jarvis Hall. He sent them a text fifteen minutes ago, but what I don't expect is for them to show up together...in Eden's Jeep. Smiling.

I've always been an irrational hot head, but she's pushed me to new heights. Got me walking around like a pubescent virgin. After she called me out earlier, I went to my local haunts to find someone else to fuck Eden Astor's face out of my brain, but it didn't work. They're all just slobbering juveniles, only wanting the same thing I want.

Which usually would be fine with me, but not today. The truth is, Eden was right. This is bigger than fucking her. My grandfather left me a threatening voicemail, asking me to check in. The old fuck is getting suspicious, and I'm not sure how long I can hold him off by saying this chick is boring.

He wants me to dive deeper. He wants me to get in her head, make her open up to me. If she has secrets, he wants to know them.

I'm the muscle, not the therapist. How in the fuck do I get her to open up to me? She looks at me like she expects more than I'm willing to give, and it's been a long time since someone has done that. *A hell of a long time.*

They walk toward us, and Barclay breathes a sigh of relief. Easy for him to do, he got some this morning.

I mentally punch myself in the face. There I go, thinking with my cock. Then again, I do my best thinking when I'm satisfied instead of salivating for it. She's got me all tied up in knots.

Barclay kicks off the door. "We ready for this?" He's all business, taking over like he's the leader of our little group. I don't care that he holds the coveted, full Knight title and we're all just lowly fucks compared to him, I bow to no one. Especially since it pisses me off that I can't tell whether or not he's another plant from a Knight. If he is, I'm going to murder his ass for taking advantage of Eden like that. Manipulation. Mind warp. Whatever it was, I will end him.

I glare at Oliver. A Mini Cooper stopped in front of Kennedy Hall earlier, dropping off a very unsteady Keegan Forbes who had to be helped to his residence hall by a bunch of English servants. Coincidence? No way.

What I'm not going to do is ask them in front of the Knight standing next to me. If he's feeding things up the line to my grandfather, I don't need him finding something like this out. Keegan was Delilah's fiancé. It's obvious why Eden would want to speak with him, even if the Knights had nothing to do with her sister's murder.

I'd also really love to know whose house they were in. The tracker I put on Eden's phone led me right to her. I suppose I'm watching her for two different reasons now.

But the tracker was for keeping tabs on her in case the Knights tried some shit. I was never going to let that happen again. Clearly, I didn't tell her about the secret app I sideloaded. She would be irate about the fact that I've basically microchipped her like a dog.

It could be worse. I could have put it subdermal. It would be foolproof that way.

I lag behind, watching the three of them as they walk across campus toward the Knights building.

Oliver and Eden stand close together, leaving room between her and Barclay.

Maybe he was a terrible lay and she's trying to send him a message? I doubt that's it. Bitches in this world talk, and I've heard plenty of stories about Alaric Barclay, the charming seducer.

When we arrive at the Knights of Arcadia, Keegan isn't outside this time. He's likely sleeping off whatever happened at that house they had him in. I have to hand it to them, I didn't think either one had it in them. Then again, someone with royalty reach has people in their back pocket to do shit like that. He probably didn't even have to lift a finger.

Eden eyes me, and I swallow at the way her gaze penetrates my thick skin as if she can see right through me to what I'm thinking. In a way, I wish she could. Get all this shit over with because when she finds out I've been sent here to watch her for my grandfather, she's going to hate me. I thought I'd have a little fun first. Use her. Abuse her. But it's turned out to be more serious than that.

A Knight standing just inside the door sees us walk in and peers down at a paper in his hands. He's a low-level Fledgling, which is why he got stuck with the shit job, but I bet he's just excited to even be here. "Eden, Oliver, you're in room six."

My mind whirs, trying to remember my own Trials

361

when they split the Pledges up. There was one particularly hellacious interrogation that lasted forty-eight hours that I don't want to repeat. My skin buzzes. Fuck that. I'm not leaving her side. They can try to keep her starving, dying of thirst, and sleep deprived, but I won't let them.

Barclay leads the way, and we find another Fledgling posted in front of room six. It's too late to give Eden pointers now. Too many eyes and ears.

"Just the two Pledges," the Fledgling says, barely looking up from his phone.

"Don't think so," I counter. "She's my charge, and I'm going in with her."

The Fledgling glances up, eyes widening when he spots me in front of them. "I was told only them."

"Then physically remove us," I bark, before stepping past a surprised Eden and opening the door.

"Hey!" the Fledgling protests.

I glare back at him, and he shuts his mouth so fast his teeth clack together.

When I turn back around, my temper flares again, but this time for a very different reason. Vincent sits at the huge oval-shaped table in the middle of the room. I slam the door behind the four of us and stare.

"Mind telling me what you're doing in here, Barclay? Cousin?"

Barclay takes the more diplomatic approach.

"Leonardo and I were tasked with making sure she gets through Trials. We're staying."

My cousin peers up, leering, before a smile breaks out over his face. "At least you passed this time."

"Oh, go fuck yourself."

This makes him laugh. There was a time when Vincent and I were close. But he fell in line when the rest of the family started to diss my father's line. Just like that. We weren't even teenagers yet, and he already knew when to follow the herd. "Please, sit," he says, gesturing toward the chairs across from him.

Eden and Oliver take a seat while Barclay and I flank them on either side. Surprisingly, Barclay has a don't-fuck-with-me-face too, and he's currently directing it straight at my cousin. His jaw twitches, though, and it suddenly dawns on me that this may not be Trials related at all. If Grandfather found out Eden and Oliver saw him with Anne-Marie, this could be bad.

Vincent doesn't speak right away. He takes his time inspecting Eden. To her credit, she doesn't flinch or squirm. She just glares right back. The thing with Eden is, she's dealt with difficult shit before. Vincent has been coddled his whole life. If he thinks he's going to intimidate her, he's wrong. She's already harder than he is. Stronger.

"Are you ready for your next Trial?" he finally asks.

"We're here," Eden states simply, not giving off any nervous vibes or insecurities. Oliver isn't either. The only tell he has is that he's leaned into Eden more, as if he can shield her from everything.

That's where Oliver has it wrong. Thinking you're always going to be someone's savior is a battle you've lost before you've even begun. Life just doesn't work that way.

"We're calling this the Favor Trial," Vincent states matter-of-factly. "It's quite easy, actually. Each Knight has a favor he needs done. To prove you're one of the team, you're going to perform the favor, no questions asked. Failure to do so will result in your elimination from the Trials. You cannot receive outside help from your team members," he adds, glaring at me and Barclay.

I grind my teeth together, wondering how Vincent's favor will impact Eden? He's such a sneaky son of a bitch. I would never willingly owe him something like this.

"What's the favor?" she asks, lifting her chin. The way she peers down at him makes my dick hard. I've been wanting to fuck him over since he left me behind, but he's currently Grandfather's second in command, which means I've had to defer to him for too long.

He pulls a folder from his lap and slides it in front of Eden and Oliver. "In that folder is the name, address, and picture of a woman. She gave birth three months ago, and I need to know the results of the paternity test she's currently keeping from me."

"Why is she keeping it from you?"

Vincent's hand turns into a fist, and I start to growl. He ignores me, zeroing in on Eden. "I said no questions asked. The other paper is the name and address of the doctor's office in which I have received intelligence confirming that the results are located."

"Then what?" Eden asks, sifting through the folder calmly, then moving it toward Oliver. "Get rid of them?"

"Just document," he responds. "The instructions are also in the folder. You have twenty-four hours to complete the favor. I'll meet you back in this room at this same time tomorrow."

He stands, buttoning his suit jacket and looking pompous as fuck. He strolls past me, flashing that signature Jarvis fuck-you smile. "Good luck."

He leaves the room, and to my surprise, it's Barclay who lets out a growl.

The three of us watch him as he loses his shit, spinning to slam his fist into the wall. He does it again and again, the skin splitting his knuckles.

"Whoa, whoa," Eden stammers. She dodges his fist coming back, reaching for it to stop its forward motion. As soon as he feels her touch on him, his body deflates.

We all just stare. I'm more than curious what this outburst means. Before I can come to any conclusions, he reaches over, grabs the folder, and marches toward the door. "We should tell him to clean up his own messes. Or not fuck someone he's unwilling to take responsibility for."

Okay, so it's the kid aspect. I wrack my brain, trying to remember if there's anything going on in the Barclay line that would make him react like this, but I come up blank. His line is squeaky clean, actually. They're one of the fortunate ones who haven't had to resort to unsavory alliances or secrets.

Or are they?

I reach forward, grabbing his wrist to stop him from leaving. "Calm the fuck down before we go out there." He turns crazy eyes on me, but I incline my head toward Eden. If he's here for the right reasons, he'll care about what happens to her, and leaving this room angry would make us stick out. "Eden and Oliver have to do the job. They're not getting out of this."

"I'm sick of this world," he pants. "Twisted psychopaths."

He's either a decent actor or he truly believes what he's saying. I'm good at reading people, and I think he's telling the truth, but I'm still not ready to make friendship bracelets with him yet.

"That makes two of us," Oliver hisses, glaring at the folder in Alaric's hand.

"So, you're here why?" I question.

"I think that's plenty obvious," he states, placing his hands on Eden's shoulders.

She doesn't flinch away, or call him a caveman, or tell him he's playing a different game than the rest of us. She just lets him do it. The longing that conjures terrifies the shit out of me. "We need to take that back to the Hall," I say, pointing at the folder. "We'll come up with a plan."

"You aren't allowed to help," Eden reminds us. She walks up to Alaric and takes the folder from him. "He said we're supposed to do it on our own."

I take the folder away from her. "He meant physically, as in not doing it for you. We can brainstorm together."

She rips the folder from my hand and stuffs it up her shirt. "You can't help."

I eye her. "If you think that's going to keep it away from me, you're very, very mistaken, Little Astor." But to show her I'm not always thinking about sex, I add, "Just take our help, at least mine. It's the smart thing to do. You don't think I've broken into places on behalf of the Knights before?"

"You mean on behalf of the Jarvises?" she throws back.

Sometimes, I don't know where that line ends and the other begins. Grandfather likes to blur it a little like he *is* the Knights.

"Just take my help," I order, sick of arguing with her.

"He's right," Barclay says. "We'll help. That's our job. We won't do it for you, but let's go back to Jarvis Hall and think about our next move."

I don't know whether it was Alaric's words or my own, but Eden backs down, returning with us to the residence hall to plan a heist that could send her further into the Knights' snare.

33

Oliver

S ometimes it pays being a royal whose face is splashed all over the tabloids. Especially when all those tabloids are available in the doctor's office that you're trying to steal information from.

Eden and I have memorized the contents of Vincent's folder. Leo and Alaric wanted us to learn how to break the security system and enter the medical office at night like ninjas, but that seemed a little too *Mission Impossible* for Eden and me.

We concocted our own plan that those two twats think is ridiculous—and it is—but I wholeheartedly believe it will work...by just using a little ingenuity.

"You ready?" I ask.

Eden fires off a text that I catch the last couple words of. She's been trying to reach her dad since last night with no luck, and his lack of response is pissing her off. Which is good. She can use that for fodder in there. "Yeah, I'm ready," she says. "Keep a straight face or this will never work."

I chuckle already. We once used a similar ruse to get us out of one of her parents' boring parties. They're particularly hard on Eden because of all the fake ass smiles, but I'm used to that kind of hell.

I jump out of her Jeep and run around to the other side, helping her out of the seat as she doubles over. We walk like that until we get to Northside OBGYN, the name inside the folder. She stumbles, but she doesn't turn it on in full force until we get inside.

"God... Jesus... This hurts," she groans as soon as we step inside.

The receptionist opposite a glass partition immediately looks concerned. "Are you okay, Miss?"

Eden leans into me, lashes fluttering.

I have my dark sunglasses down over my eyes as I peer up. "She needs help. Can you get a doctor?"

"You should probably go to the—"

Eden groans, falling, but I stop her at the last second before she hits her knees. "Please?" I ask desperately. "I was just walking by, and she was lying on your sidewalk. Something about a—"

"My tampon!" Edie yells. "It's stuck. It hurts so damn bad."

Two more nurses appear in the doorway that leads into the back of the medical practice. They take in Edie's slumped form and start asking her a million questions.

She goes ballistic. "There's a tampon. In my vagina. It's been there for a week, and I can't get it out! Please."

"Are you a patient here?" the receptionist asks. She peers between me and Edie, and I raise my sunglasses to the top of my head. "Listen, if you'll just help her, I'll pay for the expenses."

The girl's eyes widen, gaze zeroing in on my face. I make sure I'm wearing that cocky smile the paparazzi always capture. "Prince Oliver?"

I lift my finger to my lips, and Eden groans, slamming her foot down on my own. "I think I'm going into shock..." Her eyes roll, and the nurses rush me forward as I grab a basically limp Eden.

They help her into a room, leaving me with the bewildered receptionist. Now, Eden's priority is to keep them away from her vag, which is why I hear her "come to" in the other room. "Tell me how to get it out."

I peer at the starstruck receptionist, who's still staring at me. I give her a wicked smile. "Love, do you have a room more private for me to wait? The photographers have been hounding me, and I don't think carrying a girl into an obstetrician's office will do well for my reputation."

She gasps. "Oh, of course. Here. Right this way."

As I'd hoped, she leads me into the records room. The office itself is quite quaint, almost like a house they remodeled into an infirmary. The records room is cramped, with one computer in the corner and a line of filing cases.

"Don't touch me!" I hear Eden yell. My hackles rise, but I know it's part of the charade. She's probably huddled in the corner of the room. I better make this quick.

"She sounds like she's a lot of work in there. Just my luck to come across her, huh?"

"You've definitely earned some brownie points, I think."

The smitten look on her face unsettles my stomach, but Eden growling quickly captures my full attention. "Just tell me!"

A feminine voice responds, "If you'd let us examine you..."

"They might need help..." I suggest.

The receptionist slowly nods, still grinning at me

like a lovesick child. "You're probably right," she giggles. "I'll be back. Don't move."

She runs from the room, closing the door behind her and leaving me by myself. I check the room for cameras first, and then move to the filing cabinets when I find none. Everything is meticulously labeled, and I have no problem finding the drawer that holds the girl's file according to her last name.

Scanning through the other manila folders, I break into a grin when I find the one I'm looking for. I pull it out, spreading it open on top of the others. The very first paper has a lab name in the upper right-hand corner and *Paternity Test along the top*. I yank my phone out, take a picture, and then flip through the rest of the contents, taking a few more pictures just in case, before placing the folder back into the drawer and shutting it.

Eden makes more of a ruckus in the other room, and I casually lean against the cabinet, smirking to myself when Eden growls, "You don't need to touch me to help me! Who are you, Nurse Ratchett? Are you about to Kathy Bates me? This is so unprofessional."

The next thing I hear is a door banging. And...that's my cue. I open the door to the records room and step out to find Eden clutching her stomach. She winks at me, and then limp-runs from the office.

Adrenaline courses through me as she exits, leaving the nursing staff flummoxed in her wake.

"She had a set of pipes on her," one nurse remarks in frustration.

"I'm so sorry," I blurt, making myself known. "I thought she'd let you help."

"We should call the police," the other nurse suggests. "She may have been on something."

I make a disgusted sound in the back of my throat like that's probably what the issue is. "You know, I'll just pick her up and drop her off at the hospital. No need to get anyone involved."

The receptionist nods eagerly, but I'm sure she'd agree with anything I say. "That's so kind of you."

"Kind is my middle name," I smirk.

"No, it's not. It's Henry," she says, giving me a coy smile.

I give it back to her. "You got me there."

"Who are you?" one of the nurses asks, looking at the two of us like we've grown three heads.

The receptionist widens her eyes at her co-worker. "You don't recognize him? It's Prince Oliver."

The nurse looks me up and down. "No." Then she turns and leaves.

I chuckle at that. The older generation who couldn't give a shit about most anything are always good for a healthy dose of reality.

I hike my thumb toward the door. "I should get going. Thank you for trying..." I wink at the receptionist. "And thank you for giving me a place to hide."

"Here. Go out the back." She springs forward, gesturing toward the hallway. Lowering her voice, she adds, "In case any of those nosey photographers are out front."

"Excellent idea," I answer, leaning toward her as if we're coconspirators.

I follow her toward the end of the hall, and she pushes the back door open that boasts a neon red exit sign over it. I replace my sunglasses and stride from the building, giving the nice girl a "Thank you, love" before heading out into the sunlight, knowing we accomplished our tasks. No need for black catsuits and fancy technology.

The door closes behind me, and the shriek that follows makes my shoulders stiffen. I've had all sorts of reactions when people meet royalty, but that one's the most common. It never ceases to make me cringe, though.

I walk around the side of the building, hop in the driver's seat of Eden's car, and meet her around the corner. She pulls the passenger door open, and I blink at her. "Um, no."

"Oh, come on," she says, climbing in. "You drove it this far."

"It's like I'm driving a monster truck," I complain.

"Oh, get over it, Prince Oliver," she teases and holds her hand out, wiggling her fingers for the folder. "Let me see."

I pick my hip up, and she sticks her hand in my pants pocket to pull out my phone. She inputs my PIN, then brings up the pictures I took. "Some of this is Greek to me," she says, lips tugging into a frown. "Alleged Father..."—she sighs—"redacted. But whoever it is, they're a match."

"It's got to be Vincent."

"Most likely. But I can't imagine why the woman doesn't want him to know. Makes me feel like shit for having to turn this in."

I glance over. She still has my phone in her hand, but she's peering out the window, face troubled. "End game," I remind her.

She shrugs. "Yeah, I just never wanted to be the person that crawled over others to get what I want. I'm just like them."

I shake my head. I hate seeing her like this. "There's one key difference, Edie. They're doing it to keep themselves ahead. You're not thinking of yourself at all. You're doing it for Dee."

"It doesn't feel like it right now."

I reach out, placing my hand on her thigh and squeezing. She slides her gaze down, then tosses my phone into the center console before placing her hand on mine. Turning my hand around, I entwine our fingers. My phone buzzes, but neither one of us looks at it. Leo and Alaric will be wanting to know how everything worked out, but Eden seems content for the moment, her thumb gliding gently across my skin.

She tenses. "Ollie, other side of the road."

I look back at the double yellow line and jerk the Jeep to the correct side. Well, the wrong side, but whatever. Edie and I have fought about this before.

She chuckles. "You should be better at driving here than you are. How long has it been?"

"You distracted me," I protest.

She stares at our entwined hands. "This?"

I nod, and her lips curve into a bigger smile. Her gaze settles on me, and my skin buzzes in response. Glancing over—briefly this time—I notice the look on her face has changed, morphed into something fiery.

"I need something real, Ollie." She breathes out, slow and steady. "Something to show me I'm still me."

My heart constricts in my chest, then beats twice as fast. I know what she's asking. I pull off on a side road and thankfully find a remote trail into the woods that I just squeeze Eden's Jeep into.

I've barely put it in park before she's climbing across the center console and straddling my hips. She leans over, using the automatic adjustments on the seat

377

to take it all the way back and recline. Her lips hover above my neck, and the atmosphere in the Jeep charges with electricity, filling me with a desperate need.

She kisses down to my shoulder, and I inhale sharply. We never kissed before she gave in to my fantasy, and we haven't kissed since. My fingers curl around her pants, wondering if she'll follow exactly where I want her to.

I squeeze my eyes closed, hoping. If she kisses me on the mouth, I'll know she's not just doing this because she has the need to climax. She's doing this because she wants *me*.

My hands shake as I struggle with her pants. She dressed in her normal clothes today, and that's when I realize she's wearing leggings. There is no button or clasp. I grip the top, yanking down.

A ripping noise cuts through our heavy breathing, and I pause.

"I don't care," she whispers, lips moving against my neck. "Keep going."

I pull apart, ripping the material until I search out her core. Luckily, the scraps of her leggings have torn at the seam, providing the perfect access to rub her clit.

She exhales against my neck, and I raise my hips into her, wanting her to feel what she does to me.

"I need you inside me," she pants. "No teasing. No drawing it out. Just us."

She dips closer, pressing kisses against my collar-bone, then up the other side of my neck. I work on my own jeans, lifting up into her to create space so I can shove them down my hips along with my boxers.

She grabs my cock, and I exhale sharply. "It's okay, love. I'm here," I grind out. I don't need time to ready myself for this girl. My body is so attuned to hers, as if it's constantly waiting on deck to be brought into the game.

I slip the crotch of her panties to the side, and she starts to lower over me. "Hold on, Edie. You need more," I tell her, rubbing the pad of my thumb across her clit. She moves in tandem with me, then takes my earlobe into her mouth. I lift my hips, unable to help myself, and she shivers when I make contact with her folds.

"Oliver," she groans.

"Give yourself a second," I plead, knowing if she's not ready for me, it'll be uncomfortable at first. She needs that natural lube, especially since she's so riled up. She'll want to go hard and fast.

I rub her the way I know she likes as she kisses my jaw. I roll my hips again, testing. When I find her nice and wet, I don't waste time.

"Now, baby."

She grabs my cock again, centering herself before lowering in one quick movement that has me gripping her hips, trying to force her down on top of me as far as she'll go.

She cries out, letting her head fall back in ecstasy. I keep my hips still, waiting while she adjusts to me. Slowly, she brings her head back around, her hips urging mine to move with her. "I can't believe I've been missing out on this dick all this time." She drops her stare to my lips, and then like a cobra, she snaps forward, claiming my mouth.

I shove her down my cock, giving it all to her. The kiss is aggressive, almost to the point of painful as we come together. In my head, we're making up for lost time. All those instances where I wanted to devour her with my mouth come back, except I can take advantage of it now. She's mine to drag under with me. Mine to discover. I wrap my fingers in her hair, holding her in place while my tongue plunders her mouth.

She groans, long and hard, working her hips against mine in short movements that tease her clit against my pelvis.

I sneak my other hand under her shirt, searching out her curves and the pebbled nipple I know will be waiting for me. I shove her bra out of the way, pinching then pulling her straining bud, using all the friction I can until she breaks the kiss. "Oliver, please."

"You're so beautiful," I tell her. "Fuck me, you're perfect." I lift her shirt all the way up, moving forward to capture her nipple in my mouth, flicking the tip of my tongue across it as she crashes down over me.

She braces her hands on my shoulders, using me to quicken her movements. "Oliver, I'm going to come soon. I want to feel you come with me."

The moan that escapes me is the realization that I may have finally broken down her walls. I actually might have gotten to her.

When your girl tells you she wants to feel you come with her, you're going to try your damndest.

"Keep going baby," I beg as her movements become jerky.

My dick twitches, and her body shakes. Steadying her, I take over, pulsing my hips into hers, burying myself deep inside her. The squeeze of her pussy and the cry that escapes her mouth as she reaches her climax is more than enough to send me over the edge. I hold her hips still, reveling at my dick throbbing inside her until our bodies come down, spent but filled.

Edie moans in contentment, pressing a chaste kiss to my neck. I thread my fingers through her hair, heart still hammering. "You'll always be you, Eden. You don't know how to be anyone else."

She swallows, tracing her fingertips over my cheekbones. "Sometimes I just need a reminder."

I pull away, glancing to where we're still joined.

"Happy to remind you," I tell her, letting a smile play over my face.

She bites her lip, then leans closer. Surprise fills me when she brushes her lips over mine. "And you're really good at it, Number Five."

Then, she kisses me. Again.

And in this moment, nothing else matters but this. Only this.

34

Eden

*M*eeting with Vincent makes me feel exactly like I thought it would. I contacted him through the information he left in the folder, and here we sit, at the same table, in the same room, earlier this time, though. I loathe to hand over the pictures we printed of the paternity test results that he wants.

A favor, alright. What they don't mention is that sometimes a favor can make you feel like shit.

He reaches his hand out, and I barely have to move the folder forward before he's taking it from my hands. He glances briefly inside, not even long enough to see what the results are, but fast enough to see that we have something for him.

"I'm indebted to you both," he says. His face is grim today, far different from yesterday's smug fuckery look, and it makes me wonder what's happened in Vincent's world to take the ego out of him. Something horrible, I hope.

He drums his fingers over the manila folder, glancing at Ollie and me. At our backs, I feel the presence of our pissed-off bodyguards. They were definitely not happy with our unscheduled detour earlier, but what's a girl to do?

"That's not an idle promise," Vincent remarks. "Favors are an essential piece of the Knights' structure. You did me a favor, I reciprocate, providing I think it's of equal or lesser value than the one you provided for me."

There it is. The smug look is back, and I wonder what the hell he thinks is equal to finding out whether he's a daddy or not. It doesn't really matter, anyway, because accepting a favor from Vincent Jarvis is like planning my permanent stay in the Knights.

"We're finished, then?" I ask.

He nods once. "You performed well. I'll make sure the Elders are aware. How did you get it?"

I shrug. "It's a secret." After Leo and Alaric calmed down, we explained to them how we'd gotten the results, and they'd stood there speechless before cracking up. I somehow don't think Vincent would have the same reaction. "Plus, does it matter?"

"I suppose it doesn't."

I stand, and Leo moves the chair out for me. Almost like a gentleman. Odd, but okay.

My plan is to just leave the room, go back to Jarvis Hall, and take a bath to scrub the icky feelings off me, but Vincent's voice halts my plan at the door. "Leonardo? Thought you should know, Grandfather's extremely irritated with you. He wants a check-in immediately."

There's something about the way he says it that unnerves me. Check-in? What job could Leo possibly be working for his grandfather right now when he's been wrapped up in Knights shit with me?

Unless he has Leo so tight on a leash that he doesn't let him live his own life without having his hands in every part of it. Doesn't seem like Leo's style, though.

"Did you hear me, Leonardo?" Vincent asks.

Leo grunts in response, and we all leave the room, the empty hall echoing our footsteps back to us. I don't dare say anything until we're outside. The security in the Knights lair is beyond measure. You never know who's listening.

"Check-in?" I ask, finally turning toward him with a raised brow.

He shrugs. "I don't know if you've heard, but I'm a bit of a disappointment. He likes to keep tabs on me."

I press my lips together. It's not that the excuse doesn't pass, it's just the combination of the way he says it and the whole not-trusting-them talk that Oliver and I had. Despite all outward appearances of wanting to work with me, what if they're working against me?

I just can't shake the feeling.

"Awfully bold to ask questions about me when you're keeping your own secrets," he snarks.

My heart squeezes in my chest. "What are you talking about, Caveman?"

"I'm talking about how I saw a British waiter helping a distressed Keegan Forbes into his residence hall yesterday."

Oliver sighs. "Please. How could you tell he was British?"

"The accent, asshole. And they pulled up in a Mini Cooper. You think any of these twats are driving Mini Coopers?"

"We should talk about this when we get inside," Alaric notes, shifting his gaze around as we make our way across campus.

"So, I'm not allowed to talk to my dead sister's

fiancé?" I ask, completely ignoring the sensible one of the group.

"We both know it was more than talking. What the hell's going on?"

I don't know if it was me, or if it was his dumbass cousin, but something has his panties in a bunch. "Keegan and I have unfinished business regarding my sister. He was there the night she died, and I needed to know more."

"Like what?" Leo growls, prowling forward.

I stand my ground, but all that does is put us in very close proximity, which never does anything good for me. "Like ask him how she was feeling that day. Was she excited? Did he see her right before she died? Did she say anything about me?"

"I thought they weren't on good terms," Alaric questions.

"Except he says they were. He says he loves her," I pant, before throwing my hands in the air, trying to work out everything in my head at the same time I tell them. I never thought Keegan would come around to a doting fiancé, but I also trust my instincts. He wasn't lying when he told us that.

Oliver sighs, addressing the guys. "Which is why he looked like shit yesterday."

"He could barely walk."

I shrug. "He was heartsick."

Leo shakes his head slowly. "You're not fooling me."

"I don't really care what I'm doing to you, Leo. Or *not* doing to you. You're in my Knight group. That's it. You're an asshole who only thinks with his dick. Don't you have any girls to ravage? Or shitty little errands to run for your dear old Granddad? You wouldn't know a thing about what I'm feeling."

His cold stare never wavers. He blinks, and I expect him to throw me over his shoulder, walk me to the house, and lock me in my room. I expect him to reply with how he can think of me doing something more useful with my mouth other than bitching, but he doesn't.

He just leaves.

He doesn't stalk away. He doesn't march. He doesn't do it with his head down or with any emotion whatsoever. He doesn't look back or spit any parting words. He's just gone.

And I'm left in a flurry of angry bitterness with a bit of a hitch in my breath from the surprise departure. I rub my chest as he crosses the parking lot and gets in his stupid sports car. He exits the university campus the same way he walked away. No fanfare; no loud motor noises or squealing tires.

He. Just. Leaves. It's about as uneventful as it gets, but it takes a toll on me.

I don't know why. He's just some guy the Knights grouped me with, right? Someone I shouldn't even trust?

Alaric breathes in deeply as soon as he's out of sight. "Okay..."

"Okay?" I snap.

He shrugs. "What do you want me to say?"

Fuck if I know. My breath rattles around in my chest as I start toward Jarvis Hall. The stupid name above the door seems to mock me as I let myself in, then press in the alarm code.

I walk into the living room, antsy as hell. It's all of this sneaking around. It's owing people favors and not knowing what it's doing to the other people in real life. It's pretending to be anyone but myself.

Alaric checks his phone, then sits on the couch. He's quiet for a moment until he peers at me. "He's the one who found his dad, you know?"

I suck in a breath. Fuck me. And I'd just told him he'd have no idea what I was going through.

"He might understand more than the rest of us."

"Since when are you on Team Jarvis?"

"I'm not." He shakes his head. "But I've also never seen him just leave a conversation like that. Usually when people yell at him, they're sprawled out on the grass straight after or he leaves them an emotional

389

mess. I don't know how you did it, but you may have actually gotten to Leonardo Jarvis, Eden."

"Hooray for me. I'm going to bed." I start for the stairs but spin around when I hit the bottom step. "Don't follow me. Either of you."

Oliver frowns, but he does what I ask. In his blue gaze are questions he doesn't want to ask out loud, so I nod once before racing up the stairs.

I spend the next couple of hours talking myself into the fact that Leo can't be trusted while I go through Dee's boxes. I don't find anything that can be considered useful, but I do find her metal Knights box—a match to the one that contained the invitation to my first Knights of Arcadia meeting.

I peer inside it, hoping to find something, but there's nothing. It's empty.

None of this makes sense. My sister was a freaking rock star at organization. From what Holly told us, Dee recruited the girls for Devil's Night; she did their contracts and their goodie bags; she helped set up too. She should have notes lying around, file folders with invoices. Anything. She started helping my mother plan soirees when she was nine, and my mom has never praisingly insulted someone like when she announced to everyone how secretarial Delilah was.

I wish I had her phone. Like the rest of us, she was always on that damn thing. It might prove Keegan's story. It might point us toward the stalker, or whoever she had this last-minute meeting with before she turned up on the river dock, not breathing.

I pull up a note-taking app on my phone and start jotting down ideas.

Delilah's phone.

Stalker/barista?

Talk with staff at the castle.

Track down more of the entertainment.

Talk to anyone who was at the Devil's Night party who isn't a Knight.

I don't know how I'm going to do all of this without attracting attention to myself, but this is exactly why it would be easier if I was a Knight. As a Fledgling, I should get put on the Devil's Night planning party, just like her. Retrace her steps.

All of that will take time, but there's one thing I can do now: take Keegan's advice and talk to my father. He's not returning my texts or voicemails, but that doesn't mean I don't know where he lives.

I get to my feet, searching for a jacket. Oliver went to bed a half hour ago—he'd paused by my door, but when I didn't call out to him, he kept going. Checking the clock, I imagine Alaric's in bed too.

Perfect. I need to do this on my own. Family business is family business.

I sneak down the stairs. I don't know if it's because

I've just finished going through Dee's stuff or because her death is so fresh on my mind right now, but I feel raw. As if the slightest thing would slice me open and I'd bleed out all over the floor.

I will do this, I promise Dee as I cancel the security alarm and then reset it before I pull the door closed behind me. I walk briskly to my Jeep, and by the time I get in it, no one's followed me.

Taking a deep breath, I start the engine, and then roll slowly off campus, pointing my car toward my parents' house.

The drive doesn't take long, especially since I fill the time rehearsing what I want to ask. Dad always operates on a need-to-know basis, which usually suits me fine. I couldn't care less most of the time, but a potential stalker is one of those things he should've relayed to us. When my sister's safety is in jeopardy, that's a family problem.

I squeeze the steering wheel, wondering why Dee didn't tell me herself. I know the answer already, but I search for another one in hopes that I'm wrong. The truth is, she'd call and talk about family shit, and I'd blow her off. I'd blow everyone off. I didn't care. It was so much easier not to care when I was thousands of miles away.

A tear carves its way down my cheek, and I swipe at it. I don't even deserve my own misery. I should've been a better sister, which is why I'm so adamant about finding out what happened to her.

And what I really want to know from Dad is how can he not see what's in front of his face? He hasn't built an eight-figure company being stupid. He must suspect the Knights too.

Unless he knows for sure it's not...

My foot drifts off the accelerator as that thought drills a hole into my brain. I chalked up his inaction to grief and the fact that he can't seem to walk around the house without looking like a zombie. But maybe I missed the point of all this. Maybe he knows for sure it was an accident, and he really is lost in grief.

Something I should be doing too.

Maybe my mind is making shit up, trying to make sense of something that is senseless. What if it was only an old-fashioned accident?

After all, accident means something that shouldn't have happened. No, Dee didn't like the water, but she could've been on the dock. She could've slipped and fell. She could've—

The car behind me flashes their high beams. I squint in the rearview mirror, and their horn blows several times before the driver lays on it.

"Jesus. Asshole," I mutter. I peek down at my speedometer and notice I'm going thirty in a fifty-five. Oops. I pull to the side to let them pass, but they don't.

Lowering the window, I wave them on, but they stay right there, blinding me with their lights.

My heart races, my stare constantly returning to my rearview mirror. The car gets closer and closer, and with each inch they gain, panic starts to close in.

35

Eden

*I*t's the middle of the night, and I am not having any of this. I speed up. My house isn't that far away, and I know these roads like the back of my hand. I hang a right at the next street, then gun it, pushing the pedal all the way to the floor.

Gaining speed, the spooky forest on both sides flies by. The lights are a distance behind me now, and I don't know if they're following me, but I'm not taking any chances.

I take a left, then a quick right into a housing development before slowing. I keep checking my rearview mirror but don't see anyone as I exit out onto a back road. Our house is a mile down the street, so I drive the rest of the way casually.

It's midnight. Mom and Dad will be just heading to bed. Maybe. If they decide to sleep together tonight, that is.

I pull into the long, circular driveway. A large cast-iron lamp sits above the front entry, flickering like it's a real flame, but it isn't. I smile at it as a warmth spreads through me. I love this house. Always have. There are a lot of happy memories mixed in with the others here. Two sisters who grew up together. A happy, stable family...until those two sisters got older and noticed more. Then the lies about my parents' relationship started to unravel.

For everything my father is, he's still a cheating bastard. And my mother doesn't care.

How's that for family of the year?

That's when I started to despise this life. When I realized that even good things can crack. Everything can look epic on the outside, but it's only a figment of the imagination.

Like I told Oliver the other day, the only thing I want is something real. Something that transcends what I'm supposed to do if I'm a dutiful Astor. Something that won't break into a million pieces when tested.

Leo's face flashes in my mind at that moment. It's

surprising, actually, but not wholly unwelcome. A sense of loss hits me hard in the chest when I picture him walking away. I was out of line. Plain and simple.

I knew he lost his father. I was just being— Well, I was deflecting.

I push the car door open with what feels like ants crawling all over my skin. The whole situation with Alaric and Leo doesn't feel right. Here I am, talking about something that's real, and I don't even know if I can trust them. Makes me wonder how Dee ever forgave Keegan enough to let him back into her life.

I know what she'd tell me because I'd asked her before on one of the many times they were on again after being off. She'd said, "Sometimes you have to listen to your heart...even if it does end up in tatters. You can't go your whole life pushing people away."

I swallow, stopping in my tracks. It's as if she's telling me that for the first time because it's the first time I've ever actually heard her. She was saying that for me.

You can't go your whole life pushing people away.

Like I've been doing with everyone and everything. Oliver. My family. My responsibilities.

God, I'm so thick.

I enter the house, calling out for Mom and Dad. The light in the spacious foyer is on, and I take a right, heading toward the living room. I don't make it that far as Dad sticks his head out of his office. "Edie?"

"Hey, Dad," I say, stopping in the middle of the hallway.

His forehead wrinkles. "What are you doing here, honey?"

"Just wanted to chat." I glance around. The sprawling house is eerily quiet. "Where's Mom?"

"Asleep."

He steps back, so I follow him into his large office that looks out over the side yard. I scan the room, realizing I haven't been in here for a very long time. "Up late working?"

"Always," he says. "Is everything okay at school?"

I shrug, thinking the classwork is much harder than I want. But I'm sure that's not actually what he's asking. "Dad, how come you haven't answered my texts?"

He sits in his posh leather chair, and I note he's still very pale. It was dark in the hall, but all those same frail features that I noticed after Dee died are still clinging to him. "I'm sorry, sweetheart. I was going to tomorrow. Just got bogged down in work since I took so much time off after— After," he ends finally, and we obviously both know what he means. "Is it that important? I'm sorry, honey." He sits back in his chair, giving me his full attention.

"Dad, I need to talk about Dee...and the Knights." I swallow the hard lump in my throat. Talking about the Knights of Arcadia is a no-no. Or at least it has been my entire life. It was never a secret that my dad belonged to a special society. There were always whispers at parties and the pins and the cufflinks, and so many other things. But it was also implied that it was one of those things that we didn't discuss.

He shakes his head, giving me a stern look. "Now, Eden—"

"Dad," I interrupt.

"No, Eden." He stands, his chair sliding back haphazardly.

I take a deep breath to calm myself. I just need to ease him into it first. That's all. "Fine. Then can you tell me about Dee's stalker?"

"Stalker?" he asks, brows pinching.

"She got something sent to her room at Carnegie," I remind him, not backing down. "You checked on it?"

He wipes at his brow, and I spy the glisten of sweat starting to sprout. "Right. We don't know if it was a stalker or not. It was a one-off thing that never happened again. I had the contents checked for prints with my contact, and they came up with nothing. We determined it was a disgusting prank, what with the picture included. Someone jealous of her and Keegan, I don't know. Keegan was making sure she was safe."

"Did you know she argued with someone at the dock that night, Dad? A girl—"

"Eden." He stops me, face more ashen now. "What are you doing?"

His look makes me want to backtrack. "I ran into someone who knew her—who was there. She said a guy showed up that night, and they argued."

"People get in arguments, Eden. I don't know what to tell you. What happened to your sister was a tragedy. An accident," he says sternly, voice breaking at the end. "Don't let this consume you. Please," he urges.

The front door opens and closes, and Dad's gaze darts to the office door. Confusion filters through me, then panic as my father lunges across his desk to grab my hand. "Be strong, Eden. I can't help you. I—"

He pulls away a second before a voice sounds out behind me. "Ah, Alistair. Good to see you again."

I spin, heart in my throat. An Elder stands there. I can't place the voice, but he's wearing a long, dark cloak that covers his face and brushes against the floor when he walks toward me. I back up a couple spaces, but my hip hits my dad's desk, making me stop.

"Eden Astor, do you accept the will of the Knights?" A large hand reaches out to grab my wrist. I try to pull away, but the grip is fierce, strong.

"Dad?" I cry.

"Don't hurt her," he growls.

I struggle again, but another cloaked Knight strides into the room behind him. He places a bag over my head. This time, I'm not just plunged into darkness. My lids become too heavy to keep open. My breathing slows. "Dad? Dad…"

36

Eden

My first conscious observation after being drugged is that I'm swaying... upside down. My hair swings with me, dangling over water.

Panic consumes me, making my pounding head pulse with pain. My tired eyes feel like sandpaper as they rub against my drooping eyelids.

"She's awake," a familiar voice notes.

I glance over, finding a group of robe-clad Knights, but that's not who grabs my attention. It's Leonardo Jarvis, his arms crossed over his chest, looking dark and dangerous in the shadows.

He stares at me blankly. Movement catches my eye, and I take in more of my surroundings. It doesn't take me long to figure out they're all standing on a dock, water slowly rippling against wood beams bracing wood decking.

Covered lights illuminate wood posts stretching toward the ceiling joists. Arches act as windows, but they're no help in helping me discover where I am. All I see is rock on one side and water on the other.

My limbs are numb, tingling. Peering up, I immediately get a surge of pain, but I find what's holding me—a rope and a pulley that's used to bring boats out of the water. I'm strung up over moving water, and I'd bet my life this is a boat house. I've been in enough of them to know.

I'm no longer wearing the clothes I went to my house in; the skirt of a dress cascades down my body in the wrong direction. The dim lighting barely reaches my bare legs, leaving them half in shadow.

The Knights break up, beginning to line the decking on both sides of me. Panic wells inside. The more I move, the more the rope swings. Searching around, I spot a skylight. Beyond it, the moon perfectly highlights a stone turret, topped with uncommon burnt red shingles. I gasp, realizing where I am: The Knights castle. Which means the river flowing underneath me is the same river Dee drowned in.

Now what my father said makes sense. *Be strong.*

Did he know I was going to end up here? *Don't hurt her.*

Does my father think the Knights are capable of hurting me?

Because I do.

Everyone's face is hidden in shadows except for Leo, who stays in the background. My heart beats wildly, and I remember what he and Alaric told me once. The hardest Trial is about fear. Well, they hit that nail on the head, didn't they?

As the drugs wear off, the coldness seeps in. The chill in the air permeates this flimsy dress, freezing my bones. My body cramps, and I flex my fingers in and out, trying to get movement back into them.

"Bring him out," a man orders.

My body starts shaking uncontrollably. They're going to hurt me. They're going to kill me, just like Dee. Dad said he couldn't help me. He knows. He knows, and he's not going to do anything about it.

"Leo," I croak out.

If he ever thought of me as anything more than just the Pledge he was helping to get through the Trials, he'll put a stop to this, or go down fighting.

Alarm builds and builds until my chest constricts. Tears blind me as the panic attack hits. My breaths are shallow, coming rapidly, and the feeling of impending doom stampedes through me. I'm about to die. They're going to drop me in the water, and because I've been hanging upside down for God knows how long in this freezing weather, I won't be able to swim. My muscles will cramp. I won't be able to take another breath. I'll get pulled away by the current, the water so black I'll never see the topside again.

A whimper escapes me, my hands coming up to settle over my chest.

The chaos inside me is almost too much.

A gravelly, disgusted voice asks, "What's wrong with her?"

It's Leo who answers. "Panic attack."

The sound of revulsion I hear next makes my fingers clench. It must be him—Leo's grandfather. "Good thing you were following her. We'd have missed this."

I can't even react before another familiar voice hits. "Let go of me, you wanker."

"Oliver?"

"Edie? Edie, is that you?" In the next instant, there's a big commotion. "What the fuck?" A roar escapes Ollie's mouth. "Let her go."

"Ollie?" I ask again, voice breaking.

A scuffle ensues. My head whips around, trying to find Oliver, but the rope is swinging wildly now, swaying and spinning—

Suddenly, I free fall.

I suck in my last breath, a scream escaping my throat that makes my toes curl.

I jolt to a stop, whiplash ricocheting through me. A sharp pain shoots up my ankle. The dress I'm wearing slips further down, its skirt impeding my view. I can only see the water and the aged dock now, spinning in front of me. I'm so, so close. The aroma of the river hits me in the face, and I wonder if this is what Dee smelled moments before she passed.

Is this the terror she felt? The panic clawing at her?

"Help me," I gasp, closing my eyes as a bout of dizziness hits. "Please."

A few of the men surrounding me chuckle. One of them notes, "She looks so much like her sister. Ass and all."

Fury whips through me. "What did you say?" I croak. Then more forcefully, "What did you say, you creepy old fuck?"

"How dare you talk to me like that, you bitch!"

Another commotion breaks out. Fear grips me. I try to lift the skirt off my face when the swaying slows, but my limbs don't want to cooperate. Feeling in my fingertips disappears.

Oliver cries out, and I call for him again, but don't get a response.

"Leo!" I yell.

"Isn't that cute?" a voice asks. "She wants you to help her, young Jarvis."

"Will you help her?" another voice asks, mocking.

"She doesn't know," another speaks up, followed by a cruel laugh.

"Leo?" I shudder.

A chorus of laughter rings all around me. Terror sweeps me up and stars dance on the other side of my eyelids when I understand the truth. I feel myself getting queasier and queasier. I might pass out from all the blood rushing to my head and the knowledge that I've been played.

Oliver was right. Leo is one of them. I'd call out for Alaric, but he wouldn't help either. He might even be in one of those long robes, hiding his face behind his hood like the coward he is.

They're Knights, and Knights are emotionless and powerful—a horrible mix for rich people.

I'm going to die. Just like Dee.

I take in a deep breath, close my eyes again, and try to center myself as much as possible. If they're going to kill me, I'm not giving them the satisfaction of terrifying me.

"What? Nothing more to say?" a voice teases. "No one left to call for help. No one who cares to, anyway."

"You're all alone," another voice taunts. "You've been there for hours. Your muscles are hurting like hell. Your heart is beating like crazy. Do you see that river below you, Astor? It's so cold that your body will seize up. There'll be no swimming. No last frantic push to the surface."

"You'll die. Just like your sister."

My heart splinters. The shards become weapons, tearing up my insides.

Someone scoffs. "She got it easier than her sister. But I have to admit, they both make *pretty little dead girls*."

The rope unravels with a whine, and I plunge into the icy depths of the Saint Lawrence River.

Just as they promised, my body seizes. I gasp into the pitch black, river water seizing my lungs.

And there's nothing I can do about it.

The Knights have won again, but at least I'll get to see Dee soon...

————

ABOUT THE AUTHOR

E. M. Moore is a USA Today Bestselling author of Contemporary and Paranormal Romance. She's drawn to write within the teen and college-aged years where her characters get knocked on their asses, torn inside out, and put back together again by their first loves. Whether it's in a fantastical setting where human guards protect the creatures of the night or a realistic high school backdrop where social cliques rule the halls, the emotions are the same. Dark. Twisty. Angsty. Raw.

When Erin's not writing, you can find her dreaming up vacations for her family, watching murder mystery shows, or dancing in her kitchen while she pretends to cook.